THE DEATHCATS OF ASA' ICAN

And Other Tales Of A Space-Vet

ANDREW M. SEDDON

The DeathCats of Asa'ican

ISBN: 978-1-927154-44-1

Cover Design and Logo Digitization: Grace Bridges
Dog Photographs and Logo Design: Andrew M. Seddon
Space photos courtesy of NASA

"Night of the Skaggit" was published in *Misunderstood*, Rebecca McFarland Kyle and Tracy Simmons Bitonti, eds., Wolfsinger Publications, 2015.

Splashdown Books, New Zealand

http://www.splashdownbooks.com

For Olivia: The best wife in the world…galaxy…universe…

And to Kommissar Rex, CDX, RAE, the best German Shepherd friend.

And in memory of Finzi (Victrix von Boorman Haus, CXD, RAE), who traveled widely, and would have enjoyed seeing the galaxy.

Thanks as always to Colleen Drippé and Werner Lind for unfailingly helpful comments and critiques.

The quotation "The angel of death has been abroad throughout the land…" in the story *Azrael* is from a speech delivered by John Bright (1811-1889) to the British House of Commons on Feb. 23, 1855 opposing the Crimean War. Accessible at http//en.wikiquote.org/wiki/John_Bright and other locations.

OTHER BOOKS BY ANDREW M. SEDDON

Red Planet Rising (Crossway, 1995)
Imperial Legions (Broadman & Holman, 2000)
Iron Scepter (Xlibris, 2001)
Saints Alive! Vol. I: Saints of Empire (Bezalel Books, 2013)
Saints Alive! Vol. II: Celtic Paths (Bezalel Books, 2014)
Ring of Time (Splashdown Books, 2014)

CONTENTS

STARE OF THE BLACK DOG

Hughes let out a low whistle. "Quite a mess, isn't it, girl?"

He looked over at the black German Shepherd with the white patch on her chest. Victrix occupied the co-pilot's seat, as she always did when Hughes was ensconced in the command chair of *Wolf-1*.

She returned his look with her ears erect and her head cocked to one side in the way that she did when the intonation of his voice indicated a question. Hughes sensed her curiosity.

<*What?*>

He couldn't explain. Concepts such as beauty and ugliness were meaningless to even the most intelligent dog.

The earth-sized planet on the main viewscreen was shrouded by a dense blanket of hideous gray cloud, its surface features completely obscured by swirling streaks of black, brown and ochre, as if some untalented cosmic giant had used the planet's atmosphere as a failed experiment in finger-painting.

The world was named Consolation; its main settlement, Hopetown. Judging by the information in Sofi's computer banks, both names were highly implausible—or unreasonably optimistic.

There'd been no contact with the settlement since Hughes had picked up a faint distress call days ago; repeated attempts had brought nothing but silence. Still, it was worth one more try.

"Sofi, are you picking up any transmissions?" he asked.

"Negative, Dr. Hughes," Sofi—the Starship Operations and Flight Intelligence—replied in tones which always reminded him of an elderly aunt. "I detect no human-generated activity."

"Thank you," Hughes replied automatically, although it hardly made sense to thank a computer.

"You're welcome, Doctor. I should inform you that surface conditions are suboptimal for human life."

"Dangerous?"

"Not as long as proper caution is exercised."

"Good. And you're sure you've checked all frequencies?"

"Multiple times, Doctor," Sofi replied, managing to sound aggrieved.

Hughes suppressed a smile and faced the Shepherd again. "There's only one thing to do, girl. We'll have to go down and look for ourselves."

<*Work?*> Victrix's thought came to him eagerly as her bushy tail thumped the seat.

"Yes, girl. Work."

She jumped off the seat onto the deck. <*Let's go!*>

Work was what the big dog lived for, Hughes knew. He stood up and stretched. Not that he minded, himself. Setting foot on a new planet was always a welcome relief from the tedium of space travel. It was the promise of the unexpected that kept him going, as well.

A screech sliced through the silence of the fading twilight like a knife blade scraping across porcelain. The hillsides funneled the sound up the valley until it bounced, amplified, off the rock wall that formed the valley's apex, and stabbed into the brains of the two people standing below the scree on a small patch of level ground.

Jenna clamped her hands over her ears, and cast an anxious glance at her companion.

Ragnar, a head taller, but with his hair almost as long and matted as hers, didn't seem as affected by the cacophony. He shrugged. "Suckerbug."

Jenna shivered and lowered her hands as the screech faded. "Where do you suppose it could be?"

Ragnar shrugged again. "Anywhere." He slipped out of his pack and laid it on the ground. "We'd best make camp and light a fire."

"Won't that attract it?" Jenna worried.

"Maybe it'll keep it away," he countered. "Anyway, the temperature's dropping so it will probably become less active. I don't know about you, but hot food and a warm bed would suit me."

Jenna nodded. "Me too." Their energy packs had long since died as they wandered through a landscape shrouded in perpetual gloom, where hardly any difference existed between daytime and night. If only the skies would clear! She cast her eyes upwards as she unclasped her own pack, hoping to glimpse a rift in the dirty gray clouds that had blocked out not only Consolation's sun and moons, but the stars as well, making it impossible for them to know in which direction they traveled.

Perhaps, if the planet's shifting magnetic fields hadn't rendered their direction finder useless…

Perhaps what? Would they have made their way back to Hopetown by now? And if they had, would they have found anybody still alive?

Something—women's intuition?—told her no. She had a nagging suspicion that they were alone on the planet—a modern Adam and Eve, but in a dust and ash covered wasteland rather than a Garden of Eden. She tried not to think of the friends they had undoubtedly lost.

The time for tears was past. Now she had to focus on survival. But survive for what? What if help never came? Two people couldn't possibly resurrect a colony on a world as rugged and barren as this.

She sighed and began to erect their two-person tent. Ragnar collected dried pieces of the gnarled, waist-high bushes that passed for trees and coaxed a fire into life from embers that he carried in an insulated pouch.

Another screech cut through the acrid air.

"Fainter, I think," Ragnar said.

"I hope so." Jenna visualized a four-foot-long suckerbug stabbing her with its needle-sharp proboscis and draining her blood in the night. Suckerbugs were at the top of the local food chain, such as it was. No native mammalian life existed on Consolation, only insectivora and the small reptiles that constituted the suckerbugs' main diet. Something the size of humans would represent quite a feast.

She finished erecting the tent and unrolled their sleeping bags, conscious of yet another headache developing. As if she didn't have enough to deal with.

Ragnar was grilling a couple of skewers over his fire.

"Lizard meat and roots again?" she asked.

"Nothing else in the pantry," he grunted.

She stamped a foot. "I'm sick of lizard meat and roots!"

His eyes were hollow. "No choice, is there?"

"I guess not." She sat, cross-legged, beside him. "Ragnar, will we ever make it back?"

He handed her a skewer of charred black lumps, and took a bite from his own. "It could be over that hill," he replied, pointing with his skewer, "or a hundred miles away."

She closed her eyes, and her lips worked soundlessly.

"Praying again?" Ragnar asked.

She nodded.

"What for?"

"That God would send us a guide…a way out…"

He snorted. "If it makes you feel better. Otherwise, save your strength. Prayer's a waste of time. There's no one to hear you."

She didn't feel like arguing. She took a bite of meat. The lizard was rubbery but not unpleasant once you got used to it.

Light flashed across the sky, followed by the dull crump of thunder.

"Just what we need," Ragnar scowled. "This isn't a good spot if it really starts to pour."

Jenna was peering into the gloom. "Hand me the viewscope, would you?"

He rummaged on the ground behind him and passed the instrument to her. "See something?"

"On the ridge." She adjusted the focus. "I thought something moved."

He stared. "I don't see anything. Probably just bushes."

Lightning flashed again.

"I don't think so. Here, take a look."

"Where?" He took the viewscope from her.

"See that formation that looks like a pyramid? Just to the right."

"I don't—wait! You're right, there is something there." He studied the ridge. "It can't be…"

"What?" She grabbed the viewscope back.

"There's no way…" he continued.

Lightning flickered and danced between the clouds, briefly illuminating the ground.

"Dogs!" she gasped. "Those are dogs! There's a large black one, and four—no, make that five others. Where on earth did they come from?"

"Strays from the colony, no doubt," Ragnar replied. "They sure aren't native." He hefted his energy rifle. "Maybe I can pot one from here."

"No!" Jenna gasped, pushing his arm down.

He gave her a puzzled look. "Be a change from lizard meat."

"No…don't. They're too far away for a good shot," she said, trying to think of something that might convince him to refrain. "The power pack's getting low. And…and they might protect us from the suckerbug."

"Or maybe they want us for dinner instead," Ragnar countered. "Perhaps they're tired of lizard meat, too."

"Still…just don't."

"All right," he said grudgingly. He laid the rifle down. "But we'd best keep watch tonight."

"Fine," Jenna agreed. "I'll go first if you like."

"Suits me." Ragnar crawled inside the tent. "Wake me when you're ready to change."

Despite the thunder and lightning, she thought there was little chance for rain. She'd be fine remaining outside a while longer. She picked up the viewscope, tuned it to night vision, and studied the ridge again, bathed in the eerie glow of sheet lightning. The dogs were merely indistinct lumps on the ground. All but the black one. It was sitting, looking like a wolf…or a German Shepherd, she supposed. Almost, she could feel its gaze returning hers. Impossible, though. She wondered if the dogs even knew she and Ragnar were there. Perhaps by scent, if the wind direction was right.

But still…how strange.

With little indigenous life on Consolation—and most of that unpleasant—the colonists hadn't scrupled to bring dogs with them, figuring, no doubt, that any damage to the local ecology wouldn't be of any great significance. Perhaps, had they known, authorities and organizations on distant Earth would have objected, but many fringe worlds had been colonized beyond Earth's jurisdiction or capability to supervise. For the most part, such lonely worlds went their own way.

The hours passed slowly, and it was well after the gloom had passed into utter darkness when she exchanged places with Ragnar and wriggled into her sleeping bag.

She fell asleep quickly, but when she did, it was only to dream—or rather, relive what had happened those long weeks ago. It had seemed, at first, to be an ordinary day. She and Ragnar had gone on a prospecting trip, searching for a lode of the rare elements which existed on Consolation, and which were the colony's raison d'être.

It had been a clear night, full of stars, and brightened by the light of Consolation's moon. And there had been a meteor shower—one streak followed by another and another until the sky shone like a fiery stream. She and Ragnar had watched, awestruck by the sight.

And then they spotted the big meteor, blazing like a comet…growing brighter and brighter until it passed beyond a range of mountains on the horizon. And then followed the explosion—a giant fireball rising into the sky, a deafening tsunami of sound rolling across the shuddering landscape, and a pillar of cloud ascending heavenwards. The earth convulsed and writhed as a blast of hot wind swept past.

Maybe there had been more strikes across the planet's surface.

Because dawn had never come.

Their flyer—parked below an escarpment that had appeared stable but wasn't—had been crushed by a rockfall which also buried most of their supplies.

Fortunate to escape with only contusions and bruises—and possibly, she realized in retrospect, mild concussions—she and Ragnar had begun to walk…

…and walk and walk…

A scream.

Jenna sat bolt upright, her heart racing. She scrambled to the tent flap and stuck her head out.

"Ragnar—?"

He was silhouetted against the fire. "Just the suckerbug again," he said without turning around. "Go back to sleep."

"Easy for you to say." With her adrenalin flowing, she knew that would be impossible. Instead, she crawled out to rejoin him.

"No need for both of us to be up," he said.

She wrapped her arms around her chest. "Could *you* sleep?"

"No."

"Then we'll both watch."

She rested her head against his shoulder and waited for the coming of what passed for morning.

One glance at what was left of Hopetown as his shuttle circled the location had told Hughes why there'd been no response. The settlement's prefab buildings had shattered, crumbled, and melted in a devastating conflagration. All but one, which by some quirk had survived the blast and the firestorm reasonably intact. The same couldn't be said for the sole survivor, however—a middle-aged man, badly burned and injured, barely clinging to life, able to speak only a few words. That he'd survived at all was a miracle—but Hughes doubted he'd survive much longer.

Victrix had sniffed him out in a rubble-blocked alcove, surrounded by a handful of empty water containers, wrappers of emergency food, and a dead transmitter.

Hughes had been faced with a problem.

Transporting the man to the autodoc on *Wolf-1* was out of the question—he'd never live through the ascent to orbit. Hughes would have to make do with the emergency supplies on his shuttle, his far-from-adequate knowledge of human physiology, and whatever guidance Sofi could provide.

He'd have to wing it. Well. It wouldn't be the first time—and probably not the last, either.

<Go play?>

"Huh?" Startled, he'd glanced down at Victrix, who was gazing towards the door of the building. "Sure," he'd told her. "Go ahead."

The big dog had bounded off, tail streaming behind her.

<Wait.> He'd sent the thought after her. *<I have a better idea. Go search.>*

Her reply had vibrated with excitement.

<Victrix search!>

Hughes had grinned as she'd disappeared through the doorway, then sobered and returned his attention to his patient. He'd do what he could; almost certainly it wouldn't be enough.

Dawn was nothing more than a slight diminishing of the gloom.

Breakfast was raw root, fibrous and tasteless. Jenna choked it down.

"We might as well follow the valley," Ragnar said, as he shouldered his pack.

Jenna studied the rock face down which they'd scrambled yesterday. "Fine. I wouldn't mind some easier walking today."

They set off, side by side, their steps muffled by the mossy vegetation that carpeted the rough, chunky ground. As they walked, Jenna looked up at the ridge. "The dogs have gone."

"Guess so," Ragnar said. "Still think I should have tried for one."

"You could have killed someone's pet."

"*Former* pet."

The appearance of the dogs still puzzled her. Jenna had heard tales of dogs sensing a natural disaster before it occurred. Could the dogs have anticipated the meteor storm—as unlikely as it seemed—and fled the settlement before the meteorite impact?

The valley curved as it descended. They'd walked for perhaps an hour when Jenna halted at the sight of an irregular, clay-colored mound. "What's that?"

Ragnar strode ahead, and Jenna hurried to keep up. Ragnar poked at a pile of shattered chitinous plates strung together by strands of glistening slime. "The suckerbug," he said. "What's left of it."

"Must have been the dogs," Jenna said. She visualized the black dog. A German Shepherd's powerful jaws could surely crush a suckerbug's hard but brittle plates. "They helped us after all."

"Not much left on it," Ragnar commented.

Jenna shuddered. "I wouldn't want to try it anyway."

They halted at midday near where a small stream trickled from a rocky outcropping and the valley opened out into yet another expanse of sparsely vegetated wasteland.

The one consolation about Consolation was that the bacterial life wasn't inimical to humans. The red-tinged water tasted metallic, but was palatable, if just barely.

"Get up slowly," Ragnar hissed as Jenna crouched down to drink.

She did as he instructed, and turned to face the same direction. He had the rifle at the ready. "We've got company."

The dogs were there, five of them in an arc, perhaps a hundred feet away.

"Where's the black?" Jenna whispered.

"I don't—"

"Up there," she said, suddenly noticing a dark shape in her peripheral vision.

Ragnar shifted the rifle to point to the top of the outcropping. "Got a fix."

The black dog—certainly a German Shepherd, she concluded, seeing it better in the wan daylight—was standing, its head low, ears erect, gaze fixed on them.

Jenna met the unblinking stare of the brown eyes, one that reminded her of a mongoose staring at a cobra…

Something brushed against her mind. Almost like a whisper…a whisper of a sensation…

She placed her fingers against her temples. The sensation vanished. Probably just a lingering effect from the concussion. And yet…

She laid a hand on Ragnar's arm. "No."

"There are several meals there," he said.

"I think she wants to help us," Jenna said, feeling drawn to the steady brown eyes.

"What?" Ragnar exclaimed.

"She wants to help us," Jenna repeated.

"Sizing us up, more likely."

"That's not it."

"How could you possibly know that?"

"Look at her eyes."

"Her eyes?"

"They're not predatory."

"You're crazy," Ragnar said.

The black dog sat back on its haunches. It had a white patch on its chest, almost cross-like in shape, and smaller tufts on its head and neck. Jenna had the strange sensation that it was waiting for them to make a decision.

"Jenna—" Ragnar began.

"Let's go," she said.

"The pack is in the way," Ragnar said, motioning. "I was going to head that direction."

"Let's go the other way," Jenna suggested.

"But—"

"We're lost. What difference does it make?"

He shrugged. "All right. But don't make it look as if we're running."

They turned away from the immobile, watching dogs, and began to walk steadily. Jenna cast a look back over her shoulder.

The black dog studied them, until finally jumping down and joining the others.

"You're not losing it, are you?" Ragnar asked.

"Of course not. It's just…"

"Just what?"

She shook her head. "I don't know." She walked silently for a few minutes, then said, "Did you ever see that dog around the settlement?"

"Never," Ragnar replied.

"Neither did I," Jenna said.

"So?"

"I don't know."

Hughes' other task was to dig graves. There wasn't much in the way of mortal remains left of some of the settlers. Yet they deserved a decent burial. Hughes interred them all, blasting holes in Consolation's rocky ground, and reciting prayers from the Requiem Mass.

At least the settlement had been small, but that very smallness had worked against them, since the colony had been too poor to afford even a basic orbital detection system that might have warned them of the asteroid's approach and predicted its impact site.

He missed having Victrix nearby, but it was a task she couldn't have helped with or understood. Smart as she was, there were limits to her understanding.

And she was fine. Even enjoying herself. If he concentrated, he could sense her delight in freedom and of mission.

So he proceeded with his melancholy chores alone.

"I feel as if we're being stalked," Ragnar said when they camped for the night, chancing upon a shallow cave that offered some degree of protection.

"I don't think so," Jenna replied, studying the distant shapes through the viewscope.

Ragnar patted the rifle. "They'd better not come too close, that's all I can say. I'm not going to become a dog's dinner."

"I'm certain they don't mean us any harm."

"Oh sure," Ragnar scoffed. "You can read their minds, right?"

"No, I—" Jenna broke off, suddenly confused.

"Get some sleep," Ragnar said. "You're overtired."

"Perhaps you're right," Jenna agreed.

The truth was, they were both overtired, exhausted, dirty, disheveled, malnourished, and fighting off a creeping despair.

Even a good bath would have helped, but the small streams they encountered were good only for washing off the omnipresent dust from hands and faces.

She tried to sleep, but once again dreamed of death from the sky.

When she awoke, it was to find Ragnar already awake, scanning the landscape.

"You should have let me take a watch," she said.

"I meant to," Ragnar explained. "But I fell asleep." He scowled ruefully. "They could have killed us both."

"But they didn't." She laid a hand on his shoulder. "Don't be hard on yourself."

"They're in the way again," he said, returning her the viewscope and pointing. "I'd thought we should head that way."

As before, the dogs were ranged in an arc. The black German Shepherd, she noticed, was in the center, as if in command.

"Maybe we could scare them off," Ragnar suggested. "A couple of close shots, since you don't want me to hit one of them…"

"Or maybe we could do what they want," Jenna said, her attention fixed on the black dog.

"You're not serious!"

"She is," Jenna replied.

Ragnar muttered something under his breath—Jenna thought she caught the words 'crazy dog psychic'—and set about packing up their gear.

This time, as they walked, the dogs remained in sight, flanking them, occasionally angling diagonally across their path and causing them to alter their direction. The black dog was always in the lead.

Ragnar bagged another lizard-like creature; they ate half for lunch and saved the rest for dinner.

When they camped for the night, the black dog watched them from a low knoll.

"Doesn't that dog do anything but stare?" Ragnar grumbled.

"She's happy," Jenna replied.

"Oh? Because she thinks we're ready for the tasting?"

"No—not that—her body language is relaxed—"

Ragnar waved her away.

That night, lightning flickered between the clouds, and strange colors illuminated the sky.

"Which way do they want us to go today?" Ragnar frowned in the morning, hardly looking at Jenna as he wolfed down a chunk of lizard meat.

"Towards the hills, it looks like," Jenna commented, noting the position of the dogs.

Ragnar gave an exaggerated sigh as he shouldered his pack and trudged off.

They had walked for several hours when Jenna halted abruptly at the sound of a low hum. "What's that noise?"

"I don't hear anything," Ragnar said.

"It sounds like a flyer."

"You're dreaming. If anyone in the colony was looking for us they'd have done it by now."

"No, look there!"

Ragnar's expression suddenly changed at the sight of a bright spark in the sky. "You're right! It's coming towards us! Wave, Jenna, wave!" He jumped up and down, arms windmilling. Jenna followed suit.

The glint of the craft grew larger, and then descended. Ragnar broke into a run, with Jenna at his heels.

A black streak raced past them, ears back, bushy tail streaming behind.

The flyer settled to the ground. A figure emerged from the hatch and strode toward them. The German Shepherd skidded to a halt in front of him, reared up, planted her paws on his shoulders, and licked his face.

"You did it, girl!" he said. "Excellent work!"

The man straightened and faced them as they drew near. "You must be Jenna and Ragnar." He stuck out his hand. "I'm Hughes. Most people call me 'Doc'."

Ragnar seemed to be in a daze as he returned the greeting.

Jenna wasn't. She wrapped her arms around Hughes and gave him a big hug. "You're an answer to prayer! See, Ragnar?"

Ragnar recollected himself. "You're an offworlder?"

Hughes nodded as he extricated himself from Jenna's embrace. He was tall and lanky with a neatly trimmed beard, light brown hair, and a silver-gray forelock. "I was in transit to Melchior when I picked up a distress call. So I dropped into orbit and came down to see if I could help." He shook his head. "It hasn't been easy. This planet is an electromagnetic nightmare!"

He gestured toward the flyer. "Ready to leave?"

"How…do you know who we are? How did you find us?" Ragnar asked as they headed toward the craft. Jenna took his hand, nearly skipping in her delight.

"Hopetown was at the edge of the blast zone," Hughes said. "The buildings were leveled, but—"

"Were there any survivors?" Jenna asked softly.

Hughes' face clouded. "Only one that I could find. A man named Murdo. He was badly hurt and barely able to speak. He told me you two had gone off exploring." He puffed out his cheeks. "I would have tried to look for you myself, but I had to take care of him…and bury the rest. So I sent Victrix to search for you. She has a fantastic sense of direction." He patted the head of the black German Shepherd who walked proudly beside him. "Right?"

She barked.

"She's been watching us for days," Jenna protested. "But how could she tell you where we were?"

Hughes hesitated. "It's a long story…and it sounds crazy…but we're telepathically linked."

"No way!" Ragnar scoffed. "You and a dog?"

"She's not just any dog," Hughes replied. "She's genetically enhanced for intelligence and language capability."

"Every now and then there'd be mention of experiments in the news," Ragnar said, "but I never read of any successes."

"It's a rather unique situation," Hughes said.

"A couple of times I thought I felt something vague," Jenna interjected, "but I wasn't sure what it was."

"It's possible you picked up on her," Hughes said. "I've encountered a handful of people who seem to have a slight degree of natural sensitivity—or maybe it was just her body language. Anyway, when she told me that she had located you and that you were mobile but heading in the wrong direction, I asked her to direct you back."

"The dogs were herding us!" Ragnar exclaimed.

"Good thing you didn't shoot," Jenna said severely.

"She could sense your antagonism," Hughes said to Ragnar, "so she generally didn't get too close."

Ragnar scuffed his feet. "Sorry. I've just never liked dogs."

Hughes cleared his throat. "Murdo didn't make it," he said, "so when he died I thought I'd save you some walking and come to meet you."

They climbed into the flyer; Hughes took the controls while Jenna and Ragnar strapped themselves into the passenger seats. Victrix hopped onto the copilot's seat.

"Can she fly this?" Jenna chuckled.

Hughes laughed. "There are times when I wouldn't put it past her. I could tell you some stories…Truth is, I don't know what I'd do without her. She's better than any human assistant I've ever had."

The craft lifted, and the desolate landscape spread out beneath them.

Jenna shivered as a giant crater came into view, surrounded by miles and miles of ground that had been swept bare. On the outskirts of Hopetown—now nothing more than a jumble of rubble—she glimpsed a cluster of crosses, and then an orbital shuttle with its bay door open. The side of the shuttle was emblazoned with the image of a howling wolf in the center of a red cross.

Something clicked for Jenna. "WOLF!" she exclaimed. "You're the space vet!”

Hughes smiled tolerantly. “I prefer the term exobiologist, but yes.”

Ragnar frowned. “What’s ‘wolf’?”

“My ship and my practice,” Hughes explained. “Short for Wellness for Other Life Forms.”

The flyer settled gently inside the shuttle.

“I’ll take you up to *Wolf-1*,” Hughes said. “Drop you off at Melchior, if that’s OK. You can catch commercial to wherever you want to go from there.”

“What about the other dogs?” Jenna wondered. “Should we round them up?”

“I can’t stay here longer,” Hughes said. “There’s an outbreak of an unidentified illness on Melchior and they need my help—I’m late already. And my ship isn’t big enough to accommodate an entire pack. But I can have one of my vet teams here in a week or two—the dogs can survive until then. The team will monitor their health status and ensure that they’re fixed, so they won’t breed. And when a new colony is founded on Consolation—habitable worlds are valuable, even ones liked Consolation so it won’t be abandoned for long—the settlers will have friends to greet them.”

He reached over to fondle the black German Shepherd’s ears. “One can never take friendship too lightly,” he said, as she held out a paw. “Never.”

<*Treat?*>

Hughes laughed. “Reach into the compartment beside you, Jenna, would you? Somebody thinks a reward is in order…”

EYE OF THE BEHOLDER

If ever a planet deserved its name, Hughes thought, Last Chance was it. A barely habitable world in the middle of a galactic void, it had been settled by colonists who, at the end of their resources, had come across the lonely star and its solitary companion and, reluctantly but necessarily, ended their journey there. And, for some incomprehensible reason, once contact with other colonized worlds became practical and desirable, the majority had remained.

Hughes had no such intention.

He hadn't even planned on stopping until Sofi had interrupted him one day as he was reclining while listening to music. Victrix lay nearby, gnawing contentedly on a chew made of some synthetic rawhide-like material—one of a supply that he'd picked up on his last planetfall.

"Dr. Hughes?"

"Yes, Sofi?" he replied without opening his eyes.

"There's a problem with the quantum field drive, Doctor."

He opened his eyes. "Music off. Is it serious?"

"Not yet, but there's a 90% probability that it will become so in the next 6.5 standard days."

"Can you fix it?"

"Affirmative."

"Do you require any special facilities?"

"Negative. However, it is recommended that the repair be performed while in orbit around a habitable planetary body."

Hughes had nodded. It was a sensible precaution—just in case something went wrong. No one in their right mind would risk being stranded in interstellar space without a working drive and with only emergency power.

"What's the nearest inhabited planet, Sofi?" he'd asked, relaxing again.

"The only known habitable planet within 6.5 days at standard cruising speed is Last Chance, Doctor."

It was his imagination, surely, but did Sofi sound apologetic?

"Set course and initiate. Tach 5."

"Confirmed, Doctor. Enjoy your music."

Last Chance. A pity it couldn't have been Sunspot or Paradise North or StarHaven. Still, it was better than no chance. Even so, he vowed to leave as soon as Sofi's automated systems had finished their repairs.

Hughes had mixed feelings towards Earth's far-flung colonies. They provided an endless source of variety and ample professional scope, but some of them…for a native Earther, born to advanced civilization and all the amenities thereof, they could also prove to be profoundly tiresome.

But there was no choice. He felt as if he'd been marooned.

Once in orbit, he'd decided to head groundside to see what there was to see—if anything. There was no point in remaining on *Wolf-1;* he knew virtually nothing about the quantum field drive that drew power from the very fabric of space itself. Sofi could handle things.

"We'll get out of here as soon as we can, I promise," he said to Victrix as the orbital shuttle broke through a layer of greasy-appearing cloud and descended toward an undulating landscape of unrelieved drabness.

The big black German Shepherd, occupying the shuttle's copilot seat, responded with a low grumble from deep in her throat.

Hughes couldn't have imagined a more uninspired scene had he wished it. Every direction presented the same dreary olive-brown color—hills, plains, even what might have been lakes or seas. Similarly the sky, a pale, washed-out blue, lacked vibrancy.

The uninviting settlement that shortly came into view, although it had had several decades to improve its appearance, gave the impression that it lacked the will to aspire to better things.

Hughes was surprised though, after receiving landing clearance, parking the shuttle at the small spaceport, and passing through ground control, to be approached by a lean, middle-aged man in a beige jumpsuit emblazoned with a planetary government emblem on the left breast. Behind him stood an obvious bodyguard whom Victrix regarded warily.

"Dr. Hughes?" the man said. "I'm pleased to welcome you to Last Chance."

"You know of me?" Hughes replied.

Victrix transferred her attention to the newcomer, leaning slightly forward to catch his scent.

<*Friend?*>

<*Yes,*> Hughes replied. <*Be polite.*>

"Just because we're a small, isolated world, doesn't mean we're completely out of touch," the stranger said with a hint of irritation.

"Forgive me," Hughes said. "I meant no disrespect."

The man gave a forgiving smile. "My name is Fogelsong, John Fogelsong. I'm the planetary administrator."

"Pleased." Hughes returned a strong handshake. "I wasn't expecting to be welcomed by a high official."

"The encounter is somewhat impromptu, I must admit."

"Speaking of which, how does the planetary administrator know I'm here?"

"As I said, we're a small colony. My son works in ground control…"

"Ah." Hughes had learned long ago that on fringe worlds, unlike many of the major colonized planets, people actually knew each other.

"To be perfectly blunt," Fogelsong said apologetically, "I was hoping to enlist your help."

"Really?" Hughes raised his eyebrows. "I didn't receive a distress call."

"The fact is, that…well, we're not actually in distress, and it may not be in your field…" Fogelsong gestured. "But let's not discuss it here. You won't decline Chancian hospitality, I hope?"

"Not at all," Hughes replied.

"Your…ah…companion may join us as well," Fogelsong said, glancing at the dog.

Hughes smiled. "Victrix is as much colleague as companion."

"We'll be happy to cater to her needs as well."

"I'll warn you, she has a large appetite."

<*Food?*> Victrix asked eagerly.

<*You bet.*>

"This way, please." Fogelsong motioned.

Hughes fell into step beside the administrator, Victrix at his side, the bodyguard trailing behind.

"I'm still surprised that you met me personally."

"We're pretty informal on Last Chance," Fogelsong replied, walking with long, quick strides. "Pomp and circumstance is for representatives of worlds with big egos."

Chalk up points for Last Chance, Hughes, no admirer of egocentricy, thought to himself.

Hughes followed the administrator from the arrivals center to a flitter waiting outside. A few minutes' ride took them to the settlement, optimistically named 'Opportunity', and the administrative complex. Fogelsong showed them to a large, well-appointed guest suite, stylishly decorated with what Hughes presumed to be local artwork and overlooking a courtyard garden with a waterfall and flowering plants.

"You're welcome to stay on Last Chance as long as you wish," Fogelsong said. "Shall we meet in, say, one hour?"

Hughes consented, and flopped down on a delightfully spongy bed as the administrator departed.

"Nothing like the red carpet treatment," he said to Victrix who had curled up on another bed after giving the room a thorough inspection. "I wonder what he wants?"

Victrix settled down to lick her paws; Hughes took the cue and went to freshen up himself.

Dinner, served in a dining room in the administrative center, would not have been out of place on many a more populous world, even Earth itself. Left to his own, Hughes was used to a diet of fruits and vegetables. When a guest on a foreign world, he ate what was set before him.

Tonight, that meant a garnished roast of some kind of cultured meat—few worlds ate real animal anymore—seasoned with tongue-tingling spices, and side-dishes of local vegetables which tasted far better than their bland appearance implied. Dessert was what on Earth was known as a 'fool'—a concoction of whipped fruit and cream laced with a tart liqueur.

"I hope the food is satisfactory," Fogelsong inquired.

"If this is an incentive, it's a very good one," Hughes replied, patting his stomach.

"You're eager to know why I welcomed your arrival." Fogelsong directed the dining room staff—human, not robotic—to clear the dishes and depart. When the room was emptied, he said, "To put it concisely, a number of colonists have disappeared in a remote region."

Hughes blinked. It wasn't what he'd expected. "I'm an exobiologist," he protested. "Locating missing persons is hardly my sphere of expertise."

"We suspect that some kind of life-form may be responsible."

"Now that's more like it," Hughes said. He rested his elbows on the table. "Tell me more."

Victrix, who had been lying beside him enjoying a gourmet meal of her own, sat up and stared at Fogelsong.

<*Work?*>

<*Maybe,*> Hughes replied. <*Not just yet, though.*>

"Well," Fogelsong began, "here's what we know…"

Hughes pondered the administrator's words the next day as he and Victrix and one of Fogelsong's security officers, a young woman named Clare, who had a chiseled face, blonde hair, and the strapping build of a space marine, climbed out of a flyer some three hundred kilometers from Opportunity.

She wore the field uniform of the planetary security force and was slung about with weaponry—a sidearm, an energy rifle with both pulse and continuous fire modes, and others that Hughes didn't recognize. Rarely was he armed—although now was an exception—and when he was, he carried non-lethal weapons strictly for defense.

"Got enough firepower?" he asked.

She arched her eyebrows as she clipped a final item onto her utility belt. "The administrator would be remiss if he didn't take measures for your safety."

"I'm all for safety," Hughes replied, while thinking that said administrator had sent only a single officer and not a whole squad. "Right, Victrix?"

She wagged her tail.

"Do you really rely on a dog?" Clare asked skeptically.

"Best early warning system I've ever met."

Clare's raised eyebrows and pursed lips expressed her disbelief.

A narrow stream flowed sluggishly from between slumped hills.

Hughes followed its course with his eyes until the valley meandered out of sight.

"Here?" he asked.

Clare nodded. "An abandoned two-person flitter was found nearby. No trace of the occupants was ever discovered." She made a sweeping motion with her arm. "A search party similarly disappeared, as did several other people, all in this general vicinity."

"And nothing was ever found."

"No bones, no clothing, nothing."

"You'd think if there had been a natural accident, then there'd have been *some* traces."

"That's why we wonder if there might be a previously unidentified life-form." Her shoulders raised. "We hope that you—being an expert—might notice something that we missed."

"And we also hope that this isn't a suicide mission," Hughes commented dryly.

"The administrator fears that whatever it is may pose a threat to the colony," Clare replied, sidestepping his remark.

"It's a lot of territory to search," Hughes mused.

"Flyovers, both live and drone haven't spotted anything."

"Thermal scans…"

"Some false calls."

"Satellites?"

"Nothing."

"Have you tried biosensor equipped—"

"Believe me, we've tried," Clare interrupted with a curt nod.

"Well then," Hughes said. "We'll have to do it the old-fashioned way and walk. We'll do a loop, then return to the flyer. I don't want to spend the night without being close to it, just in case we have to get out of here in a hurry."

"I have no desire to be eaten, either," Clare said, stroking the rifle.

Hughes hoisted his day-pack. He motioned to Victrix. "Search, girl. Search!"

Victrix turned a tight circle, then headed up the stream, casting about in broad loops. Hughes and Clare followed.

"How will she know what to search for?" Clare asked.

"She doesn't, not specifically," Hughes said, "since we have no idea what we're looking for. But she'll alert to anything that catches her interest. Right now, she's just happy to be able to stretch her legs—she hates being cooped up on a spaceship almost as much as I do."

Hughes tuned into Victrix's emotions.

<Freedom! Ground to run on. Scents. Lots of new scents. Run.>

He grinned; some days he wished he were a dog.

The valley broadened, and ground-hugging vegetation yielded to patches of prehistoric-looking plants very similar to horsetails—still living on Earth, unchanged from the time of the dinosaurs. Animals, too small and quick for him to discern clearly, scuttled through the waving stems, ignored by Victrix after an initial inspection.

"Have you ever been off-world?" Hughes asked, making small talk.

Clare shook her head. "And I probably never will."

"No curiosity?"

"I'm gainfully employed, doing what I like," she replied stiffly.

"There are other security forces," Hughes said.

"I'm content. I have good prospects for advancement."

"Better a big fish in a small pond?"

"Something like that," she said in a tone that showed she didn't welcome further discussion. "And you…?"

"Chronic wanderlust," Hughes replied. "When I was young I dreamed about visiting every colonized world."

"Seriously?"

"Impossible, of course, especially with new worlds being constantly discovered…and, frankly, there are many I wouldn't want to visit."

"Like Last Chance?"

"It wasn't on my list," Hughes replied honestly if not diplomatically.

"It's not so bad," Clare replied in a more friendly manner. "There's beauty if you know where to look for it."

<Look! Something new!>

Hughes halted almost at the same moment that Victrix did, staring up a hillside.

"Up there," he pointed, sensing movement.

Clare activated her viewscope and studied the screen. "Tripeds," she said, handing the instrument to Hughes. "Harmless herbivores."

Hughes regarded the image. He judged the animals to be roughly sheep-sized, with short, lumpy muzzles and dirty-gray hide. More curiously, they had only a single front leg and two rear ones.

“If you want to see something interesting,” Clare suggested, “have Victrix go near them.”

Hughes regarded her with a moment’s skepticism, then sent to Victrix. <*Go check it out.*>

She bounded eagerly toward the distant animals. Hughes watched on the viewscope. The tripeds didn’t seem to scent or hear her approach until Victrix burst through the screen of horsetails. They scattered in all directions, but not by running—by bouncing. Their rear legs propelled them high in the air at roughly a forty-five degree angle and with considerable forward momentum. They touched the ground momentarily on all three legs before exploding upwards again.

Having achieved the desired effect, Victrix stopped and sat to watch the performance. How it appeared to the dog, Hughes couldn’t quite tell, the sensations he received from her being quite unusual—canine amusement—but it reminded him of a hailstorm with stones bouncing at every conceivable angle.

He chuckled. “Quite the show.”

“See. Last Chance has something worthwhile to watch.”

Hughes sent Victrix a mental command. <*Come back.*>

<*Now?*>

<*Yes.*>

<*Having fun!*>

<*We’re working.*>

<*“#$%&!!*>

Her displeasure obvious by the stiffness of her tail, Victrix trotted back.

“Where there are herbivores, there must be some kind of predator,” Hughes observed.

“Why…nothing,” Clare replied. “There are some small carnivores, but nothing big enough to take down a triped.”

“*Something* must eat them,” Hughes said. “They can’t all die of disease or injury.”

“Perhaps whatever it was went extinct, like Earth’s sabertooth cats.”

“Then why isn’t Last Chance swarming with tripeds? There’s enough vegetation to support larger numbers. No, Clare, something is thinning their ranks.”

"But if there's a creature that preys on them, why hasn't anyone observed it?"

"Perhaps they have," Hughes said slowly.

"Do you mean…?"

"It's a thought." Hughes glanced at the darkening sky. Last Chance's days were shorter than Earth's. "Let's have lunch and head back. In the morning we can bring the flyer and resume our search from here."

Despite its barren appearance, night on Last Chance wasn't quiet. Hughes never failed to be amazed at the range of sounds creatures could make. Squeaks, chirps, rustles, and noises virtually impossible to classify or describe filled the darkness. Some of them made his skin crawl.

Clare set up sensor arrays around the camp. Hughes was content with Victrix on guard. He trusted the dog's senses more than he trusted technological gadgets.

Still, he slept lightly in his sleeping pod and was glad when Last Chance's pallid sun dragged itself above the horizon.

After a breakfast of field rations they flew the flyer to where they'd seen the tripeds the previous day. The animals were nowhere in sight. But their tracks were.

<*Search,*> Hughes told Victrix. <*Find the tripeds.*> He visualized the furry bouncing creatures.

<*!!!!!*>

It wasn't hard to track them. The tripeds generally stuck to areas where horsetails flourished, and skirted rocky outcroppings. It was midmorning when they sighted the herd again, in a basin-like depression holding a murky lake.

Clare checked the coordinates. "It's not far from the last reported position of a wilderness hiker."

"We may be getting close," Hughes exclaimed. "I can feel it, can't you?"

"No," Clare shook her head. "And close to what?"

"Victrix can sense it, too," Hughes said, making eye contact with the dog, who was checking back in after making another scouting loop.

<*Something wrong. Something here.*>

"Maybe she's just picking up on your vibes," Clare suggested.

It was Hughes' turn to shake his head. "I don't think so."

They remained within visual range of the herd all afternoon, but the tripeds didn't seem inclined to venture far, merely ambling around the side of the lake. Victrix patrolled further away, but on Hughes' instructions was careful not to spook the browsing herbivores.

"It must be near here somewhere," Hughes mused.

"Why is that?" Clare asked.

"Because the tripeds like to congregate in this vicinity. See how low the vegetation has been grazed down? What better place for a predator than near its prey?"

"You're assuming there is a predator."

"Yes, but I think it's a reasonable assumption." Hughes rose and stretched. "Let's make our way back. Tomorrow, we'll start from here."

He tried to sleep that night, but once again fared poorly. His mind kept imagining scenarios of what they might find the next day. His restlessness disturbed Victrix, who normally slept snuggled beside him when on an expedition. He told himself sternly not to be afraid of monsters—but telling the conscious mind was one thing; trying to convince the subconscious was a harder task entirely.

His stomach still felt knotted with a mixture of excitement and anxiety as he and Clare started their search the next morning, parking the flyer beside the lake, which, Hughes had ascertained, contained nothing inimical to human or canine. Victrix took the opportunity for a swim in the chilly water, emerging to shake a spray of wet diamonds from her pelt.

<*Feels good! Come join!*>

<*No way. Too cold.*>

Another shake, then she barked at Hughes. <*Ready! Work?*>

"Alright," Hughes laughed, making a sweeping motion with his arm. "Go search."

The herd of tripeds had moved up the slopes of the basin to graze on some sort of low-growing reddish-green plant. A series of streams fed into the basin lake through various clefts around the circumference. Some tumbled down rocky escarpments, while others had gouged deeper channels for themselves.

<*Here!*>

Victrix barked again and headed up one such defile. Hughes paused to study the ground.

"Look," he said, "triped tracks going in—but not coming out."

Clare followed his pointing finger and pursed her lips. "Perhaps there's another way out."

"Perhaps," he agreed neutrally.

"You want to go up there?"

"Let's." He headed up the defile, but then Victrix was in front of him, facing upstream, her hackles raised and a low growl in her throat.

<*What is it?*> He asked.

<*Something bad up here!*>

<*What?*>

Hughes concentrated. All he could sense was a general unease, nothing specific—as if one predatory species was sensing another, like a wolf perceiving the presence of a mountain lion.

"What's up?" Clare asked.

"Victrix is detecting something," Hughes replied. "She's warning us."

Clare unslung her rifle. "I'm ready."

Hughes took a step forward and Victrix turned sideways to block his path.

<*No! Bad! Don't go!*>

Hughes crouched down to speak to her. "It's OK, girl. I know you don't like it, but that's the way we have to go."

He straightened, and Victrix reluctantly allowed him to proceed.

They walked cautiously, Clare with her rifle at the ready, Victrix with her tail up and nose to the ground.

"I wonder what the dog senses," she said.

Hughes frowned. "Could be a sound, could be a scent, could be a combination of things," he replied. "Dogs outclass us completely."

It was a fragrance that he noticed first, drifting down the valley on a light breeze. Honeysuckle. Or was it rose? Perhaps orange. Really, none of them, since nothing like those species grew on Last Chance.

"Do you smell it?"

Clare inhaled deeply. "It's wonderful. I've never smelled anything like it."

"I could enjoy it all day."

"I wonder why nobody's ever reported it before?" she mused.

Hughes shrugged. "Maybe it's something that only rarely blooms."

<*Wrong! Go back.*> Victrix fixed him with a pleading stare.

"Victrix is really concerned," he said to Clare.

The scent grew stronger as they progressed up the valley.

Victrix's emotions intensified. Suddenly, her hackles fully raised, she bounded away.

"Keep alert," Hughes cautioned. "Something's here."

The trickling stream rounded a bend, emerging from a small pond, surely a natural spring.

Hughes stopped and stared in amazement.

Growing beside the pond was the most gorgeous plant that he had ever seen. A thick stem, more like a trunk, of deep, vibrant chartreuse green ascended from a tangle of ropy roots toward a spread of branches from which hung a fringe of slender, silvery leaves swaying gently like a troupe of exotic dancers. Surmounting the fringe perhaps four meters above the ground, was a flower—a gigantic bloom of a deep, almost luminescent orange ringed by a sparkling rose-red border. Another spray of silver leaves shone like a halo above the blossom.

And the fragrance was almost overpowering…intoxicating…Hughes wanted nothing more than to plunge his face into the bloom and drink it in.

Nothing else mattered. Just the fragrance…the overwhelmingly lovely fragrance…

He took a step forwards.

Without warning, a heavy black form hit him full in the chest, driving him backwards and leveling him to the ground. A large paw on each shoulder pinned him. Confused, he stared into brown eyes just inches from his own.

"Victrix," he mumbled, "get off!"

The brown eyes burned into him. <*Bad! Very bad!*>

<*Don't be silly, it's only a plant.*>

<*Not!*>

Victrix's consciousness, on the borders of his own, thrust images towards him…

And suddenly, he *saw*…

And recoiled.

Victrix stepped away, off his chest, and Hughes scrambled to his feet.

The beautiful plant had vanished.

Where it had stood was a *thing*.

Not even his wildest nightmares had ever dredged up a monstrosity like that which writhed before him. Reflexively he lurched backwards, away from *it*.

It wasn't a plant at all. The roots were thick, squirming tentacles, and the trunk a bulbous body of a nauseating shade of greenish mud-brown, like something putrefying. The creature's rubbery skin crawled as if something wriggled just underneath. The fringe of silver leaves had changed into strands and sheets of mottled flesh. The divine fragrance had been replaced by a ghastly stench. And where the flower had been—a fang-ringed maw, dripping with some vile ooze.

Hughes gagged. His vision grayed, as the horror of the thing nearly overcame him.

<*Look!*>

Victrix tugged on his arm; he turned and saw Clare, her face rapturous, walking towards the creature. No, not walking, being drawn unresisting by some of the root-tentacles that had wrapped themselves around her lower legs and pulled her towards a frightful death.

"Clare!" he yelled.

She seemed not to hear him.

Hughes ran to her, grabbed the energy rifle from her nerveless hands, aimed at the base of the tentacles holding her, and fired.

Nothing happened.

He fired again, then belatedly realized that the weapon was configured to Clare's palmprint. He flung it away.

"Victrix!" he shouted. "Bite it!" He pointed to the 'root'. "Bite it!"

Victrix opened her jaws and clamped down with all the pressure of which a big German Shepherd was capable. Her teeth punctured the rubbery skin and crushed the underlying tissues. The tentacle convulsed and whipped away.

"No, wait!" Hughes ordered, as Victrix tensed to fling herself upon the thing.

The creature folded in upon itself, collapsing down with the mottled fringe outside until it looked like a tan-colored boulder, indistinguishable from the other rocks that littered the ground. The process took mere seconds.

Hughes wrapped his arms around Clare and hauled her away.

"No!" she cried. "Let me go!"

"Clare-"

"What have you done to it? Where's the plant?"

She was military-trained; she flung Hughes aside and headed toward the innocent-appearing boulder.

"Hold her, Victrix!" Hughes called, and the dog grasped the hem of Clare's pants and pulled back.

Hughes groped in his day-pack, pulled out a palm-sized neural tranquilizer, pointed it at Clare's back, and fired.

She jerked and crumpled limply to the ground.

Hughes let out a big breath.

With Victrix helping, he gripped her under both armpits and dragged her back the way they had come, until they were out of sight of the thing. He rested her with her back against a slope.

"Guard her," he told Victrix, then ran for the flyer. The creature appeared to be sessile in nature, bound to its location. He doubted it would follow them.

Panting in Last Chance's thin atmosphere, he reached the flyer. He sensed only calmness from Victrix; nothing was happening. He guided the flyer to where Victrix was standing guard over Clare, and, despite the dog's reassuring images, was relieved to find them both as he had left them. He hoisted Clare on board, waited for Victrix to jump in, and lifted the craft.

Only when they were safely away did he let out a big sigh of relief.

Clare regained consciousness as the flyer hummed its way over the undulating landscape. She studied Hughes with puzzled, disoriented eyes.

"What…where are we?"

"Heading back to Opportunity," Hughes replied. "What do you remember?"

"We saw the most amazing, beautiful plant. And then…nothing." She rubbed her forehead.

"Got a headache?"

She nodded.

"Sorry about that," Hughes said. "I had to hit you with a neuraltranq." He motioned to Victrix. "Get the med box, there's a good girl."

The shepherd wriggled to the back of the craft and returned with the desired kit. Hughes removed a cranial calmer, activated it, and handed it to Clare. "Hold this against your temple for two minutes."

"What happened back there?" she asked.

"They say a picture is worth a thousand words," Hughes replied. "So let me show you." He touched a series of sensorpads and a screen illuminated. "I did a visual memory download while you were still unconscious. This is what I saw."

The screen showed the beautiful plant with its silver fringes and giant orange blossom.

"But that's not what it looked like!" Clare exclaimed.

"I wondered," Hughes said. "How did it appear to you?"

"It was more like…like a circlet of purple blossoms. And the leaves weren't silver, they were broad and olive with golden veining."

"Interesting." He touched the screen. "Here's what Victrix saw."

The picture changed to that of the ghastly creature with its fanged maw and grasping tentacles, as seen from a dog's low perspective and less vibrant color vision.

Clare gasped. "It's…it's impossible!"

"Victrix saved me by breaking the spell it had over me. Together we rescued you from being its dinner."

The scene changed again to show the creature from Hughes' viewpoint, Victrix attacking it, and then the thing collapsing into a defensive state.

"Incredible!" Clare shuddered.

"That's what it looks like when it's not actually feeding," Hughes said. "Easy to miss, eh?"

Clare set down the cranial calmer. "I don't understand—how could we see such very different things?"

"The fragrance, I'm sure, has a hallucinogenic effect—such compounds are very common in nature. But I also suspect that there's another factor—a direct telepathic effect, a natural type of mind control which gave us an irresistible desire to approach the thing."

Clare whistled.

"A very effective, double-pronged lure affecting both the senses and the mind," Hughes continued. "We were fortunate to have Victrix along, otherwise we'd have been the next pair of missing persons."

Clare frowned. "But why was she immune?"

"I thought about that. Here's my best hypothesis. What's the creature's main prey?"

"The tripeds."

"Exactly. Herbivores."

Clare considered that. "While dogs are carnivores."

"Right," Hughes said. "The creature wouldn't want to attract other carnivores which may have once existed on Last Chance that could potentially harm it. Only herbivores like the tripeds, which don't put up much of a fight—their natural instinct, as you showed me, is to flee, not fight."

"And humans—"

"Are omnivores—part herbivore, part carnivore,—but herbivorous enough to be affected and be drawn toward the creature."

"It's a good thing Victrix wasn't deceived," Clare said.

Hughes nodded. "See why I trust her?"

"Did you kill it?" Clare asked.

Hughes appeared shocked. "Of course not! It's an absolutely unique life form. I've never encountered anything like it before."

"A very dangerous life form."

"Now that we're aware of its existence, preventive measures can be developed—warning beacons, the area cordoned off. Later, perhaps an antidote to the fragrance, possibly something to disrupt the mental effect. We don't know how many of the creatures there are. It must be studied, not destroyed. And I shall tell Administrator Fogelsong exactly that."

"At first, it was *so* beautiful," Clare said.

"They say that even the devil can appear as an angel of light," Hughes replied.

<*Food?*> Victrix interrupted with a whine.

"In a little while, girl." Hughes rubbed Victrix's muzzle.

"What does she want?" Clare asked.

"Dinner," Hughes answered.

"That's not exactly on my mind at the moment."

Hughes smiled. "I must admit that I'm a bit peckish, too."

"Well then, you must make a special one for her," Clare said. "She earned it."

Victrix rested one paw on his arm and the other on Clare's and barked.

"She wants us to fly faster," Hughes said.

"Seriously?" Clare looked from him to her. "You're kidding me."

Hughes upped the flyer's speed.

"Aren't you?"

The drab orb that was Last Chance dwindled on the viewscreen as *Wolf-1* headed outsystem. Despite his initial reluctance to visit the isolated world, Hughes was glad he'd come. It wasn't every day one got to discover an entirely new—and weirdly different—life form. That was what he liked about roaming the colonized worlds—the lure of the unexpected, even if it turned out to be dangerous.

Administrator Fogelsong had expressed his gratitude by draping a medal around Victrix's neck as she sat proudly in his office, and presenting her with an immense assortment of treats—chews and biscuits and a rubbery item made from a local tuber that she found irresistible.

"After all," he'd said, "she's the one we *really* have to thank."

<*For Victrix?*> she asked, staring at the assortment.

<*Yes, all yours.*>

<*!!!!!*>

Fogelsong's eyes had twinkled as he said, "But I'm grateful to you too, of course." He handed Hughes a computer wafer. "Here's a substantial donation to your organization. I'm sure that WOLF can find a good use for it."

"We certainly can," Hughes replied. "And if it's acceptable to you, I'm going to have one of my teams assist your researchers to investigate the creature thoroughly and do a complete planetary survey to determine how many more of them there may be."

"By all means," Fogelsong agreed. "And if you're ever in the neighborhood…"

Hughes had smiled. "I'll drop in."

And he would.

DOG IS MY WITNESS

The pads on his temples were cool, as was the voice that spoke to him from behind, just out of sight. He struggled, but the stasis field held him immobile; he could breathe and speak, move his eyes, but no more.

"It will go much easier on you if you cooperate," the voice said.

"I will tell you nothing," he gritted, straining against his invisible bonds until his face purpled.

"You need not speak," the voice continued. "Just remember. Only that."

"No."

"Bring to mind what has passed."

"I will not." And he forced down memories that threatened to bubble to the surface of his consciousness. Sport. He thought of that.

"You have been judged guilty," his interrogator persisted. "You are ordered to disclose—"

"I deny the authority of the tribunal," he replied.

An exhaled breath. "Your denial is irrelevant. What matters is that if you don't cooperate you risk sustaining permanent injury."

"I am not going to cooperate with you or anyone else!"

"It is noted that you have been warned. The consequences are your own fault."

The pads grew warmer, and he felt a tickle inside his brain.

Think of something—anything else—he told himself, and imagined setting a pack of hungry wolf-ravens on his unknown captor to claw flesh and rend bone until nothing remained but a mound of bloody pulp.

"It won't help," the voice told him. "Bring to mind the missing."

"I…will…not…" he said, as the tickle intensified, making him squirm inside.

How had they found him? How crept up on him unawares as he reclined in his suite, enjoying the panorama of space outside the clearsteel windows? How encased him in a stasis field before he even realized he was no longer alone?

Staff. It had to be one of the staff. Tsujii. Or perhaps his nosey neighbor…what was his name…?

He tried to shout for help, but received only a matter of fact reply.

"Your suite is sound-proof," the voice said. "As you yourself made certain."

"Someone will come!"

"No one will come. You requested utmost privacy for the remainder of the day."

"My dog—"

"Is shut in the bedroom. A very cute, friendly dog. Hardly the guarding type."

He knew then that he was doomed. All that was left was his will to resist. It would do no good. But yet, he wouldn't yield, wouldn't give his captor the satisfaction.

"Don't fight. Relax and give in."

The tickle intensified, growing stronger the more he fought against it, as if it wrapped tendrils around his brain, penetrating deeper and deeper.

"Remember the past," the voice urged. "Visualize it."

"Never!" he gasped. "Never."

"I'd rather not cause you any permanent harm, despite who you are."

"I'd…like to…kill…you…"

"As you killed so many others?"

He almost fell for it. Almost remembered.

"Go to the devil!"

A sigh. "Then you leave me no choice. Remember them. Where are they? Where are they?"

Colors surged through his mind, and it was if his brain exploded in a fiery supernova, and his scream plummeted into a whirling black hole to be distorted out of all recognition.

Even though he knew the colors of the nebula shimmering outside the wall-sized window were computer-enhanced, Hughes could gaze at them for hours, lost in towering black pillars, coruscating streaks of scarlet, twinkling gold highlights, and mysterious emerald swirls. Besides delighting his eyes, the sight helped distract him from the annoying discomfort of his regenerating leg.

He reached down to rub it.

At least, thanks to the miracle of modern medicine, he had a leg. It was even more of a miracle that he was still alive. What would have happened if he had died?

Contemplating the possibilities made him shiver. Raghallach II received very few visitors—he himself probably would never have gone there had it not been for a frantic call from a marine researcher who'd contracted a nasty parasite from the cephalopod-like creatures he'd been studying. Who knew how long it might have been before someone took an interest in the orbiting *Wolf-1*?

Would Sofi have detected his demise and flown *Wolf-1* to a civilized world, or would that have been beyond her programming, in which case would Victrix still be alone on *Wolf-1*, waiting patiently for someone to find her…or until she too died?

She was curled up in front of the window, tail over her nose, oblivious to the scene behind her. Despite being genetically augmented, the beauties of space were still beyond her capacity to understand and appreciate.

Hughes wiggled his toes before realizing that he didn't have any yet—the regeneration process hadn't reached that far. He would though, in time. Regeneration was worth the discomfort.

He hoped, however, that he would never have to repeat the experience…

Hughes had barely noticed it at first, just a faint pinprick above his right ankle followed by itching. Crawling up his leg was a hair-thin yellow worm, no longer than an inch, that must have slipped inside his boot while he and Victrix were exploring one of the marshlands on Raghallach II's soggy island archipelago.

Obviously, the repellent he'd applied hadn't worked.

"God help me," he murmured, dislodging the worm with a flick of his finger. It fell onto the deck plate, and he ground it beneath his boot heel.

In seconds, the bite site swelled, blistered, and darkened. The pinprick became a searing pain, and he broke out in a sweat.

He sensed Victrix's sudden tension, responding to his own, and glanced at his companion, seated, as usual, in the shuttle's copilot's seat.

<*Something wrong?*>

"It'll be close, old girl," he said through clenched teeth. "I wish you could pray."

They'd just lifted off from the planet and broken through a haze of light cloud cover. Above lay space and *Wolf-1* in orbit.

The spot on his leg was already palm-sized and purple-black with necrosis, spreading even as he watched. The reaper worm contained the most powerful cytotoxic agent ever discovered. He'd be dead in a few agonizing minutes unless its progress could be stopped. There was no time to land and seek medical help. He'd have to do it himself. If he could make it to *Wolf-1*...

He hit the shuttle controls, overriding the autopilot, and accelerating with g-stress that made his head swim and Victrix whine with discomfort.

"Warning, Dr. Hughes," Sofi said. "Acceleration is beyond normal parameters. Recommend you re-engage autopilot."

"Negative," he gasped.

The blackness was half-way to his knee.

And the sky lost its blueness and became an ebony field of stars. One of them was *Wolf-1*.

His leg felt as if it was being sawn from his body...

He bit his lip to keep from screaming.

"Dr. Hughes! You're closing too quickly!" Sofi's sharp voice jerked him back.

He was closer to *Wolf-1* than he realized. He'd kill them both flying as he was with his vision blurring and his guts knotted in a spasm.

"Sofi, initiate reverse thrust and resume autopilot for docking..."

"Affirmative, Dr. Hughes."

The shuttle slowed, and there was the familiar shape of *Wolf-1* filling the viewscreen.

He was out the hatch as soon as the shuttle slid inside the docking bay, staggering along the corridor toward the emergency medical cubicle as quickly as he was able, every step a torment, the Earth-normal gravity feeling impossibly heavy. Only one arm against the wall kept him upright. Victrix trotted alongside, her anxiety washing over him.

<Help?>

"I wish you could, girl."

The blackness was to mid-thigh, the dead flesh sloughing off in chunks. He glimpsed the white of bone.

He collapsed on the medical bed.

"Sofi, activate the robodoc."

"Systems are on-line, Dr. Hughes. Please state the procedure."

His vision grayed and his chest muscles contracted. He was going into shock. Terminal shock.

"Emergency…amputation…right…leg…at…at…" he gasped before running out of air.

Dimly, he heard Victrix whimper, felt her tongue on his cheek, and registered the hum of instruments warming up. An oxygen mask came down over his nose and mouth, and a mechanical arm positioned itself above his own.

"What location on the leg, Dr. Hughes?"

He took a gasping breath. "Proximal…femur…Initiate."

He couldn't utter another word. It was hard enough to think. *God be merciful to me, a sinner…*

The transparent door of the cubicle slid shut. He met Victrix's worried eyes one last time. They expanded into fuzzy spheres, and then the world and the pain faded and vanished.

He awoke, groggy, to find a pair of brown eyes gazing at him. It took a moment for him to realize that they belonged to Victrix, sitting on the opposite side of a transparent partition, and another moment for his mind to recall where he was and what had happened. He pushed himself to a sitting position, and the cubicle door slid open. Victrix's cold nose nuzzled against him, and he bent over to hug her.

<Victrix happy!>

"I told you it would be close," he said, his throat dry.

Only then did he look down at what remained of his right leg. The robodoc had done a neat job, he had to admit, studying the stump—the very short stump. He felt no pain, only the strange sensation that there should be *something* there.

He visualized a crutch and pointed to a storage cabinet. "Fetch it for me, there's a girl."

Victrix trotted over, pawed the cabinet's sensorpad and dragged the requested item—primitive, but still useful—to him.

Hughes slid the crutch under his armpit and made it to a standing position where he wobbled briefly before regaining his equilibrium. Then, followed by Victrix, he ambulated slowly to the flight deck, and eased gingerly into the command seat.

"Right," he said, "let's get out of here."

But where to?

"Sofi, please list the medical facilities with regeneration capability in Sector 15 alpha."

"Certainly, Dr. Hughes. My records indicate that Indrani, Svartkel, Saeger III, and Annali Station possess the requisite facilities."

"Annali Station," Hughes said after a moment's consideration. "Just the place to recuperate. Sofi, set course for Annali Station. Tach-7. Initiate."

"Confirmed and initiated, Dr. Hughes."

"How does a quiet holiday on a resort satellite appeal to you?" he asked Victrix, forming mental pictures as he spoke.

<*Swim?*>

<*Maybe.*>

<*!!!!*>

"Sofi, please make contact with Annali Station and arrange for priority regeneration." He listed the instructions.

"Yes, Dr. Hughes. I will advise you when confirmed."

He levered himself out of the command seat, even this minimal exertion draining his energy. But there was one more thing to do before going to his quarters and napping.

In the design of *Wolf-1* he'd made sure to incorporate a small chapel where he could pray.

<*Hungry.*>

Victrix's thought broke in on him as he made his way slowly along the corridor.

Two things.

He laughed. "It's been a while since you've eaten, hasn't it, girl? All right. Let me make you something special."

When she was happily munching on her kibble, he returned to the chapel.

He couldn't very well use the prie-dieu, so he perched on a chair, crossed himself, and thanked God for his narrow escape.

A voice emerged from the swirling supernova of distorted colors and sensations, repetitive, insistent.

"Where are all those who vanished? What did you do with their bodies? Where are they? Where are they?"

He forced himself to respond, to resist. "I have nothing to say."

"Picture them," the voice demanded. "See them being led away."

"It was necessary. They were useless."

"No one is useless. Where are they? Where are they?"

Annali Station had begun life as an astronomical observatory some two hundred years previously. No trace of that original structure remained; instead, the station had evolved into a massive upscale resort providing virtually all the amenities one could wish for off-world, while in sight of a stunningly beautiful nebula.

More than that, it was a world in its own right, maintaining a neutrality that was observed by all of the frequently squabbling clusters of colonized planets. It was an oasis of calm in the hubbub of human-occupied space.

Lacking close neighbors, Annali Station had to rely on its own resources as much as possible; hence the first-class medical facilities.

Leaving *Wolf-1* on station-keeping, Hughes and Victrix approached Annali by shuttlecraft. He had to admit he'd never seen anything comparable. An immense central torus was surrounded by a cloud of spherical modules connected by transparent tunnels. Lights sparkled everywhere; the station glowed like a cluster of miniature suns.

The shuttle docked in one of the larger spheres. The hatch slid aside to reveal an attractive, vaguely Oriental young woman with pale blue hair wearing a glamorous, skin-tight silver uniform—more of a shoulderless gown—bearing an official logo.

"Welcome to Annali Station, Dr. Hughes," she said in a mellifluous voice. "My name is Tsujii. I'll be your personal hostess."

"Very pleased to meet you," Hughes replied. "This is Victrix."

She acknowledged the dog with a nod. "Your suite in a Companion Animal Section is all ready," Tsujii said. "I have a transport chair for you."

"I'm sure I can make it-"

"Your comfort is our priority," she replied, the firmness of her tone indicating she wasn't going to accept any refusal. "I'll escort you to your suite. Your initial appointment in Regen is scheduled for 0300 hours station time."

"Excellent." He eased into the chair, and positioned the crutch across his lap.

"This way, please," Tsujii motioned with a slender hand, and strode along a spotless corridor.

With Victrix trotting happily alongside, his repulsor-mounted chair floated along until they reached a moving walkway leading away from the docking bay.

"This is your first time at Annali?" Tsujii inquired.

Hughes nodded. "I've often considered a vacation here, but this," he pointed to his stump, "made it acutely necessary."

"I'm sorry for your accident."

"It could have been worse."

They entered one of the transparent tunnels and for a short while seemed to be suspended in space.

"This is Module C-3," Tsujii said as they entered one of the spheres. "You're in Level 26, suite 974. There's a directory and map in your room. Transport personnel will arrive at 0245 to take you to your appointment."

"You're very efficient," Hughes said, and Tsujii inclined her head.

"We aim to be both efficient and personal."

The entrance level of the sphere was a tropical garden, ringed by palm trees and bamboo, and festooned with flowers. A fountain leaped from a sparkling pond. People relaxed on padded benches, hammocks, or just sprawled on a carpet of lush grass. An elderly couple walked with a Gordon Setter along a winding footpath, and a young boy wrestled with a Labrador puppy.

<*Play ball?*> Victrix asked.

<*Not just yet. But we will.*>

"Pardon me?" Tsujii asked.

Hughes hadn't realized he'd spoken out loud as well as telepathically. "Victrix wants to play ball," he said.

"There's an exercise garden on Level 25," Tsujii said. "Plenty of room for a big dog to stretch her legs. A lake, as well."

<*Lake? Swim?*>

<*Yes. Every day.*>

<*!!!!*>

Judging by the ease with which Victrix was prancing alongside, Hughes guessed the gravity to be slightly less than Earth standard. Victrix would love it.

His eyes slid over a young couple embracing in an arbor, and an elderly man grooming a Bichon lying on its back beside him.

And then he saw her.

"Please halt," he said to Tsujii.

The woman was in her mid thirties, he surmised, a little shy of six feet tall, moving with an easy, athletic gait. Her long hair was neither blond nor red, but somewhere in-between, and her face was finely featured. She wore a powder blue track suit that perfectly suited her slender figure.

"Who is that?" he asked.

"I'll introduce you," Tsujii replied.

"No, wait—" Hughes protested, suddenly flustered, but he was too late. Tsujii had already approached the woman and was leading her toward him.

"Dr. Hughes, may I present Miss Madeleine Dickson."

Hughes attempted to rise, but Tsujii pushed him firmly back. The lack of his leg made Hughes feel uncomfortably awkward.

"Miss Dickson is a writer," Tsujii was saying, "working on an article about some of the celebrities we welcome to Annali."

"I'm not a—" Hughes began, but Tsujii had turned to the woman. "Dr. Hughes is the founder of *WOLF*, Wellness for Other Life Forms. He's a space-vet."

"Exobiologist—"

"I'm glad to make your acquaintance, Dr. Hughes," Dickson said, extending a shapely hand.

"Just call me Hughes," he said, taking it briefly.

Her friendly smile revealed a row of perfect, white teeth. "Leina."

"Dr. Hughes will be with us for a while," Tsujii said. "Perhaps…"

"If you're willing, I'd love to talk to you," Leina said.

"I'm not much of a story," Hughes said, "but perhaps over dinner one day…? As you can see, I'm not all here at the moment."

She laughed. "Whenever you're ready. And your beautiful dog, too."

Hughes realized he hadn't been paying attention to Victrix's emotions. He trusted the dog's instincts. At the moment, Victrix was registering only positive feelings.

<*Nice lady.*>

"Call me," Leina said.

"Will do," Hughes said as she strolled away.

"Do you know—" he began.

"Her contact information will be in your suite," Tsujii said.

"You've done this before," Hughes said.

"Your pleasure is our pleasure," Tsujii replied.

As he expected, the first regeneration session was the worst—an evaluation followed by an excruciating period to establish the regeneration pattern. After that, his days rapidly developed a routine. When his sessions were over—and each day he noticed his new leg was a little bit longer—he took Victrix to the park deck for long play sessions. There was also plenty of time to catch up on reading, and sometimes even to simply relax and listen to music while looking at the stars.

And socialize.

It was on his fourth day that he placed a call to Leina Dickson and arranged to meet her, a rendezvous that took place in the restaurant on the top level of his companion animal sphere, in a circular room whose domed clearsteel roof gave the impression that there was nothing between them and the stars. Victrix curled up on a raised, cushioned platform by his side, while Leina sat across from him.

Her long hair was pulled back into a bun secured by a clasp inlaid with polished stones. She wore a ruby and diamond ring on her right ring finger; nothing on her left.

"Tell me where you're from," Hughes requested, after greetings had been exchanged, orders placed, and fluted glasses of an exotic, orange-pink drink delivered. "I can't quite place your accent." He knew better than to guess; some people, he'd learned, could be offended by a wrong guess.

"My remote ancestry is Swiss," she replied. "But I'm from Winfryd."

Hughes frowned in thought. "That's one of the Alliance Worlds, isn't it?"

"The capital planet, in fact."

"I've never visited the Alliance."

She smiled. "You, I gather, are Earth-born."

Hughes nodded. "British Isles."

"I've never been to Earth."

"That makes us even, then." He raised his glass. "A toast, to interworld harmony."

"And its local application," she added.

He noticed that she wore a gold chain around her neck, and wondered what was on the end of it.

"Will you be here long?" he asked.

She shrugged. "Until I have the information I need."

"When do you want to start grilling me?"

"The food hasn't arrived, so how about now?" She held up a hand. "But start from the beginning. Tell me how you came to found *WOLF*."

"I always had an interest in animals," Hughes began. "I think I was born with it. But my concern really started when I was about ten, and my best friend had a gahiji."

"A what?" she asked, sipping her drink.

"Gahiji are a mammalian species, native to Gudruna. They look sort of like flying rabbits, but they eat small rodents, and they're much smarter than rabbits. There was a short-lived craze for having them as pets facilitated by a loophole in certain regulations. The problem was, their biology wasn't well understood, and most of them died fairly soon."

"That's a shame."

"My friend's gahiji died, too. Just withered away. We were both heartbroken. Had a funeral in the back yard. But I decided I'd become an exobiologist and try to help all these creatures taken from their homeworlds. Because, you know, no matter how many laws are passed, people always find a way to get their hands on exotic pets. Most of them suffer from being removed from their native habitats."

"Some can be dangerous, too, I expect," Leina said.

"It's not only the animals themselves that suffer," Hughes agreed. "Eventually I discovered other people who shared my concerns. And so WOLF was born."

He went on to tell her how he'd created WOLF. How he'd rapidly discovered he had no aptitude for administration, so while retaining the title of 'president' and remaining the public face of WOLF, he delegated the running of the organization to staff on Earth.

"And so I just wander the inhabited worlds," he said, pointing to the starfield above them, "going wherever someone—or some creature—needs my services."

"Alone?" she asked.

"Not quite. I have Victrix." He suddenly realized where her question was leading. "I'm not married," he said, "although there were a couple of close calls in my younger years. But I was busy founding WOLF, and since then, always being on the move hasn't helped."

"I imagine not."

A server brought their meals, including a special plate for Victrix, which he laid on the shelf in front of her.

Hughes whistled at the sight of the layers of synthmeat. "Quite the spread. Don't get used to it, Victrix."

<Food!!!>

She began to wolf it down.

His own plate, he noticed with dismay, was somewhat less impressive, consisting of a mound of something resembling mashed potatoes veined with carrot-colored strands. It was not what he'd ordered; obviously the restaurant computers had been pre-programmed to ignore his wishes and instead provide him with the light but nutritionally complete diet the medics ordered.

"A blessing?" Hughes inquired, glancing at Leina whose artificial seafood plate looked much more appealing. She nodded, and he said grace.

Then, "You've heard about me. Tell me about Leina Dickson."

She motioned with her fork after skewing something dripping with a golden sauce and popping it in her mouth. "Well, I'm sure I haven't traveled as much as you—mostly among the Alliance Worlds. Right now, I'm working on stories about Annali Station, as you know. The Station would like to attract more business from the Alliance."

"And is there anyone…"

"Back home?" She gave a light laugh. "No. My parents tell me I'm too picky."

"Nothing wrong with that. What's Winfryd like?"

"A very lovely planet with an interesting history…"

Dinner vanished surprisingly quickly; wrapped up in conversation, Hughes could barely remember what he'd eaten; Annali Station's chefs were renowned for the quality of their creations, and he hoped that his restrictions would soon be lifted.

"Join me for Victrix's evening playtime?" he asked.

She agreed, and together they visited the park deck, Leina walking, Hughes in his transport chair. Victrix headed straight for the lake.

"You're a runner?" he asked, watching Victrix plunge into the water and swim across the lake and back. She picked up a ball and trotted over with it.

"What makes you ask?" Leina replied, throwing Victrix's ball, and watching the black dog sprint for it, throwing off a spray of glistening water droplets.

"You have that build," Hughes said.

"I won the Winfryd Alliance Marathon three years straight," she said proudly.

"That's incredible," Hughes acknowledged. "There must have been thousands of competitors."

"It's a popular run, attracting about 50,000 runners each time. I've probably lost a step since then," Leina said, "but I still like to run as often as I can, when work allows."

"That's why you're not married," Hughes teased. "The men can't keep up with you."

"Maybe when you have a new leg, you'll give it a try," Leina said playfully.

He grinned. "Maybe so."

Victrix returned with her ball. Leina threw it several more times—getting some good distance, Hughes noted.

"She'd keep you here all night," Hughes said. He yawned. "I hate to leave, but I'd best call it a day. Get plenty of rest, the medics said. Regen takes a lot out of you."

"I understand. Thank you for a wonderful evening."

"My pleasure," Hughes said. "Perhaps tomorrow I can tell you some stories from my work with WOLF."

"I'd love to hear them," Leina said, taking a path that diverged from Hughes'. "See you tomorrow."

How long had it been? How long had the voice been prompting, insisting, cajoling? How long, in this condition where time had no meaning…?

"What happened to the leaders who escaped? Where did they go? Where are they?"

"I know nothing!" He was weakening.

"You know everything. You gave the orders."

"My actions were justified!"

"They were wrong."

"I refuse to answer."

"Where are they? Where are they?"

A week passed, a week in which his leg grew noticeably, to the point where he was able to trade the transport chair for a robotic brace. Also growing were his feelings for Leina, with whom he dined on a nightly basis—and enjoying more once his restrictions were lifted. To a naturally cautious and somewhat reticent man, the turn of events was a surprise—although a pleasant one.

He told her of his life on Earth and in space, and from her he learned much of the Alliance Worlds.

She arrived late to dinner one night, looking slightly disheveled.

"Sorry I'm late," she said. "A call from home."

"Nothing bad, I hope."

"No. In fact it was expected news."

He raised his eyebrows, but she didn't seem inclined to elaborate, and he didn't press her. Her necklace had become dislodged, however, and he saw that she wore a small crucifix. He commented on it.

"A confirmation gift from my parents," she replied, and that gave them more to talk about.

Porters were moving luggage into the adjacent suite the next day when he returned from his morning regen session. Curious as to whom the new neighbor might be, Hughes loitered in the corridor until Tsujii appeared, accompanying a short, paunchy, man carrying a small white dog. A fellow of some self-importance, Hughes judged, from the newcomer's fawn-colored designer clothing, and heavy gold rings. His cheeks were jowly, and his hair and moustache silver-gray.

"Hughes," he introduced himself. He indicated his door. "Your neighbor."

The man studied him with closely-spaced blue-gray eyes that should have twinkled, but didn't. "Stanislav Tomik," he said finally, making no move to shake hands.

"Cute dog," Hughes said. "Maltese?"

"Yes."

"May I pet him?" Hughes asked.

"No." The man pulled the dog away. "He doesn't like it."

"Sorry," Hughes replied. "What's his name?"

"Felix."

"Are you staying here long?"

"If I like it," Tomik said. "Good day." He turned and entered his suite.

Hughes rolled his eyes at Tsujii, whose expression of calm professionalism didn't change.

"Well, *I* like it here," he said.

She replied with a nod and a smile.

He dismissed the man from his mind, and went into his own suite, where Victrix was eagerly waiting for him.

He spotted the man later, walking his dog, as he was taking Victrix to the recreation deck. His attention was diverted, though, by the sight of Leina jogging; too far off to call to her, he noticed only that she slowed when passing Tomik, then disappeared behind a clump of trees. He hurried as fast as his braced leg would allow, but by the time he reached the far side of the trees, she had already disappeared. Tomik was still there; Hughes waved to him, receiving a cursory response.

He thought that Leina seemed distracted at dinner that night. Perhaps the stress of writing, he supposed. Maybe she had a deadline approaching. It wasn't his place to pry, and she didn't respond to the hints he threw out.

Tomik was leaving his suite as Hughes approached his own.

"Mr. Tomik," he greeted.

"Hughes."

"I'm from Earth," Hughes said, wondering if it was possible to entice the man into small talk. "How about you?"

There was the fraction of hesitation before the man replied, "Andersen's Landing."

"And Felix?"

"Him too."

Tomik walked away.

Hughes watched him go, then, thoughtfully, entered his suite. He wasn't all that great on accents. But he'd bet a bottle of fine wine that Tomik was never from Andersen's Landing. Not that it mattered. Many people preferred to keep the details of their personal lives confidential.

"I have a new neighbor," he said to Leina over dessert the next day. "You probably noticed him when you were jogging. Older guy with a moustache and a white Maltese."

She nodded. "I've seen him. What's he like?"

"A man of few words," Hughes replied. "Told me he was from Andersen's Landing, though I doubt it. Probably some harmless old coot who doesn't want his wife to know where he is."

She chewed a finger nail.

"Something wrong?" Hughes asked.

She dropped her gaze. "I may have to leave soon. Possibly as early as tomorrow."

Hughes laid down his spoon. "I had this fantasy, that, you know…that you'd be here until my regeneration was complete."

"No…I have commitments back home."

"I understand about commitments," Hughes said.

Her blue eyes were troubled, he thought, as she looked up to meet his gaze.

"Some are harder to keep than others," she said, then forced a smile. "But we still have tonight. There's a chamber music concert in Sphere A2…"

"It just so happens that I'm free," Hughes said. "May I escort you?"

"If Victrix won't mind."

"She will. But I'll make it up to her."

There was nothing, nothing but the voice intruding into every crevice of his mind.

"Where are those transported offworld to supposed exile? Why is there no record of them being landed anywhere? Where are they? Where are they?"

He struggled to maintain his defenses. "I…say…nothing…"

"Picture them. Picture them."

Despite his efforts, images came to his mind, slipping through cracks in his resistance and then darting away. He was aware of them, but couldn't prevent them. He cursed himself for his weakness; cursed even more his interrogator.

Hughes slept poorly that night, unable to keep from thinking about Leina leaving. How could the days have passed so quickly? His teenage years were long gone—but he certainly felt like one.

Victrix woke him up earlier than usual with what he assumed was an urgent need. Not only could she physically whine, she could mentally whine as well.

"You know where the deck is," he grumbled. "Take yourself there."

<Come with.>

<Not now.>

<COME WITH!>

There was no arguing with her, he knew. She'd stare him into submission—and often, he'd learned, there was a reason for her demands.

<*All right.*>

He pulled on a jumpsuit, applied his walking brace, and followed her into the corridor. She loped away, and he hurried to catch up.

Rounding the corner, he almost tripped over her. She had halted and was watching Tomik pacing aimlessly. The man wore a curious expression, both puzzled and blank at the same time.

Victrix glanced at Hughes, then back to Tomik.

<*See? Strange.*>

"Is something wrong?" Hughes asked.

Tomik peered. "Who are you?"

"Your neighbor, of course," Hughes replied.

"No. You're one of *them*."

"One of whom?"

"Get away from me." Tomik backed up.

Hughes spread his hands. "If that's what you want."

Tomik glared at Victrix. "Is that your dog?"

"Yes," Hughes said.

"Take it away."

"Where's your dog?"

"I don't have one. I don't like dogs."

"But, Felix…?"

Tomik's expression was uncomprehending.

Hughes shrugged. "If you'll let us past, we'll be on our way."

Tomik backed against the wall, watching them warily.

"Come, Victrix," Hughes said. He studied Tomik as he walked by; the man was pale, but faint pink circles marked his temples—so faint that most people wouldn't have noticed them.

What could have caused them?

Once he was out of sight of the man, he activated the internal commlink he'd been given and called Tsujii.

"I found Mr. Tomik wandering in the hall," he said. "He seemed confused."

"A medical team will be sent immediately," she replied. "Is he drunk?"

"I didn't smell alcohol," Hughes said. Still, there were any number of illegal drugs that people used to scramble their brains. "It might be a medication reaction. Or maybe he had a stroke."

"We'll take care of him," Tsujii said, and signed off.

He was to meet Leina for breakfast, so after taking Victrix to the exercise deck, he made his way to a cafe situated with a view over Annali Station's multiple spheres.

Leina joined him shortly, looking tired, he thought, dark circles rimming her eyes.

"You didn't sleep well?" he asked.

"Hardly at all."

"Neither did I."

They ordered fruit.

"I'll be leaving later today," Leina said, picking listlessly at her meal. "I'm sorry, Hughes. I wish I could stay longer, but…"

"I was afraid of that," Hughes replied, not very hungry himself. "Not before lunch, I hope."

She shook her head. "I have some matters to attend to this morning, but we can still have lunch together."

Hughes gave a crooked smile. "When you're gone, I won't have anyone to talk to except my neighbor—speaking of whom, I found him wandering the corridor acting strangely this morning."

"Strangely? How?"

"He didn't know who I was. Acted quite paranoid, in fact. Thought that I was after him. I called Tsujii, who was going to have the medics take a look at him. I doubt they'll tell me what they find, though."

"Probably not," Leina agreed. "I'd expect them to be very discreet."

"Most cases of sudden memory loss or paranoia have a psychiatric basis or are drug induced," Hughes said. "But let's not spend our limited time talking about him."

"Let's not."

Their conversation ranged over running and music. But Hughes couldn't help but think about Tomik. It was only after he parted from Leina that he realized what the pink circles on the man's temples might represent.

He didn't think a brain could burn—but it did—the more he fought, trying to restrain the elusive images, the more it burned.

"You must cooperate!"

"I will not!"

"This is your last chance. After that…"

"Let me go! LET ME GO!"

"Where are they? Where are they?"

"They had to be removed. They HAD to. They deserved it. They opposed me."

"What did you do with them?"

He could resist no longer. With a blaze of flame, the final bastions of his resistance disintegrated. He spoke things he had vowed never—ever—to reveal.

Victrix halted outside Tomik's suite and tugged on Hughes's cuff.

"Next room, girl," Hughes said.

Victrix wouldn't budge. She stared at the closed door and barked.

<*Go in.*>

"He's not there. He's in the medical center."

<*Go in.*> Her thought was stronger.

A picture flashed into his mind. A Maltese.

"Of course!" he slapped himself on the forehead. "The dog!"

He put through a call to Tsujii. "Hughes here. Has anyone tended to Mr. Tomik's dog?"

"I don't believe so. I'll contact the kennel staff."

"I'm right here. The dog probably really has to do the necessaries. Could you let me in? I'll make sure it's OK."

"I'm sorry, Doctor, but it's against Station policy to grant access to another patron's suite."

<*Go in,*>" Victrix repeated, scratching at the door.

Hughes thought quickly. "Mr. Tomik told me he didn't have a dog. He might have hurt it in his confused state. It might require immediate assistance."

A long pause, then Tsujii said, "Please hold."

He waited until she returned. "The veterinary staff is busy attending to an emergency in another sphere. Our staff veterinarian thinks it would be appropriate under the circumstances for you to perform an initial evaluation. I'll access Mr. Tomik's suite for you."

"Thank you."

Seconds later, Tomik's door slid open, and Hughes entered, Victrix at his side. The suite was a duplicate of his own, with a large living area and a comfortable chair facing a large window. The bedroom door was closed. Victrix pawed at it; Hughes opened it, and the Maltese bounded out. Hughes noticed immediately that it was anxious and shaking.

Victrix met it, tail wagging, and the two dogs stood nose to nose for a long moment, in canine greeting. Then Victrix lay down, and the Maltese lay down in front of her.

Hughes peered past them; the bed hadn't been slept in. And his nose told him that the Maltese had already done its business.

Victrix turned away from the other dog, and sniffed around the chair.

Hughes picked up the Maltese and gave it a quick exam. Its pink tongue licked his face, and its shaking subsided.

He heard a noise behind him, and turned to find Tsujii and a kennel attendant.

"The dog seems fine," he said. "But it couldn't hold on."

"I'll handle the dog," the kennel attendant said, taking it from Hughes. "Poor little guy is probably hungry."

He departed with the dog.

Hughes exited the suite with Tsujii. "Any news on Mr. Tomik?" he asked, trying to sound casual.

She hesitated. "I can't say much, but since it was you who found him…it appears to be a psychotic break, perhaps stress-induced. Nothing organically wrong."

"Poor man."

"Sometimes people come here to escape their problems," Tsujii said. "But sometimes the problems follow them."

Almost he was tempted to tell her what he suspected, but something held him back. Victrix was eager. He wanted to know what she'd discovered.

He said, "Let's hope he gets over it, whatever it was."

They parted, and Hughes heard Tsujii contact the cleaning staff. He entered his own suite, sat on the edge of his chair, cradled Victrix's muzzle in his hands, gazed into her brown eyes, and said, "Show me."

What a dog relied on more than sight was scent, and this was hard for Victrix to communicate to him. Compared to her, he was olfactorily challenged, practically blind. So she had to translate the scent to a visual image. Gradually, a picture formed in his mind.

<*See?*>

<*I see. Are you sure?*>

<*Sure.*>

He rocked back into the chair, gave a long exhalation, then covered his eyes.

Leina was waiting for him in a quiet corner of the restaurant when he arrived with Victrix in tow and a dull weight in the pit of his stomach. A pair of glasses containing a shimmering golden liquid stood on the table.

"To toast our last meal together," she said, smiling, and ruffling Victrix's head. Her mood seemed lighter than at breakfast.

He hated to puncture it. But there was no point in prolonging the inevitable. He sat down, rested his hands on the table, and took a deep breath. "You're a downloader, aren't you?"

Her blue eyes froze.

"I saw marks on Tomik's temples," Hughes ploughed ahead. "And you were in Mr. Tomik's suite, weren't you?"

"What would give you that idea?"

"You left evidence," he said.

She regarded him steadily, without speaking.

"Your scent," he explained.

"Scent?" she repeated flatly.

"Victrix alerted me to a problem with Mr. Tomik, then detected your scent in his rooms."

"That's absurd!" she said forcefully. "I didn't take you for the drinking type, Hughes."

"I'm perfectly sober," he countered. "And so is Victrix. She's genetically modified for enhanced intelligence, and we share a telepathic bond." He waved a hand. "It's a long story."

Leina started to rise. "And an insane one!"

Hughes said, "I suppose a biosensor scan would detect your DNA and confirm it." Feigning nonchalance he took a sip of the drink. It was tart. He regarded her over the sugared rim of his glass. "Well? Are you?"

For a moment, he thought she was going to leave. But then she appeared to reach a decision and sat down again. When she spoke, it wasn't what he expected to hear.

"You've done confidential work for the Terran government, haven't you?"

"I—" he began, startled. "I can't speak about—"

"In fact," she continued, "you handled a sensitive issue for the Chief Justice of the Terran Supreme Court involving the creation of human-animal hybrids."

"How can you possibly—"

"Can *I* trust you as well?" she asked.

He swallowed, searched his heart, said, "Yes."

"Then let me tell you something more about my home system," she said, leaning back. "Winfryd has a sister planet, Hargrove, which is slightly smaller, but otherwise very similar. Both were settled at about the same time. They have always been as close as two worlds could be."

"What does this have to do with—?" Hughes began.

"Please, hear me out," Leina said. "Some twenty years ago, a dictator came to power on Hargrove, by the usual means—exploiting people's fears during a time of uncertainty. And he maintained power by the usual means—corruption, bribery, a secret police dedicated to himself alone, the elimination of opposition."

"I've never heard of this," Hughes said.

"With the number of worlds in the colonized galaxy," Leina said, "I'd be surprised if you had."

Leina took a drink from her glass, and set it down again. "My sister married a computer scientist from Hargrove, who was active in the opposition. One day, they and their three small children simply disappeared." Her blue eyes dimmed, as if she was looking into the past. "A mutual friend sent us the news. I used to stand outside my house and look up at Hargrove, and wonder what had happened to them."

Hughes made a sympathetic murmur."And they weren't the only ones.

People disappeared by the thousands. And then, not content with Hargrove, the dictator threatened to invade and annex Winfryd. That was a step too far, and the Alliance Defense Forces finally intervened and defeated the dictator and his military. My brother was an assault ship pilot. He was killed in the military action."

"I am so sorry," Hughes breathed.

"Unfortunately, the dictator and many of his leading cronies avoided detection and escaped. We've been hunting him for nearly a decade."

"I still don't see—"

"Mr. Tomik is not a harmless old coot. He's a brutal killer. And his name isn't Tomik. It's Roald Ingvar."

Hughes pursed his lips.

"We learned that he had taken refuge in the Confederation of Planets. Our relationship with them is prickly at best. We have no extradition treaty with them. The Alliance Governing Council considered sending a team of space commandos either to kill or capture Ingvar, but didn't want to risk worsening relations, or even starting a conflict with the Confederation for violating their sovereignty. Also, we didn't want to make him a martyr on one hand, or return him to Hargrove where he still had followers, on the other.

"Then we obtained intelligence that Ingvar was coming here, to Annali Station. But Annali is neutral, so we didn't wish to violate their neutrality, either. Another plan was devised."

She pointed to her temple. "Yes, I'm a downloader."

Hughes said, "I've downloaded visual memories from myself and Victrix. I've heard rumors of more sophisticated procedures."

"What kind of rumors?"

"Of secret government downloaders—also called mindbreakers—destroying men's minds."

"And is that what you think I am?" she flashed. "Do I strike you as the kind of woman who would harm an innocent old man and then lie about it?"

Hughes was taken aback. "No, I—"

"I don't know what goes in on in Earth's territories," she interrupted, "but let me tell you about the Alliance Worlds. We are not savages or unethical monsters."

"I never said—"

Again, she didn't let him continue. "The Alliance has highly developed downloading technology, far in advance of that of other worlds. We're proud of it. And we use it only in the interests of justice."

"Tell me more," Hughes asked quietly.

More calmly, she said, "I'm an official downloader for the Alliance Department of Justice. Normally I work with victims or witnesses of crime, in order to improve their testimony. I do not break people's minds. The procedure is done voluntarily, and harmless if the subject cooperates."

"And if not?"

"There's a risk of inducing mental disorders. I know what you're thinking," she continued. "But I'm here as an official agent of the Alliance Council because of my expertise. I was selected to take this assignment and I accepted."

"I hope it wasn't to get revenge."

"No!" she snapped. "In order to learn the truth."

When he didn't reply, she reached out to lay a hand upon his. "Can't you understand? If all the Alliance—if all *I*—wanted was revenge, Ingvar would be dead by now. Or I'd have deliberately ruined his mind. What you see—the way he is now—is because he wouldn't cooperate. He wouldn't face—or reveal—the truth. Some people refuse to admit the truth, Hughes. They insist they've done no wrong, despite the evidence of their atrocities. They become twisted, believing they're above the law, above right and wrong. But you can't deny the truth forever. You can't hide or suppress it indefinitely. Eventually the truth will be revealed. And it will either set you free or it will break you."

Hughes remained silent for a moment.

"You're not convinced," she said sadly.

"I want to be," Hughes said. "I really do."

"Information on Roald Ingvar is readily available," she said. She reached into a pocket and removed a small metal disc which she slid over to him. He picked it up, and a hologram of Leina's face formed over his palm, and above it an official seal bearing the words 'Leina Dickson, Senior Intelligence Specialist, Alliance Department of Justice'. The hologram faded after a moment and he returned the disc to her.

"Senior Intelligence Specialist," he said. "You looked me up, didn't you? That's how you knew."

"Of course," she said, "once I realized that…" She looked away. "That

I was beginning to have…"

"What about being a writer?" Hughes asked, shifting his position.

"Also true. I was a war correspondent during the conflict on Hargrove. I've also published a couple of novels under my own name. As God is my witness I'm telling you the truth."

He couldn't contain his surprise. "You came here in the open, using your real name?"

She nodded. "The truth is the best cover. When I get home, I'll write up the stories I've heard here—yours included, if you'll allow me. There's nothing to connect me to Ingvar." She shrugged. "Annali officials don't know that Tomik is Ingvar—that they're harboring a wanted war criminal. And if they found out, they wouldn't want it to become known. They'd seek to avoid embarrassment. So if they did become suspicious, they wouldn't do anything. They want business from the Alliance. They'll blame Tomik's mental breakdown on age or stress."

After a moment, he asked, "Did you get what you wanted?"

She brightened. "I think so. The recordings will need to be analyzed. But I believe that we'll learn what happened to many of the missing. It will bring closure to the survivors, and put an end to a painful chapter in Alliance history. And there's something better than that."

"Oh?"

"Have you ever heard of Earth having secret outposts, prison planets?"

He nodded. "Rumors."

"Exactly. There have been unconfirmed hints that Ingvar didn't murder all his opponents, that many of them were shipped off-world, to prison planets or labor camps. We've never been able to locate any of them. But now, with the information I obtained, I think we might have a chance."

Her hand tightened on his arm. "Just think, Hughes, maybe my sister and her family are still alive. Wouldn't it be wonderful?"

He laid his hand on top of hers. "I pray that it is so, Leina."

Absently, Hughes reached down with his free hand to stroke Victrix's ears.

"So now you know." Leina withdrew her hand and took a deep breath. "I've confided in you, Hughes. No one on Annali Station was to learn of my mission."

"I'm honored by your trust."

"I wouldn't have told you if I hadn't learned about your own secret dealings."

"Not as secret as I thought, obviously."

"What is?"

"You won't—?

She shook her head. "Don't worry. Funny, isn't it? Despite all the planning, I hadn't factored in the possibility of encountering a canine detective and her equally perspicacious master."

Hughes was forced to smile. "Pure happenstance," he said. "If I hadn't been Tomik's neighbor, I'd never have known."

"Do you really think it was chance?" Leina wondered."

"Or was God taking an interest in us?" he concluded for her. "I don't try to guess the designs of the Almighty." He swallowed. "But I can't help but wonder if perhaps He meant for us to meet."

His heart warmed as her lips turned into a pleased smile.

"Well then," she said, "What are you going to do?"

"Do? With what you've told me?" He picked up his glass again and twirled it around, watching the irridescent liquid swirl. "To be perfectly objective for a moment, my evidence, being second-hand—or paw—from Victrix, wouldn't be admissible in court. And I expect the suite has been thoroughly cleaned by now. If there were traces of your DNA there, they could have come from me, as we've been spending time together—off my clothing for instance."

"And subjectively?" she asked hopefully.

"Subjectively, I don't wish to do anything." He met her gaze. "Your secret is safe with me. In fact, I admire you. And I hope…I hope that you can save some of your people."

"Pray, Hughes. Pray hard."

"You have my word." He signaled for a server. "Are you ready to eat?"

"Ravenous."

"Me too," he said, realizing that his appetite had returned.

They ordered, then Hughes said, "I'm going to miss you, Leina."

"And I, you."

<*She go?*>

He glanced down to where Victrix was looking up at him. She'd been so quiet he'd almost forgotten she was there.

<*Yes.*>

<Victrix sad.>

Leina was watching him curiously.

"Victrix is sorry you're leaving," he said. "She says she'd like to see you again."

"Only Victrix?"

He felt his cheeks warm. "I'll be counting the days."

"As will I."

"But I'm a wanderer…I never know where I'll be next."

Her smile widened. "Don't worry. Gathering information is my specialty. I'll find you."

A pair of black paws landed on the table. Victrix, standing on her back legs, looked from Hughes to Leina.

"You have my word on it," she said, laughing, and leaning over to hug the German Shepherd. "I would never lie to a dog. Especially not a telepathic one."

THE DEATHCATS OF ASA'ICAN

They were almost through.

Almost there.

Almost home free.

Relax, Hughes told himself. Breathe slowly and deeply. Nothing was going to happen. Nothing.

He tried once more—and failed, again—to let go of the tension coiled up inside him. *Almost* wasn't good enough. Not in exobiology, not in love, and most assuredly not in interstellar space.

"Scan, Sofi?" he asked.

"All clear, Dr. Hughes. I detect an elevation in your heart rate and respirations."

"I'm fine."

"Are you experiencing any subjective symptoms?"

"I'm *fine*," he replied curtly.

He gnawed on his left thumbnail while alternating his gaze between the starfield on *Wolf-1*'s main viewscreen and the plot of the ship's position: Nearly—but not quite—at the end of a route that was interestingly, though unnervingly, called the Gauntlet.

"Still clear?"

"Yes, Dr. Hughes. I will alert you if there's any change," Sofi replied, managing to sound piqued. "May I suggest—"

"No!"

The odds were in his favor…

Victrix was sitting beside him, her black muzzle aimed at the viewscreen, her ears erect, her brown eyes locked in a penetrating stare, the ball she'd been playing with having rolled away, unnoticed. She couldn't know—or comprehend—exactly what worried him, but she could share his anxiety. Or was it her own anxiety that he was receiving, adding to his own? He wasn't certain. Sometimes it was hard to disentangle his emotions from hers.

Wolf-1 had been clipping down the Gauntlet for days, traveling as fast as Sofi deemed prudent along a corridor of space deemed "exceedingly dangerous" by the navigational program. The corridor wound through a stellar nursery, and all around—courtesy of computer-enhanced images—were swirls and columns of gas and dust, illuminated by the light of newly-born stars.

Yet those condensing physical elements weren't the danger.

Perhaps the navigational program exaggerated...

"Sofi, how long until—"

"Three point five hours, Dr. Hughes. A mild sedative might help—"

"NO! And don't ask me again."

"Very well, Doctor."

Three point five hours.

He repeated the number to himself. Only a little longer, and *Wolf-1* would be through.

Victrix's nose twitched.

He had a momentary impression of sudden pain, followed by anger—

His gaze shot back to the screen.

At first, he saw nothing. And then—

A spot where the distant stars were distorted and twisted... and then they vanished into a sworl of enlarging blackness...yet it wasn't black, because its edges scintillated, like flickers of jagged, multi-hued lightning. It reminded him of an aura preceding a migraine.

The coruscations became the outline of a form, and suddenly *something* was there, directly in front of *Wolf-1*, twisting and writhing out of nowhere—a maelstrom of shifting patterns and forms that always seemed just on the verge of coalescing into a nightmare shape but never quite did.

Victrix barked, snapping Hughes out of a momentary paralysis. He realized that Sofi had been speaking

"Proximity alert, Dr. Hughes," Sofi was repeating, her calm tones contrasting sharply with his own sudden panic. "Initiating avoidance maneuvers."

"Confirmed," Hughes said, gripping his armrests out of stress more than any real need.

Wolf-1 veered away from the disturbance, the ship's electromagnetic shields flaring under an onslaught of radiation and sub-atomic particles. *Wolf-1* wasn't a warship, built with multiple levels of shielding to defend against weapons—just enough to protect its human and canine occupants from the normal levels expected during interstellar travel.

Could they outrun whatever it was, Hughes wondered? *Wolf-1* was fleet enough for his purposes, but not overly so. Fight? Fight what? How could you fight something without even knowing what it was? And with what? He'd always resisted having weapons added to *Wolf-1*…

The thing was right in front of them again.

"What is it, Sofi?" he asked.

"Unknown, Dr. Hughes. I have nothing comparable in my memory banks."

So much for this mission of mercy, Hughes thought. Perhaps it would be their last…

He'd been surprised when the request had arrived from the Planetary Health Officer of Asa'ican. Somehow, the name rang a faint bell, although he couldn't recall hearing of the planet before—not that that in itself was unusual. But what *was* unusual was that Asa'ican belonged to the Association of Free Worlds, a distant and little known planetary grouping that had been colonized, forgotten about, and then rediscovered only within the past few decades—and which, by all reports, preferred to be left alone by the rest of the inhabited galaxy.

Forgotten worlds weren't uncommon, although it was unusual for a whole planetary grouping to exist beyond the knowledge of other systems.

Regardless, there was, it seemed, an outbreak of some kind of strange illness. The official, a woman named Larella, had informed him that local medical experts had made no progress in combating it. Perhaps he, as a pre-eminent exobiologist…?

Hughes could never resist a challenge.

After making sure Larella understood that he usually cared for non-human lifeforms, and that dealing with humans wasn't his specialty, he agreed to come.

Only after he was underway did he learn about the Gauntlet. And that despite the dangers it was the only practical way to reach Asa'ican and the Free Worlds.

He'd taken risks before, as well. But could he have taken one risk too many? Annali Station suddenly seemed a long time ago, and very far away. And Leina—perhaps he'd never see her again. Would she ever learn what had happened to him? Would he even merit a brief mention in a newsfeed?—"Founder of WOLF disappears on humanitarian mission…"

For years, Hughes had worn a small Celtic cross that he'd acquired in Ireland. He loved the stories of the interactions of the Celtic saints and animals—including wolves, which seemed especially appropriate once he'd selected 'WOLF' as a suitable acronym for his organization. Many of the saints had been pilgrims. Hughes raised a hand to the cross's worn surface, wondering if his own pilgrimage was over.

Because no matter which way *Wolf-1* turned, the anomaly was always in front, drawing ever closer, warping space, and straining *Wolf-1*'s systems.

A tiny whimper escaped from Victrix's nostrils.

"I'm sorry, girl," Hughes began, glancing down. "I hate for anything to happen to you—"

He broke off and grabbed his head as something like a soundless scream stabbed from one temple to the other. His eyes watered.

Then it was gone, leaving behind a sensation as of an echo.

"What was that-?"

"Proximity alert, Dr. Hughes," Sofi said.

"I know, I know—" he started, before it registered that another blip had appeared on the scan screen, approaching at high speed.

The thing seemed to hesitate, then, as if forgetting about *Wolf-1*, turned to confront the new threat.

He told himself not to anthropomorphize. It was bad enough to do it with animals, but with a spacial anomaly…

"Visual, Sofi," Hughes said. And then, "My sainted aunt…"

Approaching was a warship, decidedly old and outdated, probably sold to one of the Free Worlds by a more wealthy system, yet still spaceworthy.

Once in range, it opened up on the spacial disturbance with its main weaponry—

—and the distortion appeared to fold in upon itself. Then, as it had come, it twisted, and with a final flicker of multihued light, disappeared.

Hughes hadn't realized he'd been holding his breath. He exhaled.

"Incoming communication, Dr. Hughes."

"Put it on screen, Sofi."

"This is Free World StarCruiser *BlackSun*," said a heavy-browed, square-faced man wearing a light green uniform. His accent was so thick that Hughes had difficulty understanding him. "Are you all right?"

His voice shaky, Hughes replied, "Fine, thank you, Captain…"

"Brockham. You're lucky we were on patrol in this vicinity," the captain continued, a hint of reproach in his tone. "Plenty of ships have entered the Gauntlet and never come out."

"I'm glad you prevented us from becoming one of them."

The man glanced aside. "You ID as civilian vessel *Wolf-1*."

"Correct. My name is Hughes. I'm *en route* to Asa'ican to meet with Health Officer Larella."

"Please transmit your authorization and clearances."

Hughes did so.

"Everything appears to be in order," the captain concluded after a few moments. "You may proceed. You shouldn't have any further trouble."

"I hope not," Hughes replied. "I really hope not."

He was still feeling drained by the encounter some hours later, when, after achieving orbit around Asa'ican, the shuttle bearing him and Victrix dropped through a layer of low-hanging clouds to reveal a landscape of field-covered rolling hills that reminded him gut-wrenchingly of England—although with slightly different hues—as if, perhaps, painted by an Impressionist. Asa'ican was obviously not one of the marginally habitable planets that made up the vast bulk of human-colonized worlds. The first arrivals here had been lucky. No wonder their descendants preferred to keep their world to themselves.

After landing at a small but functional spaceport on the outskirts of Asa'ican's capital city, Tawhita Tauranga, a chauffeured flitter took him to the governmental complex, where a functionary directed him to the Planetary Health Officer's office.

Larella was about Hughes' own age, with short brown hair and a kindly, round face. She looked, Hughes thought, quite attractive, despite the spotless white uniform she wore—undoubtedly a relic from the days when white coats were associated with the medical profession.

"Thank you for coming, Dr. Hughes," she greeted, her accent nearly—but not quite—as impenetrable as the captain's. "You and…"

"Victrix," Hughes replied, patting the big dog on the top of her head. "My assistant."

Larella's eyebrows rose. "'I'd assumed you'd have a human companion."

"You'd be surprised at how much help a dog can be."

"I don't recognize the breed."

"German Shepherd," Hughes said. "Very popular on old Earth. Bred for both intelligence and physical presence."

"Is she enhanced?" Larella asked suspiciously.

Hughes nodded. "Is there a problem?"

Larella frowned. "Enhanced animals are not permitted on Asa'ican. We have dogs here, descended from those brought by the original settlers, but genetic enhancement is prohibited."

Hughes, who'd seen the unfortunate results of far too many genetic experiments, said, "A prudent policy."

Larella looked mildly surprised.

"I rescued Victrix from a research facility," Hughes said.

"So you weren't responsible for her enhancement?"

"Not in the slightest."

Larella drummed her fingers in thought. "I'm not sure—"

"We're a team," Hughes interrupted. "A package deal. Both or none."

She thought for a moment longer. "I suppose then, under the circumstances, I'll have to make a temporary exception for her."

"Understood. Thank you."

"I hear you almost didn't make it to us," Larella said. "I'd hoped to provide you with an escort, but the military wouldn't cooperate."

"What attacked us?" Hughes asked, accepting the change of subject.

She raised her shoulders. "Theories abound, but no one really knows for certain."

"Surely there must be *some* idea…"

"All we can say with any degree of confidence is that it represents some kind of multi-dimensional phenomenon that erupts unpredictably," Larella said. "The name varies on different worlds," she added, pouring two drinks of some pale blue liquid from a carafe on her desk and offering one to Hughes. He sipped it, enjoying a cool tingle on his tongue. "On Halfrida they call them Morderkatz. On Othmann they're referred to as Raumtigers. Here, we know them as DeathCats." She shrugged again. "I suppose somebody with an overactive imagination thought they saw a resemblance to felines."

Hughes took another swallow of his drink.

Larella continued, "Our weapons have some effect, but in what way…" she let the sentence hang. "For some reason, most eruptions occur in the Gauntlet. Which," she said, giving a small smile, "has certainly limited the number of unwanted visitors."

"In that case," Hughes said, returning the smile, "I'm glad to be among the invited."

"We don't want you here," a harsh voice interrupted. Hughes swung around to see a young man framed in the doorway. He looked to be about fourteen or fifteen standard years old, Hughes guessed, with the same color hair and roundish face as Larella. But unlike her gray eyes, his were hazel, and his expression was hostile.

Victrix sprang to her feet, hackly, facing the young man.

<*Sit!*>

Victrix grumbled but obeyed his telepathic command. She regarded the newcomer warily.

"Don't be rude, Linddun," Larella said sharply. "Dr. Hughes is my guest." To Hughes, she said, "My son, Linddun."

"Pleased," Hughes said, rising and extending his hand. The boy ignored it. "You're an Earther. I don't like Earthers."

"Linddun!" Larella gasped.

"I'm sorry to hear that," Hughes said.

"You killed my father," Linddun accused, turning on his heel.

"My husband died of the Withering," Larella explained to Hughes. "The illness I contacted you about."

"We never had it here before you Earthers came," Linddun rasped, speaking over his shoulder as he strode out the doorway. "You brought it to us."

It was with a sense of profound relief that Hughes stretched out in the guest quarters that Larella had arranged for him. The day had provided more than enough emotional strain. Victrix curled up contentedly on a plush mat beside his bed, and was soon snoring gently.

It took Hughes considerably longer to drift into sleep, and when he did, it wasn't restful for long. A vague half-sleep was disturbed not by visual dreams, but by emotions—at least, that was what they seemed to be.

Loss.

Despair.

Anger.

Determination.

All washed over him in succession, although permeated by something else—he couldn't quite determine what—something utterly foreign.

And then there were the sharp things, skewering through the blackness—and it was they—somehow—that caused the loss.

Loss.

Despair.

Anger.

Determination.

The scratching of Victrix's twitching legs against the side of the bed roused him to partial consciousness, and in that moment of partial clarity he realized that the dreams and emotions weren't his.

They were coming from Victrix.

Fresh air and blue sky overhead.

It didn't get much better, Hughes thought, as he and Victrix strolled though the city the following morning along streets shaded by thick-stemmed vines artistically fashioned into spirals and arches and figures that he guessed might represent native fauna.

The quaint architecture had been designed, he surmised, more for aesthetic impression than for functionality. The Free Worlds had—inevitably, given their isolation—lagged behind the technological progress that Earth's domain and the other larger planetary affiliations enjoyed. So walking through the city was like taking a walk in the not-too-distant past.

The Free Worlds had, however, been making up their deficit by purchasing materials and technology at a ferocious pace. And so the difference was probably not so marked as it had undoubtedly been decades ago.

Victrix enjoyed it also, alert to all the new sights and smells—and passersby were equally curious about her, regarding her with unconcealed stares. While there were plenty of other dogs of various colors and conformations, Hughes saw nothing that resembled a Shepherd.

"Tell me about the Withering," Hughes requested when he was seated in Larella's spacious office.

"Well," Larella replied, after organizing her thoughts, "here's the abbreviated version. It's also called Litowski's Disease, or more commonly NMD—neurocephalic metamorphic degeneration. It begins insidiously, and is invariably fatal, with death occurring after several years. It's popularly known as the Withering because victims slowly waste away—but it's accompanied by a host of neurologic symptoms including hallucinations and eventual insanity."

Hughes listened as she recited a substantial list of associated symptoms.

"What's the cause?" Hughes asked. "I assume—since you requested my help—that it's an alien organism of some kind."

She nodded. "We believe so." She touched a pad on her desk and a screen on the opposite wall illuminated. "They say a picture's worth a thousand words. This is a scan of the spinal cord of a recent patient with early disease. The color's artificial, of course."

Hughes whistled at the sight of a purple mass with tentacle-like extensions spreading fungus-like over the spinal cord.

"Microsurgery can't remove it?"

"No. In fact we can't even biopsy it."

"You can't—"

"No. Because there's nothing there."

Hughes stared. "That's absurd! You can scan it but not physically find it?"

"Exactly." Larella folded her hands. "You see why we need your help."

"Let's try a different tack," Hughes said, steepling his hands. "How do people contract it?

"We don't know. It just seems to happen sporadically. There's no vector we've been able to find."

"Then where's it from?"

She spread her hands. "It's slightly more common on Asa'ican than the other Free Worlds. That's the best I can say."

"You're not making this easy."

"If it was easy, we'd have figured it out already," Larella replied with a touch of asperity.

"Pardon me," Hughes said. "I didn't mean any disrespect. It's just that…I've never heard of anything like this before."

He stroked his beard. "Maybe you're searching in the wrong place. Was what Linddun said correct? Did the disease arrive after the Free Worlds were rediscovered?"

"Partly," Larella said. "There were a few cases during the years after initial colonization, but when those died out, no new cases occurred until after New Contact."

"So it's possible."

"Please forgive my son," Larella said. "He's not a bad kid, but he took his father's death very hard."

Hughes waved a hand in reassurance. "Don't worry about it."

"He's very smart, actually. He loves science. I'm thinking he might make a good epidemiologist one day."

Hughes only half heard her, his mind already working. "I'll need all the data you have on the Withering, including what treatments have been tried."

"It's at your disposal." She motioned. "I also have a laboratory requisitioned for your use. And as many assistants as you need."

"Right now, all I need to do is study, and think."

And exercise Victrix, he might have added as the Shepherd made it very clear that a short walk in a city was not enough for an active dog who had been cooped up in a starship for longer than she deemed appropriate.

<*Go play!*> She insisted, tugging on his pants leg nearly hard enough to pull him over.

<*All right.*>

The files Larella had given him looked daunting. Well, he hadn't expected anything else. So despite his eagerness to begin work, an outing before settling down to mental exertion might not be a bad idea.

Although he enjoyed exploring new cities, most often it was the countryside that beckoned him—and Victrix, he knew, would never pass up the opportunity for a swim.

He took a rental flitter some miles out from the city, to where a small river—which he was assured was perfectly safe—meandered between fields on one side and vacant land covered with low-growing bluish vegetation on the other.

There, he found a comfortable perch on some rocks while Victrix splashed and brought him a length of some flexible, stick-like plant for him to throw.

He was curious, but today detected no remnant of the emotions that had come to him in the night. Victrix was simply Victrix, happy to be playing, and undisturbed.

Well, strange things happened, and the mind was susceptible to so many influences.

But a dog wasn't a human, the canine mind not the same as—nor as complex as—the human mind.

And so he found himself unable to totally dismiss those strange emotions.

And what, he wondered, as he pitched the stick yet again for Victrix to chase, were the 'sharp things'?

The next days developed a predictable routine—hours of study broken up by occasional excursions with Victrix. In the evenings he'd locate a suitably appealing restaurant and sample the local cuisine—some items of which he enjoyed, while others were quite unpalatable.

And at night…if he was lucky he'd sleep well, but frequently his mind would be following a train of thought and not allow him as much rest as he would have liked. Most of those trains went nowhere. Others seemed promising at the time, but when morning arrived he realized their flaws.

At least there was no recurrence of the strange emotional dreams, although they still perplexed him.

Finally, he reached the end of the data files Larella had given him.

"Any luck?" she asked when he went to report on his progress.

"Your people have been very thorough," he said. "Very thorough indeed."

She accepted the compliment with an inclination of her head.

"And yet I wonder…there's something missing, but I don't know what."

"A hunch is at least a starting point," Larella said.

"I wouldn't say it's even that."

"What next, then?"

Hughes said, "Have you heard the old medical joke, 'If all else fails, examine the patient,'?"

She chuckled. "I'll arrange it. There's no lack of them at the moment."

"But first, I'd like to talk to your son."

"To Linddun? Why?"

"Because I'd like to enlist his aid."

The expression on her face was impossible for him to read. "I'll call him."

Linddun arrived at Larella's office a little while later, looking disgruntled and irritated. He was sweaty, wearing some kind of garish athletic gear, and chewing on an orange-colored fruit.

"Your mother tells me you're very talented," Hughes said. "I'd like to ask for your assistance."

The young man's face tightened. "You want *my* help?"

"Yes."

"Why should I do anything for *you*, Earther?"

"Linddun!" his mother exclaimed. "Be polite!"

"Don't you want to help find a cure for the Withering?" Hughes asked.

Linddun scowled. "It's too late. My father's dead."

"What about the other people who are—or who will be—infected? Don't you want to help them? They're *your* people."

Linddun pondered that. "I suppose so."

"Good! Since you say that off-worlders brought the Withering to the Free Worlds, I want to see proof. Can you correlate all cases of the Withering, from when the Free Worlds were colonized to the present, with arriving vessels?"

Linddun nodded. "It should be easy enough—we're only looking at a few decades, since there were no cases in the hundreds of years when we were left alone."

Hughes ignored the barb. "And I want to know the originating worlds of the arriving ships."

Larella said, "I can arrange for the authorization to access the Interworld Commerce files."

"Military and private, too," Hughes added.

"Whatever's not too highly classified."

"I can live with that," Hughes said. "Can you have them for me soon, Linddun?"

"It shouldn't take long," Linddun said.

"And while you're at it, can you create a list of all reported appearances of the DeathCats?"

"The DeathCats?" Linddun exclaimed. "What do they have to do with anything?"

Hughes shrugged. "Probably nothing. But they're unique to this area. One of them almost did me in."

Linddun muttered something under his breath.

"Have you ever seen one?" Hughes asked.

Linddun shook his head. "No. But I wouldn't mind the experience."

He turned towards the door.

"Thank you," Larella said to Hughes, when Linddun had departed. "That was very considerate of you."

Hughes smiled. "You saw through me very quickly."

She came to stand beside him, and touched his arm. "Anyone could have run that correlation for you. You could have done it yourself."

"Perhaps."

"Forgive me if I say you're not very convincing."

"In my experience, there are different types of patients," Hughes said. "Linddun is one of them."

The patient that Larella arranged for him to examine wasn't a young man—neither was he old—but he looked prematurely aged, what was left of him: A shrunken husk, now no more than a shell holding the pitiful remnants of a mind. He lay on a bed, attached to life support machines. His eyes were tight shut. Despite his comatose state he looked like a man in pain.

"Can you believe he was once President of the Federal Council?" Larella commented.

"How long ago?" Hughes asked.

"Two years."

He blew out his breath from between pursed lips. "It's unfortunate that we don't know the incubation period of whatever this is."

"By the time people present with the Withering," Larella replied, "it's either with the sudden onset of back or nerve pain, or, if they delay seeking help, then with more generalized symptoms and wasting. But you're right—we don't know how long the organism has been in their bodies before it begins to cause symptoms."

Hughes studied the scan image on the screen beside the man's bed. The entire spinal cord and brain were enveloped in strands of alien substance.

"Even if we can figure this out," he mused, "it might be too late for him."

"Probably so," Larella concurred.

Hughes had met the soon-to-be widow accompanied by a pair of young children as they'd entered the hospital.

"Do your best," the woman had said after Larella had introduced him. "Please."

He'd murmured assent; now he felt pressure. Could he help this doomed man? And even if the man lived, would his mind recover?

He realized that he'd been staring at the screen, and not paying attention to Victrix. The black Shepherd had put her front paws on the bed, and rested her muzzle near the man's cheek.

It looked sweet, and comforting.

<*Listen!*> Victrix insisted.

He rested a hand on her head, and tried to tune into her sensations. At first, he detected nothing unusual. He closed his eyes to concentrate, performing the mental equivalent of trying to detect one musical tone amidst a cacophony of others.

Then he heard it—faintly, as if from a great distance. A sound that wasn't a sound, but that reminded him of a sound—high-pitched, perhaps, plaintive, like a cry or a wail. But it was like nothing he'd ever heard—or experienced—before.

<*Hear?*>

<*Yes.*>

Hughes cringed inside, the mental noise scraping across his nerves. He couldn't stand it for long—what the victims must endure…

He broke away, opened his eyes, and looked up at Larella.

"It's crying," he said, puzzled.

"What is?"

"The organism. It's really weird."

"Dr. Hughes," she said heavily, "I expect more from you than bizarre statements."

"Victrix senses it," Hughes replied, straightening and meeting Larella's gaze. "She's telepathic. And for some reason she's able to detect things—thoughts, emotions, sensations—from some non-terrestrial organisms."

"And she tells you this?" Larella sounded incredulous.

"Yes," Hughes replied. "That's why she's my assistant instead of my pet—because of our telepathic bond."

"I don't believe it," Larella said flatly. "Prove it."

"All right." Hughes motioned to Victrix to get down off the bed, then picked up a data pad from a table and extended it towards Larella. "Take this and write down a task for Victrix to do—don't say it out loud so she can't hear you. Make it within a dog's physical capabilities. I'll read it and mentally tell her what to do."

"Without looking at her. Without any physical movements."

"Right." Hughes sat down and swiveled the chair to face the wall.

Larella bent over the pad for a moment and then handed it back to him. Hughes read it silently.

<*Victrix, take this to the man in the next room and come back with him.*>

<*Work?*>

<*Yes, it's work. Understand?*>

<*Victrix understand!*>

Victrix nudged him with her muzzle, then took the data pad in her mouth. She turned, crossed the room, and reared on her hind legs to slap the sensorpad by the side of the door. Tail high, she trotted out. A moment later the door opened again to reveal a puzzled-looking young man carrying the data pad in one hand, while Victrix led him by his other sleeve.

"Did you want to see me, ma'am?" he asked.

Larella chuckled. "No, Peralta, it was just a test. You can go back to whatever you were doing."

Shaking his head, the young man departed.

"Satisfied?" Hughes asked.

"For the moment, at any rate," Larella said, "unless you're some kind of magician. I can understand why you'd want Victrix to accompany you."

"As I said, she's an invaluable assistant. Got a treat?"

"Uh…"

"It's all right." Hughes fished in his pocket for a dog biscuit.

<*Good work!*>

<*Go play?*>

<*More work first.*>

"Are there more cases in this facility?" he asked Larella.

"Dozens," she replied. "Perhaps more. It's recently become a mini-epidemic." She studied him intently. "We don't eliminate people just because they become sick and incapacitated as I understand they do on Earth."

"My job as an exobiologist is to heal whenever possible," Hughes replied. "If it's all right, I'd like Victrix to listen to more victims."

"If you wish," Larella replied. "You know, I'd rather expected you to use the lab I arranged for you…"

Linddun had a very self-satisfied expression plastered across his face the next time that Hughes saw him. He and Victrix were sitting outside, enjoying a light lunch in Larella's company when the youth approached them across a shady plaza.

Victrix trotted over, yanked the data pad from his hand, and carried it to Hughes.

He tried not to smile, noticing that Larella was doing the same.

"Here you are," Linddun said, his voice stony. "As I said, you offworlders brought the Withering to us."

Hughes set down his lunch—a pastry shell filled with local vegetables—and scanned the data. Linddun sat next to his mother, beside a statue of some planetary notable.

"In broad outlines, it fits," Hughes concluded. "What's most interesting are the times when the first colonists discovered the free worlds, and then again on re-discovery, when only a few ships arrived. A case of the Withering was detected within a few months after the arrival of a significant proportion of vessels. Later on, as the number of arrivals increased, so did the number of cases, although it's impossible to pin down a specific case to a specific arrival."

He scanned further down. "I don't see where there's a correlation to any specific world."

"I didn't, either," Linddun said.

"Which doesn't surprise me," Hughes said. "I've accessed numerous data bases and been unable to find anything resembling the Withering on any other world."

"Which means…?" Larella prompted.

"That if the causative organism hasn't been detected on any of the Free Worlds, and not on any outside worlds—"

"That it's somewhere in-between," Linddun interjected.

"Exactly," Hughes said. "And there's an awful lot of space in-between."

His mind went back to the man in the hospital. A lot of space, and not a lot of time.

He scratched the side of his nose. "The reports say that radiation helped."

Larella shook her head. "Not really. Only very briefly. The organism just comes right back. Sometimes after a few hours, usually only a few minutes."

"I'd like to observe a treatment."

"We don't do them anymore, since there was no permanent effect."

"I'd still like to observe one. With Victrix."

She gave him a sharp look. "Another hunch?"

"Sometimes you have to play them."

"I don't think the former president's wife will object."

It wasn't long afterwards that Hughes was standing in an observation room with Larella and Victrix at his side. On the other side of the partition the withered man lay in a treatment unit.

<*Listen to him,*> he told Victrix.

<*Again?*>

<*Yes.*>

<*"#&#!!*>

<*Do it!*>

This time, he heard the high-pitched keening sooner. He clenched his fists and nodded to Larella. She relayed an instruction to a technician.

Hughes studied the computer-enhanced scan as twin beams of radiation hit the thing twined around the man's spine. For a moment nothing happened, then the keening scaled to a higher pitch that agitated every nerve in his body. Just when he thought he couldn't endure another second, the fungoid mass writhed, and then vanished. The keening stopped.

The technician halted the treatment. Hughes wiped sweat from his brow. Victrix was staring at him, her own pain visible in her eyes.

<*Good girl!*>

<*Listen?*> The thought was tired, resigned.

<*One more time.*>

Hughes didn't have to wait long. A few minutes later the mass reappeared.

As did the keening.

<*Enough. Stop now.*>

<*Treat?*>

Hughes rummaged in his pocket.

"See," Larella said. "Just what I told you."

"But I learned enough," Hughes said.

"What did you learn that we haven't?"

Hughes feigned a mysterious look. "In due course, Larella. In due course."

That night, the emotional dreams returned.

Loss.

Despair.

Anger.

Determination.

And the sharp things.

The sharp things that must be destroyed.

Instinctively, his hand reached down to rest upon Victrix's head.

His subconscious wove and unwove strands together through the night, creating and destroying new patterns, until finally one pattern survived.

And when he awoke in the morning, Hughes was convinced that he knew.

Larella was on a secure commlink when Hughes and Victrix arrived at her office as soon as he thought it polite to do so.

Her face was set in rigid lines.

She glanced at Hughes as he entered, and gestured him towards a chair.

She listened for a few more minutes, then said, "Thank you, President," and cut the link.

"What's the matter?" Hughes asked. "Anything you can tell me?"

She tapped her right index finger on her desk. "The Council is debating what can be safely disclosed to the public without creating panic."

"That serious?"

She nodded slowly. "Potentially."

"If it's something classified, then treat me like anybody else."

"But you're not," Larella said. "You're an offworld expert here at my request. You deserve to know. And if you want to leave, you are free to do so."

She took a deep breath. "DeathCats are gathering at the opening of the Gauntlet, something they've never done before. Our scientists are worried that such a clustering may pose a threat to the planet."

"That's exactly right," Hughes said.

Larella exploded from her chair. "*What?!* How can you possibly know—?"

"Not for sure," Hughes said, also rising. "I'm extrapolating from my experience with other species."

"Other species? What are you talking about?"

"Certain behaviors," Hughes replied, "are very much alike."

She looked at him as if he'd lost his mind. "Our Navy is preparing to intercept them," she said at last.

"They mustn't do that!" Hughes exclaimed, shaking a hand in negation. "Not unless your Free Worlds are prepared for a disaster the likes of which you can't imagine."

Larella's face was red. "Hughes—!"

"I've got an idea," Hughes said. "But we've got to move quickly."

"To do what?" she said through her teeth.

"To see if I'm right or not." He gripped her arm. "It might sound insane, but I want you get our patient on my shuttle and up to *Wolf-1* as quickly as possible."

"In his condition? He may not survive."

"He's going to die anyway. Look, it's worth a chance. It might be his only hope. Ours also."

"Or it might not. Look, Hughes," Larella said, making an effort to speak calmly, "you haven't said one thing that makes sense. Why should I trust you?"

"Because he's the exobiology expert," Linddun said, his voice dripping sarcasm.

Hughes hadn't heard the youth enter. Neither, apparently, had Larella. Her eyes flashed as she whirled around. "Would you quit coming in like that? How much have you overheard?"

"Enough," Linddun said. "You brought him here. Do you take his advice or not?"

"That's quite enough, young man! If I want *your* advice—"

"And if we're going, I want to go too," Linddun added.

"I haven't said that anyone is going," Larella snapped. "And if we were, it's too dangerous. The DeathCats—"

"I'm part of this team, aren't I?"

"Well, I suppose so, but—"

"Then let me come."

Larella hesitated.

"Let him come," Hughes said. "And Larella, you must trust me on this. I think I know how to avert catastrophe."

"Can you guarantee it?"

"No."

Dreams and the sensations received by a telepathic dog? Who could guarantee anything on that basis?

She passed a hand over her eyes. "Linddun's correct. I guess I'd better back you up. I just hope I don't regret it."

"Me too," Hughes replied.

Asa'ican was a bright jewel circling its sun as *Wolf-1* headed outsystem. One of the advantages of working with a government minister, Hughes had learned, was that things could sometimes be made to happen very quickly. It hadn't taken long for the former president to be transferred to *Wolf-1* and be installed in the medical bay.

Victrix sensed the humans' excitement, and sat practically quivering with eagerness. Larella was awash with tension. Linddun had eagerly explored the ship before returning to the bridge.

Hughes prayed silently.

Risking his own life was one thing—risking that of Larella and Linddun, and the ex-president, quite another.

Second thoughts flooded his mind. Could his crazy idea possibly be right? If only it could be tested—but he couldn't come up with an alternative way.

It was almost with a sensation of relief that Sofi reported picking up the handful of capital ships that constituted Asa'ican's navy. And beyond them—

Hughes and Larella gasped in unison, while Linddun mouthed what Hughes guessed to be a local curse.

The sight of one DeathCat had been awesome enough. There weren't words to describe the seething mass that roiled and distorted space into ribbons of coruscating colors and gravitational vortices.

What could a handful of aged ships hope to achieve against so many?

"Incoming communication, Dr. Hughes," Sofi said.

"On screen, Sofi."

The semi-familiar face of Captain Brockham appeared.

"What are you doing, Hughes?" he barked. "Get that ship out of here!"

"Whatever you do, Captain," Hughes said, "don't fire on the DeathCats."

"Look, Hughes, I'm in charge here. I don't take orders from civilians like you."

"He's under my instructions," Larella said, stepping into pickup range. "We need to move closer to the DeathCats."

"That's foolhhardy, Minister!" Brockham made a slashing movement with his hand. "I don't know what he's told you—or exactly what's going on—but I can assure you it's not safe here."

"I hope I may be able to stop the DeathCats," Hughes said.

"Let us pass, Captain," Larella said. "Consider that an order. I've cleared it with Minister for Defense."

Brockham clenched his teeth. "If you go beyond our perimeter, you're on your own. There'll be no rescue this time."

"Understood, Captain," Larella said.

Wolf-1 passed the waiting warships and edged closer to the seething mass of DeathCats.

Loss.

Despair.

Anger.

Determination.

Sharp things. Destroy the sharp things.

The wave of emotions channeled through Victrix hit him like the hammer of Thor. He forced them away.

"Let's go." Hughes led the way to the medical bay, where they stopped outside. In the room, the man lay on a multi-purpose table conformable to fit many different species. His respirations were shallow. He looked about as close to death as it was possible for a person to be.

Hughes met Larella's gaze.

"Sofi," he said, "shut down quantum field drive."

"Shutting down, Dr. Hughes."

He took a deep breath. "Zero gravity in the medical bay."

"Confirmed."

The man rose slightly off the table, held close by the restraints.

For a long moment, nothing happened.

Then, from near him, a spot of blackness appeared, rippling with colors on the edges.

Larella's breath hissed.

"How's it going to get out of the ship?" Linddun wondered.

The thing pulsed brighter. Then it twisted, and was gone.

"Like that," Hughes said. "Through whatever dimension it normally inhabits." He motioned to Larella. "Scan the president to make sure. Sofi: Restore gravity to medical bay."

"Restoring."

Larella hurried inside.

Hughes dropped to his knees and locked eyes with Victrix.

<Do you hear it?>

<Victrix hear.>

And there it was, a faint sound, growing fainter, but this time not a cry, but something that if he had to give it a name, sounded joyous.

<Think, Victrix. Show them…>

He brought to mind many of the things, rising from the planet's surface, and being released.

And he imagined dogs, like Victrix, surrounded by puppies.

And he thought of humans and their children.

It was a lot for a dog's mind to conceive—even one with genetically enhanced intelligence. But she didn't have to understand—only visualize and project the images, to be a conduit for Hughes.

<*Show them. Show them. No hurt. We meant no hurt.*>

<*Victrix show.*>

She was doing her best, Hughes knew. But were the images clear enough? And if so, were they intelligible to the completely alien DeathCats?

<*Show them!*>

Were the emotions lessening?

"Larella," he called, at the same time trying not to lose his focus on the images for Victrix.

"The medscan's clear," she replied. "It's gone!"

"Excellent!" Hughes responded. "And if I'm right, this time it's gone for good. Call your people on Asa'ican. Have them load all patients with the Withering onto whatever ships they have available. Bring them out here, and do just what we did."

"Incoming communication, Dr. Hughes."

"Audio, please, Sofi."

A man's heavy voice said, "Hughes? Brockham. The DeathCats are moving back. I don't know what you did, but whatever it was seems to be working."

"Don't follow them, Captain. Let them go."

"Copy. Out."

Hughes gave Victrix a hug.

<*We did it, girl!*>

He sensed her pleasure.

<*Go swim?*>

<*For as long as you like.*>

Then, as he rose, a pair of arms wrapped themselves around him. Startled, he returned Larella's hug.

"You're a genius!" she exclaimed.

Hughes laughed. "Hardly."

"You didn't get to be famous for no reason. How do you do what you do—when no-one else can?"

"A lot of times," Hughes said, "other people have already asked most of the questions. What I do is to think of the questions they haven't asked. When I was young my mother was always telling me that I asked the strangest questions. It's my—gift, if you will—to sometimes be able to look at things from a different angle. To be able to connect things that don't seem to be related."

He ruffled Victrix's ears. "Plus, I have help."

Then he held out a hand towards Linddun. "Your assistance was a great aid."

The young man paused. Hughes could imagine his conflicting emotions—possibly he'd even hoped that Hughes, the Earther, would fail. Finally, he took Hughes' hand tentatively and returned the handclasp.

"Maybe our patient will recover," he said, flashing a quick smile.

Larella coughed gently.

"There's hope," Hughes said. The president had opened his eyes, and seemed to relax. But whether or not that portended a recovery…? "Pray that it might be so."

"I'm still not sure I understand," Larella said later, when *Wolf-1* was approaching orbit above Asa'ican. "How did you figure out that the Withering was due to the DeathCats' young?"

Hughes grinned. "That's where Victrix helped a lot. Once I realized that the emotional dreams I was having were originating with the DeathCats, and then that the organism involved in the Withering was also giving off emotions, I figured there had to be a connection.

"And then, when I saw how the organism temporarily disappeared under the effect of radiation—exactly the same way as the DeathCat I saw retreated to another dimension—I was certain that they were related. It seemed too much to be mere coincidence.

"In retrospect, I guess it was a good thing I encountered the DeathCat on the way here. Otherwise, I might not have connected the two."

"But there were more than telepathic feelings involved," Larella said.

"It's only a guess, mind you," Hughes said, "but consider these facts. The DeathCat appearances occur mostly within three areas of the Gauntlet.

Voids, actually. And there have been no cases of the Withering on worlds in other planetary groupings—specifically not those worlds where ships originating in the Free Worlds have gone. So if, as appears certain, the Withering is brought here, it has not been taken away."

"Why not?"

"My hunch is that it's due to the structure of the Gauntlet itself. I suppose a ship captain could verify this, but from my reading it's much easier for a ship to come down the Gauntlet towards the Free Worlds than it is to go the other direction—something to do with the way space is warped and the effect on the dimensions involved. I don't understand it, frankly. But I think an analogy would be paddling a canoe downstream versus upstream."

"I don't see the link."

"What I propose is happening is that as ships come through the Gauntlet they pass these areas of void where the DeathCats dwell. For some reason the young are dragged away—possibly by our quantum field drives. Once in the area of a planetary system they're under the influence of gravity and are unable to break free. Some end up on the surface of a planet—possibly they latch onto a human as a surrogate host or energy source. Others I suppose fall into the sun."

"Cosmic roadkill," Linddun interjected.

"Exactly. And the reason that they aren't pulled out of the Gauntlet in the other direction is because our ships are going upstream, as it were, so the spacial distortions pull the young away from the ships and back towards the voids."

"Amazing," Larella said.

"Your people can take it from here," Hughes said. "Probably the simplest solution is to find alternative routes for ships that don't take them through the voids. If we don't threaten their young—because that is how they perceive it—the DeathCats won't threaten us."

"Mother love," Larella concluded.

"Precisely," Hughes said. "It doesn't matter what world you're on, it's never a good idea to anger a protective mother with young."

NIGHT OF THE SKAGGIT

BioScience Professor Eshkol Steinmetz yawned and pushed back his chair from his workstation. The display on his computer screen faded and died. The daytime activity and sounds of the Sultan Planetary Institute of Science had long-since lapsed into the drowsy hum of instruments on routine settings for the night or running programs that needed no human input. As if that wasn't enough evidence of the lateness of the hour, a glance through the window revealed a star-speckled night sky above the twinkling lights of Lexa's Ridge.

He should have gone home hours ago, but his current project was far too interesting—and potentially rewarding. If he could solve a hundred year old mystery—and he was on the verge, he was sure—professional advancement and fame would be his. Even so, enough was enough. He couldn't do his best work while barely able to keep his eyes open.

He rose, stretched, left his office, and headed down the deserted main corridor of the bioscience research wing. With his mind still distracted by work, and senses dulled by fatigue, he almost missed the faint scratching that came from behind a closed door.

He stood stock still to listen, holding his breath.

Had there really been a noise? Surely not. Not from this particular lab. No one but he and his research assistant had clearance to enter this lab, and she'd left hours ago.

A maintenance robot? That had to be it. He relaxed and took one step away—

But there it was again. A definite scratching, this time accompanied by a strange, high-pitched mewing.

He shivered, suddenly cold. Surely his assistant couldn't have been so careless—

His first instinct was to summon Security. But what if some trigger-happy officer responded? He dare not risk it.

He edged forward and palmed the sensorpad. The door whispered open, and he crept inside, halting halfway across the threshold. The scrabbling stopped abruptly.

He peered into the dimness, waiting for his eyes to adjust to the subdued glow of blinking status lights.

He saw nothing, heard nothing. And yet he knew it was there, somewhere.

It was only the barest flicker of a shadow, just enough to register in his peripheral vision, something black emerging from the darkness. He twisted his neck to look up, raised his arms, when the black something struck him from above, felling him to the floor.

He felt a moment of fear.

A spasm of pain.

And then nothing.

<Wet. Dark. Room. Room. Room. Green. Small. Smaller.>

Hughes, sitting on a row of weathered granite blocks that had once been part of the wall of a building, closed his eyes and focused his mind on the images coursing through Victrix's brain. Sometimes the technique worked better than others; he hoped today would be one of those times.

He tried to blot out the dull roar of the nearby surf, the scent of salt spray, the fitful sunshine peeking through serried ranks of cloud, and the dull hardness of his perch. Instead, he was a dog…a genetically engineered and augmented black German Shepherd, a dog with greater than canine intelligence, a dog who—like him—had been subjected to experiments that rendered her telepathic, but who at heart was still a dog…

…seeing with a dog's eyes, experiencing with a dog's senses to the limited extent that a human mind could appreciate them…

…and he was there…

The chamber was square, made of tightly fitted stone blocks, green with lichen and moss-like plants. Water dripped down the walls and splashed underfoot. A few streaks of wan daylight filtered through cracks in the roof while repulsive lumps of some squishy material glowed weirdly on the ground. It smelled of dank and decay, like rotting sea-wrack. Chitinous and worm-like creatures clicked and slithered in the shadows.

The room opened into a corridor…then another room, just like the first…more corridor…another room…

Strange lines—patterns—on a wall. Carvings? If so, unlike any he had ever seen before.

The ceilings were low, the corridors narrow…too low and too narrow for a human…

<…the distorted image of a human, too tall and ungainly to fit in here…>

He sensed canine humor…

…steps going down, descending into blackness…

…the passageway choked by rubble and plant growth…thick stalks and rubbery bulbs…the water level rising…

<Too dark. No room.>

He sent a thought: *<Don't go further. Come back.>*

Hughes allowed the connection to fade, and once again found himself sitting on the stone wall within sight of the sea. Around him were the tumbled remains of several buildings, the structures disappearing into the waves. To his right, an arched entryway still stood; and it was into this that Victrix had gone, descending into subterranean passageways.

As he studied the entrance, waiting for Victrix to reappear, the sound of the waves washed over him. He had been born within sight and sound of Earth's North Sea, and the sea was a part of his soul…as much a part as the green hills of Herefordshire to which his parents had moved when he was nine.

Victrix appeared, green strands dangling from her head and wrapped around her stick-up ears.

Hughes laughed, and waved a hand towards the breaking waves. "Go and wash it off."

She barked. *<You too?>*

Her eyes shone with eager hope.

Hughes hesitated—the water was cold—then acquiesced.

<Only for a minute.>

The beach was deserted. He stripped to his shorts and followed Victrix into the skin-tingling, breath-taking waves. Together they splashed and frolicked. Hughes wondered if the builders of the ruins had enjoyed swimming, or if they regarded the ocean as an enemy.

Victrix brought him a stick in her mouth, and he flung it for her to retrieve. He knew how this went—she could fetch all day. But already he was covered in goosebumps, and his toes were numb. He headed for the shore, realizing belatedly that he hadn't brought a towel. He dressed anyway.

Victrix pestered him repeatedly to throw the stick, and he obliged her.

The world was called Sultan—pronounced locally as "Sool-tahn". To Hughes, the name conjured up images of the Arabian Nights—sheiks in flowing robes, bejeweled, half-naked belly dancers, heavily laden camels plodding across desert sands. But Sultan was almost as far from that as it was possible to imagine.

Its continents were rain-deluged mountains, their slopes carpeted with lush vegetation, separated by valleys of soggy meadows. It was a world of silent, dripping forests, where living plants grew almost as quickly as dead ones decayed.

It was also a geologically active planet—the ocean and shoreline not as innocent as they appeared. Tsunamis had often pounded the coastline in response to earthquakes. There were no modern towns or settlements along the coast.

As interesting as Hughes found the forests of weirdly shaped, moss-covered trees—and Victrix was delighted to romp through them—what fascinated him more were the ancient cities. Sultan was one of the few colonized worlds possessing evidence of advanced civilization. Half submerged, the ruins dotted the shorelines of the major continent, mute testimony in stone to a vanished race.

Nobody knew what had happened to their builders, although perhaps the evidence of elevated radiation levels from a cosmic ray burst in the long distant past provided a clue. Whatever the cause, the cities had been abandoned and left to the mercy of rising sea levels.

Hughes had jumped at the chance to explore the closest such ruin, not far from Lexa's Ridge. The builders had obviously been of diminutive stature; he was pleased that Victrix had been able to be his eyes in parts of the ruin he otherwise wouldn't have been able to reach.

The possible carving intrigued him. What had the unknown builders been like? What had they hoped, dreamed, feared? Had they been intelligent enough to think of reaching for the stars? Those were questions for the archaeologists to debate—for him, only to speculate and wonder.

And as he wondered, he recalled that Leina had also been interested in ancient races. He'd heard nothing from her. How was she doing? Did she even remember him? Perhaps she'd been ordered by her superiors in the Alliance Department of Justice to have no further contact with him.

Should he have followed her to the Alliance? At the time it hadn't seemed such a good idea. He'd needed time to reflect, to let the emotions cool, to verify what she'd told him—just as she, for her part, had checked out his background. He'd even located and read with enjoyment one of her novels.

Perhaps he should have attempted to contact her—but she'd implied that she would seek him out.

Victrix poked him with the stick, and he realized she'd been waiting for him until her patience—never long—had expired.

"Last throw," he said, pitching the stick as far out as he could.

Victrix was cold; he didn't need to see her shivers to tell that. But she'd never admit it. When she emerged from the ocean he motioned toward the flitter.

"We'll come back again."

<*Promise?*>

<*I promise.*>

The city of Lexa's Ridge lay well inland, far from the hazardous coastline, on a mesa surrounded by endless forest. Hughes looked forward to exploring the city in greater detail, but first he had a patient to take care of.

As president and founder and chief exobiologist of WOLF he considered it his prerogative to decide which cases he'd take personally. This was one of them. "Kie-voolch," he muttered, letting the alien word run across his tongue. A kyvwlch—an extremely rare, exotic creature imported at great expense from Ceithin by the ferociously wealthy director of a commercial cruise line, lay near death.

The local veterinarians had been baffled. Not surprising, since hardly anyone would ever encounter a kyvwlch, no matter how long their career. Hughes was fortunate that he had—the more rare and exotic a creature, the better. He made it his business to be informed about the exotica of many worlds.

When he'd first laid eyes on the kyvwlch, the intelligent, bird-like creature had been nothing more than a motionless clump of lusterless feathery appendages.

"Spare no expense," the magnate had said, and Hughes had nodded in understanding. Such an intelligent creature became more of a companion and friend than a pet—even to people who lacked the enhanced bonding that he and Victrix shared. Normally, he'd have taken the patient up to his state-of-the-art facility on *Wolf-1*.

But the magnate had demurred. "We have first-class facilities here."

Sultan was a highly advanced colony; after inspecting the facilities, Hughes agreed that they *were* first class, and so he'd been granted use of a suite in the veterinary center, as well as a highly competent staff to assist him.

The case had been challenging—made more so by the kyvwlch's near-terminal condition. Had he been called earlier, he could have worked at a less-pressured pace. As it was, several days worth of extensive testing and head-scratching had resulted in a diagnosis—the kyvwlch's condition was due to the lack of the rare-earth element holmium, common on Ceithin but virtually non-existent on Sultan. Correct the deficiency and the kyvwlch would make a full recovery as its metabolism slowly recovered. Most interstellar ships used the element in their quantum drives, so it wasn't hard to procure a few micrograms.

As he checked on the creature in its modified bio-support unit, he was pleased to see that its vital signs had improved already, and that it was beginning to move spontaneously.

It was with a pleasant degree of self-satisfaction that he headed to the magnate's mansion, where he had been allocated a guest suite far in excess of his usual accommodations.

"I'm pleased to report that I've determined the problem, and that the kyvwlch is responding to treatment," he said, meeting the magnate and her husband in their arboretum. "I anticipate a full recovery."

"That's excellent!" the magnate beamed, rising to clasp his hands.

"You don't know how relieved I am. Just name your price, and it's yours."

Hughes felt his face flush. "Let's wait until it's totally out of the woods," he said, and went on to detail his findings and treatment regimen.

"You make it sound simple," she said, "but none of our local experts could figure it out."

"Sometimes it's just a matter of knowing what to look for," Hughes said. "Not only are species different, but planets are, too."

"Regardless, you've certainly earned our gratitude. Hasn't he, Enrique?" she said, glancing at her husband, who had remained silent and seated.

The man gave a distracted nod.

Hughes looked from husband to wife. "Is something wrong?" he asked. "Have I come at a bad time?"

She gestured with a ring-bejewelled hand. "Tell him, Reeky."

The man raised troubled eyes. "There was an…incident at the Institute last night. A senior researcher was seriously injured, and the skaggit was stolen."

"Reeky is on the board of directors," the magnate expanded. "Naturally, he's upset."

"Naturally," Hughes echoed, pulling up a chair and sitting down. "What's a skaggit?"

"A native animal," Enrique replied. "Believed to be the last of its kind. It's been on display in the Institute museum for…I don't know how long. Maybe a hundred years."

Hughes blinked. "It's dead, then?"

"Oh no, it's quite alive. Kept in a habitat unless it's removed for research purposes. Each new generation of budding scientists takes a crack at studying it."

"And this researcher—"

"Professor Eshkol Steinmetz."

"—was studying it?"

Enrique nodded.

"Was there anything special about it? A reason someone would want to steal it?"

"Other than being one of a kind, nothing that I know of."

"Surely there's a gene map."

"I expect so. No one's actually cloned it, though, as far as I know. I could be wrong."

Hughes rubbed his chin. "So it was presumably stolen by someone wanting an absolutely unique specimen? There are plenty of unscrupulous collectors out there."

"I'd think it would be hard to get it off world," the magnate said.

Hughes shook his head. "Not necessarily. A bribe to an inspector. A freighter captain not overly scrupulous about his cargo. There are professionals who deal in illegal interworld transport."

"I'm sure our planetary security forces are aware of the possibilities," she replied casually.

"I hope so," Enrique said dully. "I hope so."

Hughes dreamed that night of lost cities and vanished races.

Or perhaps Victrix did and they shared dreams.

Sometimes it was hard to tell.

But these dreams, he was certain, were his.

They made a welcome break from chasing rabbits and sticks and fetching balls.

Rebma Zetnom couldn't suppress a shiver as she and her roommate Maurelle left their dormitory just as dawn was lightening Sultan's overcast sky, and entered the acre of woods that separated their building from the Institute. Normally she enjoyed walking the scenic path, but today…something didn't feel right, and she snugged her jacket tighter around her neck.

"What's the matter?" Maurelle asked.

Rebma shook her head. "Just a funny feeling."

"Shame about Professor Steinmetz."

"I can't believe anyone would attack him." Rebma wiped the corner of her eye.

"What about your project?"

"I don't know," Rebma said. "It's his project, really. I'm only an assistant. I suppose it will be on hold until he recovers. Or maybe administration will assign me to someone else as my advisor."

"Just pray it isn't Duschova. She's a witch, let me tell you."

"You think they'll find out who did it?" Rebma wondered.

"Sure. But who would steal the skaggit?" The path forked. Maurelle turned left. "See you at lunch?"

Rebma waved a hand. "Usual place. Not that I'll be hungry..."

Maurelle disappeared from sight.

Rebma scuffed listlessly through fallen leaves, listening to the sounds of nocturnal creatures bedding down for the day and others awakening to take their place. She could identify most of them by sound. A tree-hopper there, a leaf-lizard over there, something big up there—

She halted.

Something big?

She peered into the foliage. There shouldn't be anything big. But the scratching she'd just heard...

She couldn't see anything beyond green vegetation.

She shrugged and moved on.

A large piece of the green detached itself and plummeted toward her. She had no chance to run. Only time to emit a startled half-squeak half-gasp before the thing hit her. Twisted, she fell awkwardly against a tree trunk. Pain spasmed through her neck and shoulder, and then her head struck a gnarled root and all went black.

But not before she felt a puff of warm breath on her face.

It was late when Hughes awoke, enjoying the luxury of not having to get up early. Victrix, too, snored at the foot of the bed.

A voice command cleared the window, which had been darkened for the night. Rain sluiced down from dark, low-hanging clouds, dotting the ground with large puddles.

"Good thing we went exploring yesterday," Hughes commented.

Victrix opened her eyes, looked out the window, gave a low grumble, and closed them again.

"I still have to go and check on my patient, though," Hughes added, rising and dressing.

"Stay and sleep, if you want," he said to Victrix as he left the guest suite. Victrix stayed put. Hughes smiled. She had never been a morning dog. Some dogs woke up with boundless energy. Not Victrix.

He found Enrique staring morosely into a mug of coffee in the breakfast area.

"I hope the tremor last night didn't bother you," Enrique said.

Hughes shook his head. "I didn't even notice it."

"Just a small one. Probably won't even make the news."

Such things, Hughes gathered, were so common as to be ignored most of the time. Surely not enough to make Enrique look out of sorts.

"Did anything else happen?" Hughes asked as he made himself a cup of tea.

Enrique rotated his mug between his hands. "A graduate student was attacked in the woods near the Institute early this morning." He raised his head. "The police said the wounds appeared to be caused by some kind of animal."

"An animal?" Hughes echoed, locating a pastry and parking himself across the table from his host.

"So they say," Enrique replied skeptically.

"So not related to the attack on Professor Steinmetz?"

Enrique sipped his coffee. "The strange thing is, she was his project assistant."

"Curious."

"Bad publicity for the Institute," Enrique said. "Two attacks in two days."

"If you need my help…"

Enrique waved a hand. "Thanks, but I'm sure our animal control people can handle it."

"The offer's open. In the meantime, I'm going to check on the kyvwlch."

"Effie."

"Pardon me?"

"That's what she calls it. Effie. Named after a great-aunt." Enrique took another gulp of his coffee. "Don't ask me. I don't get it either."

Hughes spent the majority of the day at the Veterinary Center, since, after taking care of the kyvwlch, he'd been invited to give a series of lectures on exobiology as well as consult on a number of cases.

He returned to the mansion late in midafternoon to settle down with a novel. It wasn't a bad way to spend a rainy day.

Except that Victrix wanted to go for a run in it.

And wouldn't take no for an answer.

"Get away!" Jurg Karolek snarled, aiming a kick at a tan-colored, ferret-like creature that twined between his ankles. The cantrix emitted a shrill squeal and darted off into the gathering twilight. "Horrible thing!"

"What's with you?" his companion, Lachel, inquired as they headed toward the gleaming white buildings of the Institute.

The rain that had drenched the city for most of the day had finally blown over, leaving the trees dripping and the buildings glistening with a wet sheen.

Karolek's scowl deepened. "What do you bet they're going to blame me that the skaggit's gone?"

"You?" Lachel, a head shorter than his coworker, looked up at the bigger man. "You had nothing to do with it."

"They'll say that I left the enclosure unsecured or something."

Lachel snorted. "Nonsense!"

"Been working there twelve years, I have, and has there ever been a problem?"

"You're conscientiousness itself," Lachel soothed.

"I admit that I never liked the thing," Karolek continued. "And maybe I teased it once or twice—"

"Once or twice a shift," Lachel interrupted. "You think none of us noticed? You tormented the creature."

"But I never hurt it, did I? At least not so any of the white coats ever found out."

"True enough."

"And I haven't even been near it since they moved it into the research lab."

"So there's nothing to worry about."

"Mind you," Karolek continued, "I'm glad that it's gone. Perhaps now they'll give me a better job."

"I always thought taking care of the skaggit was pretty cushy," Lachel said.

Karolek shook his head. "Besides making sure it didn't escape, there was always something strange about it…the way it looked at me. Creepy."

"I didn't know you had such an imagination."

"I wasn't imagining anything! The creature was weird. Weird."

Lachel recoiled from the intensity of the other man's rejoinder. "Whatever you say. I never went near it myself."

"If you had, you'd have known."

Lachel didn't reply, and the two men approached the service entrance of the Institute.

Karolek came to a sudden halt. "Did you see that?"

"See what?"

Karolek stared at a stack of recycling bins. "I don't know. I saw something move. It was long and red…like a big cantrix."

"A big red cantrix?" Lachel burst out in a laugh. "Have you been hitting the retsma again?"

"I only drink after work—not before," Karolek rasped, balling his fists. "I tell you, I saw something."

"All right, all right," Lachel said. "You saw something."

Karolek motioned toward the door. "Go on in. I'm going to check it out."

"Have it your way."

Lachel disappeared through the entrance, and Karolek made his way cautiously to the bins, peering between and behind them.

Nothing. Only shadows created by the building's exterior lights.

Irritably, he kicked the closest bin, eliciting a dull, hollow thud.

"Where are you, you miserable creature?"

He kicked another bin, harder. "Get out here!"

Another kick.

And then he heard it, the plaintive, flute-like song of a cantrix, but deeper, more resonant.

"Hah. I knew it."

He rubbed his palms together. Cantrixes were common, but one like this—obviously an unusual specimen, perhaps a mutant—might be worth something. He shifted a couple of the bins. Where was it?

"Come to daddy," he crooned.

Another few notes answered him, coming from above.

He looked up. One of the higher bins had its lid partway open.

"There you are," he whispered.

He gripped the edge of a lower bin and hauled himself up, then repeated the maneuver to reach the second tier. He lay flat on the edge of a higher bin from where he could see down and into the partly-open container. He edged open the lid further and peered inside. At first he saw nothing but wires and electronic junk to be recycled. Then his gaze lit on a red ball curled in a corner, and a pair of glittering oval eyes.

He reached inside to try to grab it—cantrixes were harmless animals, virtually defenseless. His fingers brushed fur.

He was unprepared for the red streak that flew towards him and wrapped itself around his head, for the teeth and claws that latched into his scalp and chest. A garbled scream died in his throat as incredibly strong digits constricted his airway. Pulled forward by the weight of the creature, he tumbled headlong into the bin.

"Karolek! Where are you?" came a voice he might have recognized as Lachel's if blinding pain hadn't overwhelmed his ability to hear and respond.

His eyes! His eyes!

"You're late for work, you stupid idiot!" Footsteps came close and receded. "I knew you'd been drinking."

Karolek's legs twitched and were still.

Victrix shoved her cold wet nose in Hughes's armpit.

<Wake up.>

"Huh?" he mumbled, his mind sleep-clouded. "It's the middle of the night." He tried to roll away.

<*Someone coming.*> She shoved harder.

"Ah, all right." He swung his legs off the bed. "Light on."

He blinked in the sudden illumination, then shrugged into an old-fashioned dressing gown—he never traveled without one—and cinched the belt.

Victrix pawed the door activator panel, and it slid aside to reveal Enrique with a hand upraised to knock.

"You're still awake," he said, sounding surprised. "Good. There's been another attack. Um…the Director is downstairs."

<*Work?*> Victrix's ears perked up.

<*Looks like it.*>

<*Let's go!*>

"Victrix says we're ready to help," Hughes said, as the black German Shepherd barked, pushed past Enrique, and headed downstairs.

Two strangers waited in the living area—a tall, swarthy man with bushy eyebrows and short, curly hair, and a stocky woman wearing a black and silver CityPol uniform. Enrique performed introductions—"Doc Hughes and Victrix, meet Director Siyeh and Commander McRae."

"Pleased," Siyeh said, extending a long-fingered hand.

"This is highly unusual," McRae said by way of greeting, leaving her hands by her sides.

"Consider Dr. Hughes as a civilian consultant," Siyeh said. "The Institute will cover his expenses."

McRae glowered. Victrix, sitting, fixed a warning glare on the woman.

"What's happened?" Hughes asked.

"An animal attendant at the Institute was found in a recycling bin after he failed to show up for work," Siyeh explained. "He was nearly exsanguinated and horribly mutilated—face almost entirely ripped off."

"By an animal?" Hughes guessed.

"The wounds are consistent with an animal attack."

"Did security cameras catch the incident?"

Siyeh glanced at McRae before answering Hughes. "This is Sultan, Doctor, not Earth where you can hardly go the bathroom without being captured on camera. Here, we value our privacy and our freedom. There are only a few security cameras in the most vital areas. The exterior of the Institute is not one of them."

Hughes pursed his lips. "Did any of the victims get a look at what attacked them?"

"Professor Steinmetz glimpsed some kind of dark-colored animal-"

"So he wasn't assaulted by a thief stealing the skaggit?"

"That was the initial premise," McRae said stiffly. "It is still a possibility."

"But you don't believe it."

"It seems more likely that the skaggit was left unsecured and escaped."

Siyeh cleared his throat. "The student—Rebma Zetnom—swears it was green and jumped from a tree. And Jurg Karolek mumbled something about a giant red cantrix during a brief spell of consciousness."

"Am I meant to assume that Sultan's wildlife is going on a murderous rampage?" Hughes said to McRae.

She flashed, "It's not funny! People are afraid to walk in the vicinity of the Institute. If anyone else gets hurt, there'll be panic."

"I never said it was funny. But it's certainly strange."

"It's possible that the animal attacks are completely unrelated," she said. "It's also possible that the skaggit is behind all of them."

"But the vastly different descriptions…?"

McRae dismissed the comment with a flick of her wrist. "Witnesses can be notoriously unreliable. Steinmetz saw something in the dark. Zetnom was distracted by foliage. Karolek was a known drinker."

"Hmmm." Hughes swiveled back toward Siyeh. "Is there any connection between Karolek and the other victims?"

Siyeh said, "He was one of the attendants in charge of the skaggit."

"All roads lead to the skaggit, it seems." Hughes stroked his chin. "What were the researchers working on?"

"Something to do with skaggit metabolism, I believe."

"Nothing to do with toxins or disease?"

"Not to my understanding. Besides, we've been studying the skaggit for a hundred years—if it had any dangerous transmissible pathogens I think we'd have known it by now."

"This is getting us nowhere," McRae said harshly.

Hughes ignored the interruption. "Do any of these descriptions match that of the skaggit?"

Enrique answered by crossing to a computer and returning with a holocube, which he handed to Hughes. "See for yourself."

The skaggit was, Hughes thought as he activated the cube, unlike any creature he'd ever seen. The best analogy he could devise was the unlikely cross between a praying mantis and a small bear cub. It was slightly smaller than Victrix but with the long, ungainly limbs and neck of a mantis. Its body was covered in a bluish-gray fur except for the limbs and head, which were leathery-appearing hide with faint yellowish veining. Its eyes were large and round with horizontal oval pupils, set in a snub-snouted face with a small mouth. The front limbs had prehensile digits; the rear ones, stubby claws.

"It's totally harmless," Siyeh said to his unspoken question. "There's never been a problem with it."

"So these attacks—assuming the skaggit is behind them—would be out of character for it?"

"Totally."

"Well?" McRae demanded. "Do you think you can solve the case that's baffling us?"

Hughes ignored the sarcasm. "The skaggit holds the key. Finding it is paramount."

"There's been no trace of it since the initial disappearance," McRae said. "But we're still inspecting every departing ship."

"A wise precaution," Hughes said. "I don't wish to disparage your animal control personnel, but I'd like to look for it myself."

"Suit yourself," McRae said. "It's your time and the Institute's money you'll be wasting."

"With your permission," Hughes said, "I'd like Victrix to examine the attack sites."

"The dog?" McRae goggled. "Look, our people have the most up to date scanners—"

"I don't doubt it," Hughes said, "but yes, the dog."

"Here?" Hughes asked the officer detailed grudgingly by Commander McRae to show him the incident sites, as he and Victrix stood in an innocent-appearing patch of woods near the Institute.

"We found the woman right under that tree," the officer, a young, bored-looking man named Pinchot, said, pointing.

<*Search,*> Hughes told Victrix.

<*What for?*>

<*Anything unusual.*>

"We found nothing here," Pinchot commented, as Victrix put her nose to the ground and sniffed around the tree, "other than blood from the victim."

"Maybe not," Hughes replied, "but I doubt the scanner exists that possesses the sensitivity of a dog's nose."

"Tracking a man is one thing," Pinchot objected, "but tracking something unknown…"

"That's where a dog has an advantage over a scanner. Along with a dog's nose comes a dog's brain. And intuition. A scanner can detect innumerable organic compounds, but it can't determine what constitutes a scent."

"It sounds so…so…"

"Old-fashioned?"

"Exactly. Besides, and I don't mean to be insulting, a dog is still just a dog."

"That's where you and I disagree," Hughes said. "Victrix is not just any dog."

He watched her circle the area.

<*Anything?*>

<*Lots of scents.*>

<*Remember them.*>

Victrix came and sat in front of Hughes. <*Done.*>

Hughes gave Victrix a pat. "Let's go to the next site."

"You're finished?" Pinchot sounded disappointed.

"We're only just beginning."

Hughes and Victrix repeated the procedure at the service entrance where Jurg Karolek had been attacked.

"Last one," Hughes requested.

Pinchot hesitated. "Professor Steinmetz was attacked inside. I don't know…" He cast a meaningful glance at Victrix.

"Victrix is my assistant."

"I'd best call Director Siyeh." Pinchot tapped a commlink attached to his collar and put through the request. When Siyeh came on line, he said, "Dr. Hughes wishes to see Dr. Steinmetz's laboratory and the skaggit enclosure. With his dog."

"Permission granted. I'll meet you there."

Hughes gave a small smile.

Pinchot accessed the doors and admitted them, leading them down spotless, gleaming corridors.

"It was right here," he said, pausing, "at the entrance to this lab. He was blocking the door."

Victrix took what looked like a cursory sniff.

"And?" Pinchot asked.

Hughes met Victrix's brown eyes. Then he said, "Let's go to the skaggit enclosure."

Pinchot beckoned. "It's this way." He led them out of the non-public area of the Institute into the museum section. A few adults and children meandered through the exhibits.

Hughes made a mental note that he'd have to come back for a proper visit. Especially to see some of the artifacts retrieved from the ancient cities, and a holographic representation of what one such city might have looked like in its prime.

Siyeh was waiting for them just beyond a sign that read 'Skaggit Display Closed'. "Welcome to skaggit-land," he greeted.

The skaggit enclosure was a ten-meter transparent cube. Hughes rapped his knuckles on it. "Clearsteel?"

"Take a military-grade weapon to blast through it."

Hughes studied the habitat. Stone blocks imitated ruins, and trees extended upward from neatly-trimmed underbrush towards a ceiling that mimicked the sky, with holographic clouds moving past an equally unreal sun.

"We attempt to recreate both weather and seasons," Siyeh said proudly.

Well-worn paths threaded through the low plants. The skaggit obviously had its routes.

Victrix whined softly to attract Hughes's attention.

<Go inside?>

"She'd like to enter," he said.

Siyeh raised his eyebrows. "No harm in that, I suppose." He led them through a security door into a corridor that ran behind the enclosure. Siyeh halted before a double set of security doors, entered a passcode, and waited for a retinal scan and palmprint.

"Who has access to the enclosure?" Hughes asked.

"Myself," Siyeh said, "the assistant director, and the attendants. The passcode is changed regularly."

They passed into the enclosure, and watched as Victrix padded through the underbrush and sniffed the fake ruins.

"It seems virtually burglar-proof," Hughes commented.

"The skaggit wasn't stolen from here, if that's what you're thinking," Pinchot said.

Hughes frowned. "Where, then?"

"It was being temporarily housed in Professor Steinmetz's lab," Siyeh clarified.

Victrix returned, sat in front of Hughes and raised a paw.

<Go find?>

He could sense the excitement in her voiceless query.

<All right. Be careful, OK?>

<Victrix careful.>

He visualized the skaggit so she'd have a mental image as well as the scent.

"Thank you," he said to Siyeh. "I think we're now ready to go skaggit hunting."

Pinchot snorted.

"Let me know if you locate it," Siyeh said. "I wouldn't want anything to happen to it."

They retraced their steps out of the enclosure; Siyeh accompanied them back to the staff entrance.

Her tail high, Victrix bounded away.

"You just let her run off like that in a strange city?" Pinchot asked.

"She can take care of herself," Hughes replied. "If she encounters any difficulty, she'll let me know."

"Do you really think she can find the skaggit?" Siyeh wondered.

"If anyone can, Victrix can," Hughes said, as the dog disappeared from sight.

And yet, he knew he would worry, as he always did, when she was working alone. The dog was probably more than a match for the skaggit, but he didn't want her taking chances.

"She'll find it," he said, almost in a whisper. "She'll find it."

Victrix didn't return to the mansion that night, but Hughes didn't sense any concern from her. He tapped into her varying moods—excitement, frustration, disappointment, renewed hope, and finally satisfaction. He received dim images of city streets, and then endless forest.

Sleep didn't come easily to him, even though he made sure to seek the intercession of St. Francis on her behalf.

He was still partly awake when another light tremor shivered the mansion, and when finally he fell asleep, it was to dream of a misunderstood hungry wolf…a terrorized town…and a saint who brought peace between the two…

St. Francis and the Wolf of Gobbio. He wondered dimly what had brought the old story to mind.

Victrix didn't return the next day, either, leaving Hughes in a prolonged state of nervous apprehension. He busied himself by doing further consultations and visiting the museum.

It wasn't until late in the afternoon when he felt the brushing of Victrix's consciousness against his own. An image of the ruined city near Lexa's Ridge flickered through his mind.

<*Come,*> Victrix said.

<*You come here,*> he replied.

<*No. You come to Victrix.*>

He sighed. Victrix could be very stubborn. But she must have a reason.

<*I'm on my way.*>

"Where are you going?" a startled Enrique asked as Hughes hurried out of the mansion.

"To meet Victrix," Hughes replied.

"Did she find the skaggit?"

"Ask Director Siyeh to be ready when I return," Hughes said as he dashed out the door. He clambered into his flitter and lifted off.

Afternoon shadows were lengthening when he set the craft down near the archway—how long ago now it seemed that he and Victrix had explored it! A warm front had moved through, and the temperature was remarkably pleasant.

There was no sign of Victrix, although he sensed her presence nearby. He walked over to the archway.

Sitting in its shadow was a familiar figure. Hughes crouched down in front and extended a hand. Suddenly, he froze, and shivered. It looked like Victrix—exactly like Victrix, even down to small tufts of white fur where in her youth she'd been bitten by another dog—but it *wasn't.* The eyes weren't the warm, loving, brown ones he knew…instead, he saw in their depths something totally inhuman—in*canine* he corrected himself.

Alien.

Slowly, he withdrew his hand, resisting an instinctive impulse to spring up and run away. He stayed where he was, enduring the scrutiny of the alien eyes. He knew better than to show fear.

Instead, he gave a low whistle. "So that's what we're dealing with," he murmured to himself. "I should have guessed."

<*Victrix,*> he sent a questing thought, <*where are you?*>

<*Here.*>

Calmly, deliberately, he turned his head. Victrix—the real Victrix—sat in a patch of darker shadow, from where, he observed, she could easily intervene.

<*Good work, girl.*>

<*Victrix find!*>

<*You did.*>

<*It friend.*>

<*A friend? Sure?*>

<*Look.*>

He met Victrix's stare and allowed his mind to draw closer to hers. And as he did so, he felt the touch of something unearthly. It took him a moment to realize that the creature had some telepathic ability as well, and that apparently Victrix could mediate it. He allowed himself to relax and invited the skaggit to share its thoughts.

Images flooded his mind.

A city, dimly glimpsed, hazy as if shrouded in mist…an ancient city, but not ruined, not dead…

Figures moving through the streets, the corridors, the rooms…the city alive… he could almost feel the pulse, the vibrancy of civilization…

But the figures were blurred, indistinct, as if only vaguely remembered…

Racial memories, perhaps, Hughes surmised, since the skaggit was surely far too young to have experienced life in cities dead for millennia upon millennia…

He wished he could see clearly, for other creatures moved among the larger ones, accompanying them…

Had the skaggits been the dogs of the vanished ones?

The larger figures disappeared, and there were only skaggits, inhabiting cities fallen into decay and ruin…yet despite the loss of the great ones, there was still a sense of community, of belonging…

Until, as years and generations passed, their numbers dwindled; slowly, inevitably, they slid towards extinction, until finally, and that not so long ago, only one remained…

The ruins became a place of loneliness, of despair, and eventually bleak acceptance…

Suddenly, strange, new beings came…

Despite being distorted by perspective and the different optical wavelengths of the skaggit, Hughes recognized humans.

Hope. Perhaps the loneliness would end, and a new bond be forged…

It approached the humans…

Hughes gasped as a wave of violent emotion flooded over him—sudden fear, betrayal, pain, anger…

The surge of passion subsided, and Hughes recognized the habitat, felt its walls that not even the sharpest claws could scratch, walls that were not a home, but a prison…

And time passed, years and years and years…

No energy, no will to Change…

Faces, peering in. An endless routine of pacing along short, repetitive trails. Food that never varied. Boredom, never-ending boredom…

Periods of fear and pain, when it would be taken from the habitat, pinned, studied…

Hopelessness…

Despair…

Resignation…

Until the anger rose again…more pain…teasing, torment, mocking…

And something snapped.

Hughes felt the skaggit's despair boil into rage and a thirst for revenge…

And then, when it wasn't expected, an opportunity for escape came…

He felt anticipation as it lay in wait for the three who had harmed it most recently, satisfaction as teeth and claws sank into flesh, as tongue tasted blood, as cries of fear subsided into moans…

Yet it could not—would not—kill…

It looked upon what it had done…and was there regret, remorse?

Yet now it was free. Free to roam the old places, to live alone until it died, unloved and unwanted…

The connection snapped.

Hughes rocked back onto his heels.

The Victrixes—both of them—still sat, unmoving. Hughes stretched out his hand toward the skaggit again. This time, he didn't pull it back. He rested it on top of the skaggit's head.

"You poor creature," he murmured, "you poor, poor, creature."

It had happened years ago, back when he was still in training, attending an educational session on Far Horizon. He'd been running late to a scientific seminar, and was relieved to see a number of open places on the busy flitter landing pad. He set his craft down and jumped out.

A slowly moving object caught his attention, and he paused, squinting in the bright sunshine. Finally he identified it as a pygwhit, a native creature vaguely resembling a terrestrial armadillo, but with six legs, a long tail, and a varicolored dorsal fin. They were amiable animals, that some people kept as pets.

Obviously it had strayed from its normal feeding grounds in the surrounding grasslands.

Other flitters landed, and Hughes thought briefly that he should remove the creature from danger. But then, he'd be late for the seminar. And the professor hated late arrivals. So he'd hurried on, thinking he'd remove the pygwhit after the seminar.

But there was to be no second chance. When he returned to his flitter after enduring an excruciatingly boring presentation, the pygwhit—what was left of it—was in almost the same location as when he'd first seen it. With a sense of sickness within him, he'd crossed over to the mangled remains.

The pygwhit hadn't stood a chance—a descending flitter had mashed it into the ground.

The sight remained burned into his memory all these years later. And he could never shake the sense of regret. It would only have taken a moment to save the pygwhit, and yet he hadn't been willing to take that moment. Because of his inaction a living creature had died an unnecessary death. He'd vowed never to make that mistake again.

Now, years later and lightyears distant, Hughes paced around Sultan's tumbled ruins, hands clasped behind his back, conscious of Victrix watching him, both her eyes and her erect black ears swiveling to follow him.

<*Help it.*> Her thought came to him.

<*I'd love to. But how?*>

The skaggit wasn't a pygwhit that he could just lift up and carry into a field. Or onto *Wolf-1*.

And then an idea flashed—from where?—into his mind. He wondered if perhaps God had sent it as a way for him to atone for his prior sin of inaction.

It was insane. But it might work, because he was certain of one thing: The skaggit was a metamorph—a shape-shifter. And apparently—incredibly—Siyeh and the staff of the Institute *didn't know*.

Hughes formed a mental picture for Victrix.

<*This is what I want. Can you see?*>

<*Victrix see.*>

<*Show your new friend. Show it.*>

He thought she was getting the idea—and so was the skaggit.

Without warning, the ground heaved. Hughes staggered, catching himself on an angle of stone to keep from falling. Another tremor shook the earth, stronger than the first. He clutched the rock, ripping his fingernails. Dust cascaded from the ancient archway. As the tremor faded, Hughes backed away.

As he did so, he turned towards the sea, and watched, fascinated, as the sea retreated, exposing more and more of the ancient, sunken city. Eventually, the sea withdrew all the way to the horizon, and the encrusted buildings marched towards it, finally disappearing into the sand of the sea floor.

He was so mesmerized that at first he didn't realize the significance of what he was witnessing.

And then understanding hit him, and he swung about and raced for the flitter.

<*Victrix, come! Run fast. Fast!*>

He heard an echoing mental impulse, but not directed at him. <*Come with Victrix!*>

Two shapes flashed past him and leaped into the flitter. He reached it seconds later, and bundled in even as a giant wave rose behind him and crested towards the shore like a monstrous bird of prey looming over a helpless ground-dweller.

He lifted the flitter and gunned the engine, heading for higher ground and safety.

In the rear viewscreen he watched the tsunami slam ashore, smashing the time-worn arch, tumbling the building stones as if they were child's toys, splintering the trees above the tide-line. Even over the strained hum of the flitter's laboring engine he heard the snapping of trunks, the rumbling of boulders, and a massive, wet roar.

Then the wave, its power spent, subsided into a churning froth of foam and debris.

"Too close for my liking," Hughes said to himself, decelerating the flitter to a more normal cruising speed. "Enough beach for me for a while."

<*Swim! You promised!*> Victrix was annoyed. Well, a dog might understand a bigger than normal wave, but not the danger of a tsunami.

<*There will be other beaches on other planets,*> he thought, trying to be conciliatory. <*This one is not safe.*>

<*Don't forget!*>

<*I won't.*>

Hughes found a small crowd waiting for him at the mansion—the magnate, her husband Enrique, Director Siyeh, and Commander McRae met him at the door.

"Did you find the skaggit?" Siyeh asked.

"First things first," Hughes began, the anger that had been gradually building up in him on the flight back finally reaching venting point. "You didn't tell me the skaggit was a highly intelligent social being!"

Siyeh looked perplexed. "It didn't seem important."

"Not important?" Hughes snapped. "Didn't you—didn't *anybody*—spare a single thought for that creature being locked up, alone, for a hundred years?"

"What could we do?" Siyeh pleaded, spreading his hands. "It was the last of its kind…and the habitat is more than adequate-"

"It's no more than a fancy jail. You kept the skaggit imprisoned for a hundred years to be tormented by researchers and staff. Would you do that to a human?"

"It's an animal!" Siyeh flared, red-faced. "And our researchers abide by the strictest guidelines for animal welfare."

"So just because it's an animal, you think you can do whatever you want to with it? It's a living being with feelings and emotions," Hughes retorted. "Did you ever consider what the skaggit might want?"

"Spare me the sentimental drivel," Siyeh gritted. "How could you possibly know any of this?"

"Through Victrix," Hughes replied. "We're telepathically bonded."

"Ridiculous. Telepathy doesn't exist."

"It does," Hughes countered. "I might forgive you for being ignorant. But not callous."

McRae broke in. "So you *did* find it?"

"Victrix did." Hughes faced her. "As we suspected, the skaggit wasn't stolen, it escaped, injuring Professor Steinmetz as it did so. How it escaped is for Director Siyeh's people to determine."

"Where is it?"

"Victrix tracked it to the ancient city. We escaped just before a tsunami hit—your instruments undoubtedly registered it. Forget about the skaggit. You'll never see it again."

"So I can reassure the populace?" McRae persisted.

"If you're convinced the skaggit was responsible for all three attacks, then yes," Hughes said. "If not, then let your animal control people look for a green blob and a giant red cantrix."

McRae turned and stomped off.

Siyeh let out a long breath. "The Institute will still pay you—" he began.

"Forget it," Hughes replied harshly. "I don't want your money."

"You'll take ours though, won't you?" the magnate said. "For your work on Effie?"

Hughes nodded. "My usual fee. Now, if you'll excuse me, I'll get my bags and leave."

Siyeh had disappeared when he returned.

The magnate and her husband followed him out, Enrique with his hands clasped behind his back and eyes downcast.

Hughes slung his bags into the flitter.

"You've found a new dog," the magnate observed, looking into the craft.

Sitting beside Victrix was a black and tan German Shepherd.

"A stray," Hughes replied. "I thought I'd give him a home."

"He's a fine-looking animal."

"I've named him Rex," Hughes said, petting the dog while looking into eyes that, to his mind, weren't quite canine.

"I can't believe that such a beautiful creature would be unloved," the magnate marveled.

Hughes gave a resigned smile. "Sometimes people can't see what's right in front of them," he said as he climbed into the flitter. "Funny that way, isn't it?"

SHADOWDOGS

"Incoming communication, Dr. Hughes. Priority One."

Dimly, through sleep-haze, Hughes recognized Sofi's voice. "Leave me alone," he mumbled into the sheets. "I'm sleeping."

"Incoming communication, Dr. Hughes. Priority One," Sofi said more insistently. "Please acknowledge."

Hughes yawned and rolled over. Something crunched under his pillow. He groped under it and pulled out the broken remains of a dog biscuit.

Victrix…! She had stashes of treats all over the ship. Under his pillow was one of them—a place that Rex, who seemed generally quite content in canine form, typically ignored.

"Dr. Hughes, would you please wake up and answer me? There's an incoming Priority One communication!"

This time, the words registered, and he sat up and rubbed his eyes.

"Doctor Hughes!"

"All right, already, Sofi! I'll take it on the flight deck." He hated taking calls in his bedroom.

Who could be calling him with an emergency? He swung out of bed, nearly stepping on Victrix's tail as he did so, shrugged on a jumpsuit and headed for the flight deck. Victrix followed.

"Open channel, Sofi," he said, leaning on the back of his seat.

The screen illuminated to reveal a narrow-angle view of what was obviously a warship, and a stern-faced young man wearing a gray military uniform with tan shoulders that Hughes couldn't identify.

"This is Alliance Starcruiser *Defensor*," the young man said in clipped tones. "You are requested to reduce to sublight speed and prepare to be brought aboard."

Hughes gaped. It took a moment for him to find words. "This is the civilian vessel *Wolf-1* on a humanitarian mission to the Covenanting Worlds," he protested. "I am authorized to pass through Alliance space."

The young man didn't blink. "You are requested to reduce to sublight speed and prepare to be brought aboard," he repeated.

Hughes glanced at the NavScan screen. Nothing. For all his sensors showed, *Wolf-1* was alone.

"I am an unarmed civilian vessel on a humanitarian mission," he said. "Kindly state the reason for your request."

"Denied," the young man said. "You will please follow instructions."

Hughes sighed. Arguing with military—no matter what planetary grouping they were affiliated with—was rarely productive. "Copy. Reducing to sublight."

The transmission ended, and the screen returned to showing a starfield. Hughes swung around into the seat. "Take us to sublight, Sofi."

"Confirmed, Dr. Hughes."

Wolf-1 transitioned to normal space. And there, transitioning in sync and blotting out the stars, was a massive warship. Hughes whistled. He had little knowledge of warships, but had no doubt that not only could *Defensor* reduce *Wolf-1* to atoms in moments, but also out-run the smaller ship, all the while possessing sophisticated shielding that made it invisible to his scan while traveling faster than light. It probably matched anything Earth herself could space.

"Incoming communication," Sofi reported again.

"On screen."

The same young man said, "Release your helm to remote control."

"Copy."

Hughes leaned back and glanced at Victrix. "What could an Alliance warship possibly want with me?"

Under remote guidance, *Wolf-1* closed on the larger ship. Hangar bay doors opened, and Hughes spotted several small vessels—shuttles, scoutships, and assault ships, most likely. *Wolf-1* eased inside. A docking link swung out and engaged.

Hughes stood up. "Let's go and introduce ourselves."

Rex was sitting by the airlock doors, having come in so quietly that Hughes hadn't noticed his arrival. He pursed his lips.

"You'd best stay here, boy," he said. At the moment, he wanted to concentrate on his and Victrix's impressions and reactions, and not be distracted by the skaggit—who, for all his years in captivity, had spent very little time in human society. Hughes was still learning how to read the skaggit's body language.

Victrix followed him along the link, while the doors shut out a sad-looking Rex. It was quite amazing, really, how the skaggit had adjusted over the past months to his new life as a faux German Shepherd. Hughes had spent many hours training him, and the intelligent creature had responded eagerly and well—although more than once Hughes had found the skaggit morphing from one bizarre shape to another, as though reveling in his ability.

Victrix padding alongside, Hughes exited into a large arrival platform on which stood four people. Two wore the same style gray and tan uniforms, the third an olive green one, and the fourth a black cassock with a red sash.

The first uniformed man stepped forwards and extended a hand. He was tall and lean—aristocratic, even—with dark hair flecked by silver and piercing blue eyes. A gold sunburst framed by two cobalt stars at each of the four diagonal points glittered on his collar. "Dr. Hughes. I am Star Admiral Georg Henrick. Welcome aboard *Defensor*."

Almost automatically, Hughes returned the handshake. "I admit that I'm not used to being halted in space by military ships. I'm on a mercy mission—my clearances are in order—"

The admiral raised a hand. "I apologize for the peremptory manner of this meeting. There's no problem with your clearances. Everything will become clear in short order." He motioned toward his companions. "Ship commander Captain Wilhelm Druck, Special Operations Field Group Leader Sonja Velika, Cardinal Nahiossi Hohnihohkaiyohos."

The captain was shorter, stocky without being fat, brown-haired, with drooping eyelids. The Group Leader's steely eyes regarded Hughes seriously from a strongly-set face framed by closely cropped red hair. Her form was lithe and muscular.

Hughes greeted the first two with polite nods, and received the same in return.

He bowed to the cardinal—white-haired, with high cheek-bones. "Your Eminence."

"May the blessing of our Lord be upon you," the cardinal said.

"This must be Victrix," the admiral said, looking at the black German Shepherd. "May I?"

Speechless, Hughes nodded, and the admiral bent over to allow Victrix to sniff his hand, and then he petted her head. "A fine looking dog, isn't she?" he said to the Field Group Leader. "Perfect conformation."

"Excellent," Velika said shortly.

Hughes sought for the dog's emotions and found only calmness—she, at least, wasn't detecting any hidden animosity.

"Let's go where we can talk more comfortably," the admiral directed, leading the way across the platform into a conference room, where five chairs were arranged around a table. A mug sat in front of one. Admiral Henrick waved Hughes towards it. Victrix curled up at his feet with a bored sigh, used to the drill when among groups of humans.

"Irish breakfast tea, with cream."

"You know a lot about me," Hughes said.

"We know everything about you," Henrick replied, sitting down. "That's why you're here."

Hughes sipped his tea. "I find that somewhat disconcerting."

"It was necessary, to be sure that we could trust you."

The ship vibrated faintly—the sensation of a starship attaining supralight velocity.

"Where are we going?" Hughes asked.

"I'm afraid I can't tell you," Henrick replied.

"What *can* you tell me?" Hughes asked, beginning to feel irritated.

Henrick cleared his throat. "The matter is sensitive…and embarrassing to the Alliance."

"*What* matter? I assume that you want my assistance—"

"Indeed we do. You have perhaps heard that Pope Gregory XXIX has done the Alliance the honor of a visit."

"I heard something, yes."

"But what you don't know—what almost nobody knows—" the admiral cast a distressed glance at the cardinal—"is that His Holiness has been abducted."

The room was spartan, chiseled out of solid rock, and, she suspected, ancient. She wondered briefly what race might have carved it and why. But however old the chamber was, the door was modern—and impenetrable.

The room had a bed, hygiene facilities, and a light that illuminated in nine-hour cycles. Meals appeared regularly, brought by a young man who neither spoke nor made eye contact with her.

Otherwise, she never saw nor heard her captors.

And there was nothing to do but think and pray.

"Kidnapped?" Hughes exclaimed, jerking upright.

The admiral nodded. "We can't go into more than general detail."

The captain spoke for the first time. "Following a state visit to Winfryd, the pope was to visit my homeworld, Aurora, but never arrived. The papal ship was later discovered with its communications and drive disabled. Several Swiss Guards were killed."

"An inside job?" Hughes wondered.

"Why would you think that?" the Group Leader flashed.

"It stands to reason," Hughes replied. "I doubt that Alliance security would simply let kidnappers waltz up to the papal ship and whisk the pope away."

Admiral Henrick motioned. "How it happened does not concern you."

"All right," Hughes said. "What am I to know other than that he's vanished?"

"We know where he's being held."

The captain said, "A rebel group known as the Sons of the Dark Dawn operates in the Alliance. We're certain they're responsible."

"So if you know who has him, and where he's being held," Hughes said, "where do I come in?"

"Because of this," the cardinal said, illuminating a viewscreen to show an image of the pontiff.

Gregory looked to be about seventy, although he could have been decades older. His features were vaguely Hispanic, and he was rail thin. Gregory appeared tired and slightly disheveled.

"I am being treated well," Gregory said. "I expect that plans are being made to rescue me, but I expressly order that no lives be risked in the attempt—"

The cardinal halted the transmission. "I cannot go against His Holiness's express instruction," he said.

"Is the transmission authentic?" Hughes asked.

"Without a doubt," the cardinal replied.

"We're ready to launch a rescue operation," the Group Leader interjected forcefully. "And the Alliance Council won't object."

The admiral spread his hands. "You see my dilemma," he said. "How to rescue the pope without risking lives."

"A sticky wicket," Hughes said, "to use an old Britishism. Negotiations?"

"Out of the question," Admiral Henrick said quickly. "Their demands—which don't concern you—are impossible to fill. And the Alliance does not negotiate with terrorists."

Startling him, Victrix rose to her feet, a low growl in her throat, her hackles rising. Hughes glanced around, saw nothing. <*Down, girl! Behave.*>

Grumbling, she subsided.

"But I still don't see where I come in," Hughes said.

"Beneath the pope's voice was another one," Henrick said, "that was detected when the message was carefully analyzed. It said two words—'Hughes' and 'Victrix'. It took our intelligence service to discover who Hughes and Victrix were."

Hughes smiled slightly. "I've never worked in the Alliance. I'm not surprised you didn't know who I was."

Again, Victrix was on her feet, hackly.

<*Down!*> Hughes repeated firmly. "I apologize," he said to the officers. "She's not normally like this. I don't know what's gotten into her."

He met Victrix's brown gaze.

<*What's the matter with you?*>

<*Not alone.*>

<*What?*>

<Others here.>

Almost, he had the sensation of being watched…He glanced around the room, past the curious expressions of the others.

<There's no one else here. Now stay put.>

<%^$##!>

"But why us?" he asked.

"We didn't know at first, either," the admiral said, "until we researched you and learned of your bond."

"I'm getting more confused by the moment."

"You and Victrix form a unique team."

"Surely, if it's a dog team you want, you have your own military-trained ones."

"But you and Victrix are the only human-dog telepathic team."

Victrix was up again for the third time, growling.

Something brushed against his leg. Startled, he glanced down.

There was nothing there.

Shaking inside, he put his hands on the table and rose to his feet. "What is going on here?"

"Meet the Shadowdogs," Admiral Henrick said, also rising, "with whom you'll be working."

The ancient walls weren't totally soundproof. Whoever had turned the chamber into a prison cell hadn't noticed—or had discounted—a crack at floor level in one corner. Perhaps it was a natural flaw in the rock, or perhaps some long-distant earthquake had created it.

But through it, with her ear close to the ground, she discovered she could hear Pope Gregory engaged in prayer. And through it she could converse with him, keeping her voice low just in case anyone was listening outside the door.

She'd heard him being told by their captors to make a message stating that he was all right, and that no rescue was to be attempted. She'd heard them boast how and why any such attempt would be doomed to failure.

And the idea had come to her in a flash, and she'd whispered through the crack, hoping that her voice would be loud enough to be recorded but quiet enough that her captors wouldn't hear her.

There was no way to know if she'd succeeded.

And it was only the pope's presence close by that helped her retain her sanity as day followed indistinguishable day.

Special Operations Field Group Leader Sonja Velika handed Hughes a viewscope. He trained it down a rugged sandstone canyon to where a shallow river and the canyon walls blended into an eye-twisting shimmering haze.

Several days had passed, and *Defensor* had entered orbit around a planet whose name he'd not been told.

He passed the viewscope back. "What is it?"

"EDF. An electromagnetic disruption field. It renders us totally blind and deaf."

"Them too?" Hughes wondered.

She nodded. "We can't probe past it, but they can't scan out, either."

Hughes rubbed his chin. "Doesn't *Defensor* have the power to neutralize or blast through it or something?"

She gave him a scathing look. "Of course. But they've threatened to kill the pope the instant we try to disable or penetrate the field."

"Do you believe their threats?"

"They killed the chancellor of Sajag during a rescue attempt. They're responsible for the deaths of upwards of ten thousand people during the past decade. Yes, we believe them."

She paced a circle, and Hughes followed, conscious of the planet's slightly greater than Earth-normal gravity that made his thighs ache—he needed more exercise, for sure—and breath come harder. Nearby, Victrix sniffed in crevices and under fern-like vegetation.

"Just who are the Sons of the Dark Dawn?" he asked.

"A terrorist group from Honza that claims their planet was illegally annexed by the Alliance, despite the fact that the majority of the population has voted repeatedly for Alliance membership. They want to secede and set up a highly rigid, theocratic government. They have no scruples about killing anyone who opposes them.”

Velika took a breath. “Their leader is a renegade ground forces officer. He claims to have stolen the specs of an advanced surveillance system and to possess heavy weaponry—both within the realm of possibility.”

“I see,” Hughes said slowly. “You’re banking on the fact that telepathy can’t be detected.”

“If it even exists.”

“You don’t believe it does?”

“I’m skeptical.”

“I don’t blame you. I used to be as well.”

“It was Admiral Henrick’s idea. Frankly, I think he’s shooting at the wrong asteroid.”

Hughes stared down the canyon. “We’ll need to get a look inside before we determine a plan of action.”

“Whenever you’re ready.”

“Can we get closer to the field’s perimeter?”

She nodded. “There’s a small side canyon that enters about fifty meters from the field. We can set up a base there.”

“Then let’s do it.”

‘Miserere mei, Deus, secundum magnam misericordiam tuam.”

Have mercy upon me, O God, according to your loving-kindness.

She only needed to hear the first few, faint words from Pope Gregory to be able to recite them along with him; alone in their separate cells, yet they could still pray together.

“Et secundum multitudinem miserationum tuarum, dele inquitatem meum.”

How long ago had she memorized them? She couldn’t remember. They were words she’d known since childhood.

“Amplius lava me ab iniquitate mea, et a peccato mea munda me.”

Perhaps she’d learned them from hearing them sung; composers across the centuries had set them to music.

“Quoniam iniquitatem meam ego cognosco, et peccatum meum contra me est semper.”

The words flowed over her, bearing her along as if she were a fallen leaf on a stream.

They brought her comfort; comfort that she needed, not knowing who had captured her, or why, or if she'd ever leave this prison alive.

The planet's orange sun hung just over the canyon rim, casting lengthening shadows into the depths, and highlighting the indigo river with orange ripples.

"A few more minutes, I think," Hughes said, standing on a flat outcropping just above the river. The EDF shimmered about ten meters away. He averted his gaze; looking directly at the field made his eyes feel as if they were being wrenched out of their sockets. "We'll take every little bit of help we can get."

Velika nodded. "The warm front helps, too. Makes her heat signature, minimal as it is, harder to detect. She'll probably register as a mouse-sized rodent, if at all."

Hughes glanced to where a seemingly disembodied pair of brown eyes regarded him curiously. If Victrix opened her mouth, he'd glimpse a flash of teeth and tongue, that was all. She reminded him of the Cheshire Cat. He was tempted to reach down and make sure she was really there.

Waiting just behind them at the base camp was a squadron of similarly outfitted canines: The Shadowdogs. One of the Alliance Defense Force's secret weapons. Velika had sketched the details for him.

They were a team of superbly-trained German Shepherds, canine assault troops, equipped with combat suits—like the one Victrix now wore—made of a highly-advanced light-conducting metametal that rendered them invisible but for eyes and mouth. They carried an assortment of weaponry, and each dog was remotely directed by a skilled handler.

"They're better than robots," Velika explained, "because they can think and respond with a capacity for intelligent disobedience that no artificial intelligence can match." She sighed. "But we can't risk transmissions from their handlers being detected, not if the terrorists have the detection equipment they claim to have."

She regarded Hughes steadily. "We can't make any mistakes. We have to get it right the first time, or the pope is dead."

"So there's no pressure on Victrix and me," Hughes said wryly, trying to counter the anxiety he felt.

"You're civilian," Velika replied tartly. "It's my head—and the admiral's—that are on the block."

"Understood."

"I have my doubts about this, Hughes."

"Well, if anybody had told me I'd be working with a team of invisible dogs, I'd have been skeptical, too."

She almost smiled. "Fair enough."

The sun pitched below the rim, low-hanging clouds turned to gold and crimson, and the canyon descended into near-darkness, lit only by bioluminescent plants creating weird, blotchy patches on the canyon walls, and the eerie-green glow of the ferns.

"Good," Hughes said. "Now she'll be invisible for sure. But she'll still be able to see and scent."

He crouched down to Victrix's eye level, silently praying that their connection would be strong enough to accomplish the task. He had seen through her eyes before, but it wasn't always easy.

Velika pulled a sealed pouch from a pocket and handed it to him. "A piece of the pope's clothing, as you requested."

Hughes opened it, and held it for Victrix to stick her muzzle in it. "Sniff, girl."

She did as instructed, then he said, "Now go find."

<Victrix find!>

<Be careful. Don't go near people. Look and come back.>

<Victrix look.>

She bounded off, but paused uncertainly just outside the EDF.

Hughes lowered himself to a sitting position with his back against a comfortably eroded hoodoo. "This may take a while," he said to Velika. "Please don't disturb my concentration."

"Got it."

Hughes stared above the canyon rim to where the first stars of night twinkled and a pair of small moons whipped in a close orbit. He tuned out the distant conversation of the troopers clustered around the military flitters, the gentle chuckling of the stream, and the rustling of the ferns. He felt Victrix's mixed enthusiasm and caution as she waited for his command.

And then he saw the EDF through her low field of vision. It wasn't as eye-rendingly bad as what he experienced with human eyes.

<*It's all right. Jump through it.*>

Victrix took the shimmering wall in a bound.

A sharp pain stabbed through Hughes's head, followed by a strange, disorienting sensation. But the connection held, and then he was seeing rocks and shadowy underbrush, and felt the ground moving rapidly underfoot.

Victrix didn't register them, but he thought he glimpsed sensors and weapons emplacements. To Victrix, they were "cold things"—things that humans made but which had no significance to a dog, being formed of uninteresting metals and plastic. She made no move towards them, and so he didn't correct her.

The canyon opened out into a forested expanse rather than the narrow confines that Hughes had been expecting. The giant forms of otherworldly trees rose above ground-hugging ferns.

<*Nothing.*>

<*Keep trying. Find him.*>

Victrix began to circle.

<*People.*>

She was scenting them.

<*Careful. Stay away.*>

<*No see Victrix.*>

Hughes worked the nails of his left thumb and index finger. She was invisible, he reminded himself, with a heat profile like a mouse—nobody could mistake her for a human. She carried no weapons, no electronics. She was, basically, a ghost.

And then Victrix slowed to a walk and he saw humans in a clearing, perhaps a half-dozen of them.

Victrix halted, nose to the ground. She pawed the dirt.

<*Victrix find!*>

<*Excellent. Where is he? Show me!*>

She threaded her way through what appeared to be a compound of some kind, keeping to the shadows of what Hughes interpreted to be fortified and camouflaged prefabricated buildings.

His fingertips and lips tingled. He'd never have had the nerves to be a criminal or a spy.

Then she turned and approached the looming canyon wall. Hughes wondered where she was going, but then noticed a pair of doorways inserted into the rock.

<*There!*>

<*Which one?*>

She began to move closer, then paused. A man strode over from the compound.

<*Stay!*> Hughes commanded.

The man approached the doorway on the left, placed his hand on a sensorpad, waited while it opened, then motioned. Another man emerged, wearing a white garment. He fell into step beside the first man.

<*Follow them!*>

Victrix trailed the pair as they made a circle around the compound, staying well inside the perimeter of the EDF. After a few minutes they returned to the canyon wall, the man in white passed through the door which slid shut behind him, and the other man walked away.

Pretty casual, Hughes thought. They obviously weren't expecting the elderly pope to cause any trouble. Gregory probably wasn't the escaping kind.

<*Come back now.*>

<*Now?*>

<*Yes. You can swim in the river.*>

<*!!!*>

He allowed the link to fade, and rubbed his forehead. Such a long period of intense focus always gave him a headache. He rose and stretched.

"Well?"

Hughes started. It was Sonya Velika. He'd been so absorbed that he'd forgotten her presence.

"Victrix located the pope," he said. "And I think I know how we can rescue him."

"At once?"

He shook his head, regretting the movement. "This time tomorrow night." He explained briefly.

"I'll notify the admiral."

<*Swim?*>

Hughes jerked at a sudden nudge against his leg. Two disembodied brown eyes looked up at him. He laughed. "You're quite the sneak, Victrix.

Let's get you out of that suit, so you can swim properly." He yawned. "Then I need to get some rest."

"Is anything happening?" she whispered, her lips close to the crack in the wall.

"Nothing," Pope Gregory's voice came back. "They don't speak to me at all. But they seem calm."

"Oh." She couldn't keep the disappointment from her voice.

"Be patient, daughter."

"I just wonder when…or if…"

"God's time is not ours."

"But it seems so long…"

"Sometimes trials last for a few days, sometimes for years. But morning will come again."

"If only, Holy Father, if only."

"Don't give up, daughter. Despair is from the Evil One. I'm sure the Alliance authorities are doing what they can. And if they fail…whether we live or die, we are the Lord's."

"Aren't you afraid…even a little?"

"He has no hope who never had a fear. I believe it was an English poet who said that. Besides, these men can harm only the body. Not the soul."

"It's hard not to be afraid."

"It is. But take it from someone who has been on the receiving end of seven assassination attempts. Or is it eight?"

"I'll try. Good night, Holy Father."

"Good night," Pope Gregory replied.

She kept her head by the crack and listened as he recited his evening prayers.

The scene was almost identical the next night, except that more troopers arrived in military flitters, wearing armored combat suits and carrying energy assault rifles. Somewhere amongst them—Hughes could hear their eager whines—was a team of Shadowdogs, stripped of their weapons and commlinks.

Velika radiated tension, the muscles of her lean face taut; Hughes expected that he did, as well.

And what a time to be fatigued, on top of everything else! Rex had woken him in the night by playing one of his favorite games. Shapeshifting into something with sucker-like appendages he'd hang onto the ceiling and then drop a ball near Victrix—THUMP—thump—thumpthumpthumpthumpthump—before retrieving it with an incredibly long prehensile tail. Victrix, not amused, would bark, upon which Rex would do it again—and again—until finally Hughes shouted at them to stop it.

Velika scowled as he approached.

"Problem?" Hughes asked.

"A message from Cardinal Hohnihohkaiyohos. It seems that Pope Gregory is an animal lover as well, and he's not sure that the pope would approve of the use of dogs in warfare." She stared hard at Hughes. "We're going through with the attempt anyway."

"I think we can pull it off."

"Good." She looked past Hughes. "What's that other dog doing here?"

Hughes followed her gaze to where a black and tan German Shepherd stood next to the suited and nearly invisible Victrix. He wasn't sure why he'd brought Rex along—a hunch, or intuition, or the pleading look in the skaggit's eyes. "That's Rex, my other dog. Consider him as back-up." No need to tell Velika of the skaggit's shapeshifting skills.

"There isn't a spare suit, and we don't have time to take one off one of the other dogs," she said curtly.

"He won't need one."

She gave him a questioning look, then beckoned to a waiting soldier. "Trooper Vitver is one of the dog handlers. He'll recall the squadron."

Hughes frowned. "How? With the EDF…?"

The trooper held up a small object. "A dog whistle. Primitive but effective, and unaffected by the EDF."

Hughes grinned. "Sometimes simple is best."

"Let's get into position," Velika said. "It will be dark in a few minutes."

Hughes dropped to his haunches, and put his hands on either side of

Victrix's head, feeling the smoothness of the invisible metametal beneath them.

<*Do just what I told you. No playing.*>

<*Victrix know.*>

<*Good girl.*>

He made the sign of the cross over her. <*God help you.*>

<*???*>

He smiled. <*I know you can do it.*>

"What are you doing?" Velika asked.

"Just a prayer," Hughes replied.

She pressed her lips together.

"I've heard that there are no atheists in foxholes," Hughes added.

Velika waved the comment away. "Are you ready now?"

Hughes stood. "Ready, Group Leader."

"Good." She turned away from him to issue orders to her troops.

Hughes crossed to the same hoodoo and made himself comfortable. He pointed beside him. "Rex, down and stay."

The sun slipped below the canyon rim, and the twin moons began their nightly passage. The ferns glowed with green light.

"I'll give you a signal," Hughes said to Velika.

"Standing by."

"Let's hope that their routine is the same." He patted Victrix. "Go, girl."

She turned and instantly vanished from sight. Hughes sought for her images.

Nothing.

Not a flicker.

His fingernails scraped along the rock.

Tense. He was too tense. *Settle down, Hughes. Breathe deeply. In and out.*

A jolt of pain followed by a wave of disorientation rattled him. Victrix had penetrated the EDF. So she was in the forest of giant trees and ferns. Ferns. Imagine ferns.

In and out, in and out.

Ferns. Where were the ferns?

His heart hammered. What if he couldn't make the connection? What if there was something wrong? What if the Pope was going to die because of him? What if—?

Stop it!

In and out. In and out. Breathe slowly, deeply, think of ferns…

Ferns!

There they were, gloomy in the gathering night, their fronds waving as if performing a sensual dance.

He relaxed, and simply allowed himself to observe Victrix's progress.

This time, Victrix went directly to the doors in the cliff, and waited.

Nobody came.

Had last night's walk been an aberrancy, rather than a routine? He felt the anxiety coming back.

"Well?" It was Velika's voice, spoken softly near his ear.

"Nothing yet," he replied.

And then a man strode out of the darkness. But was he heading for the door? He had to be.

He was.

The door opened and Pope Gregory stepped out. The two men took the same path as before.

<Follow them.>

<Victrix know!!>

Her answering thought sounded petulant. Sometimes she didn't like to be reminded of what to do.

Pope Gregory and his guard circled the compound, approached the fern forest.

"Now!" Hughes said, almost breaking his own concentration, and Velika snapped a command. Hughes waited a few moments, then sent a message to Victrix.

<Go, girl!>

He had a sensation of the ground becoming a blur underfoot, then a feeling of flight as Victrix launched herself into the air, then an impact as she slammed into the guard, ploughing him hard into the ground. The man grunted as the wind was knocked out of him.

Victrix grasped the hem of Gregory's cassock and yanked the stumbling pontiff away from the guard. The man gasped something, and other men came running even as Victrix pulled her charge into the fern forest.

She glanced back, long enough for Hughes to see the pursuing terrorists closing on the aged pope. And then they were flying in all directions, knocked off their feet as the squadron of Shadowdogs smashed into them. He could only imagine what they felt at being suddenly assailed by a fury of invisible opponents. Bursts of flame erupted from impacting rifle fire, but the shots were wild.

<Bring him, girl. Bring him!>

The pontiff, too, must have been amazed at an invisible force hauling him away.

Another wave of disorientation, and there was Pope Gregory in front of him, staggering and lurching. Hughes scrambled to his feet as Velika and a pair of troopers ran to Gregory.

The pope blinked, bewildered. "What's going on?" he panted.

"You're safe. Other explanations can wait," Velika said. "Get him out of here and up to *Defensor,* she commanded the soldiers. "Move it!" The soldiers turned, supporting Gregory by the arms.

"Recall the Shadowdogs," Velika ordered, and trooper Vitver put the dog whistle to his lips and blew.

"Wait!" Pope Gregory wheezed. "What about the journalist?"

"What journalist?" Velika demanded.

"The one who was captured with me."

"I don't know anything about a journalist. My orders were to rescue you. Please, Your Holiness, go with my men."

The troopers hurried the pope away.

Hughes's mind raced. A journalist. Someone from the Alliance who knew of him and Victrix, who'd whispered a secret message to get him to come.

Impossible.

It couldn't be!

He felt the blood drain from his face.

"Group Leader!" he exclaimed. "We've got to go back."

"No."

"We must rescue—"

"We've got the pope. That was the extent of my orders."

"But—"

"Look, Hughes. We're going to deal with these terrorists. Now that the pope is safe, *Defensor* is going to blast that EDF, and we're going in. I want you out of here. *Now.* Do you understand?"

Hughes clenched his teeth.

<*Go back in,*> he sent to Victrix. <*Take Rex. The other door.*>

He sensed, rather than knew what she was doing. Rex bounded past him.

Velika whirled. "Where are they going?"

"After the journalist."

"I gave you an order!"

"Five minutes. Let us have five minutes."

She looked as if she would explode. Then she said, "That's all. Then this area is becoming a battle zone. If you want to be a casualty, that's your choice." She turned away and issued orders. "All units, move back to a safe distance from the EDF. Prepare to engage. Handlers, get the Shadowdogs armed and commlinked. Make it fast!"

Hughes sought desperately for Victrix. This time, despite the adrenalin coursing through him, he made the connection easier. She was racing toward the cliff, Rex beside her…as far as he could determine, the skaggit having morphed into something low and dark. He glimpsed humans scrambling to take up positions.

And then a thought chilled him.

How were they to open the door?

An armed Shadowdog could have blasted it open. Unless, of course, the chamber had been rigged to kill the occupant if forced entry was attempted.

He groaned. There was a way. There had to be.

Someone stood near the doors. A guard.

Suddenly, an idea came to him. But would it work? Would Victrix and Rex understand?

<*Take him down and hold him.*>

That was easy.

The man slammed to the ground under the weight of a big German Shepherd at full speed. Victrix pinned him with her fangs at his throat.

Now the hard part.

Hughes sent her a picture. <*Tell Rex.*>

<*???*>

He tried again, doing his best to visualize what he wanted. It was awkward, not being able to communicate directly with the skaggit.

<*Understand, Victrix, you must understand…*>

She was sitting on her cot, hands folded. She'd been praying, but then thought she'd heard…what? The sounds were faint. Men shouting? The discharge of energy weapons?

For a moment she hoped…

But perhaps they were just having a party. Letting off steam, as bored men will do.

Then the door slid open.

She jumped to her feet.

Something stood in the doorway, framed by the light of her room against the night behind.

It moved inside.

She screamed.

To Hughes's relief, Rex appeared in Victrix's peripheral vision. He placed his right front paw on the pinned man's hand…and even through Victrix's eyes, Hughes could see it change shape as Rex's leg elongated into human form.

<Good! Now open the door!>

Both dogs knew that trick.

Rex crossed to the door, reared up and pressed his paw-hand onto the sensor pad.

But how good was his mimicry? Did it extend to palm print detail? Hughes held his breath.

The door slid open.

Rex entered, disappearing from Victrix's view.

Then a woman emerged, fright plastered across her face.

<Help Rex. Bring her.>

Victrix left her prisoner, and, as she had with the pope, grabbed the woman's clothes in her jaws and pulled her towards the cover of the forest.

The woman was an athlete. She ran.

Weapon fire burned close by. The guard was on his feet, snapping off shots.

Hughes didn't have to issue a command. This time, it was Rex who took the man down.

He couldn't hold the connection. Hughes jumped up, dashed to the EDF and was there when she staggered through the visual distortion. He scooped her up into his arms. Rex—looking fully canine—leaped through the EDF moments later.

"Leina! It *is* you—"

"Hughes! But…"

"Out of here! *Now!*" Velika and a trooper hustled them both towards a flitter.

Hughes dropped Leina into the passenger seat, and himself into the control seat. Rex jumped on board, and he spotted Victrix's eyes looking over his shoulder.

He gunned the engine, lifted off, and sped down the canyon, even as a bolt of blue fire descended from the sky. The EDF disintegrated with a flare of unleashed energy that crackled and flared past the fleeing flitter and filled the air with the harsh tang of ozone.

"Wh-What happened?" Leina murmured.

G-forces pushed them into their seats as one of *Defensor's* orbital shuttles lifted off the planet's surface to take them back to the waiting starcruiser.

"What do you mean?" Hughes asked, unable to take his eyes off her. To meet again…like this…it was unbelievable.

"I was praying in my cell, when the door opened and this…this *thing* came in…it was…I've never seen anything like it…it was sort of like a squashed dog but it walked upright, and it had one arm like a human…I ran past it, but then something else dragged me along…I thought I'd gone mad!"

Hughes blushed. "I'm sorry…I had no way to warn you. Victrix was wearing an invisibility suit. And I forgot to tell Rex to—"

"It wasn't Rex, Hughes!" she exclaimed, staring at the black and tan shepherd. "I know a dog when I see one!"

"It's a long story," Hughes said. "I'll tell you later."

"You'd better."

He put an arm around her shoulders, and held her trembling form close.

A medic—easily identifiable by the white bands on the shoulders of his Alliance Defense Force uniform - was waiting for them as the shuttle docked.

"I'm fine, I really am," Leina protested.

"Orders, Miss Dickson," the medic replied.

"Best go with him," Hughes said. He whispered in her ear as the medic walked ahead. "But don't mention anything about what you saw…"

She shuddered. "I'm not letting the shrinks put their instruments on me…" She coughed. "You look like the one who should be seeing the medics."

Hughes grimaced. "I've got the headache to end all headaches…"

The mood in the briefing room was completely different from when Hughes had first been brought aboard *Defensor*. Besides the military officers and Cardinal Hohnohohkaiyohos, Leina, Pope Gregory, and Victrix and Rex were present—Victrix sitting beside Hughes, while Rex nestled against Leina, to whom he had taken an immediate liking.

"A successful outcome," Admiral Henrick said. "The pope—and Miss Dickson—rescued, and the terrorists brought to justice."

Hughes mused that Leina didn't know that rescuing her hadn't been in the plans. He didn't think he should tell her.

"Alive or dead?" Pope Gregory asked.

"A mixture of both. Those who could be safely captured and who didn't commit suicide will stand trial."

Gregory looked tired, but otherwise no worse for wear. Henrick continued, "We're going to rendezvous with a fast light cruiser, Your Holiness, which will transport you to Aurora, so that you may continue your visit. If you still want to…"

"But of course," Gregory beamed. "I must complete my engagements. My secretary will no doubt be busy revising my schedule."

"Excellent. The people of the Alliance will long remember your visit." He turned to Hughes. "*Defensor* will drop *Wolf-1* near Covenanting Worlds space. I believe you'll find that you'll not be much delayed."

Hughes inclined his head. "Thank you."

"And then, there is the matter of compensation. You and your companions have rendered an invaluable service not only to His Holiness, but to the Alliance and myself personally."

Hughes held up his free hand. "The privilege of serving is all the reward I need." He squeezed Leina's hand. "That, and to be reunited."

"But it's not all you're going to get," the admiral said. He motioned to Captain Druck, who approached the dogs. "Since this is a confidential affair, I am not authorized to present official honors. However, I am happy to award Victrix and Rex with honorary Alliance Defense Force service medals."

Captain Druck placed the medals around the dogs' necks'. Although she couldn't know exactly what it meant, Hughes sensed that Victrix was very pleased with herself. He sent her a mental smile.

"While I would like to be able to award you the Alliance Cross for outstanding service, you'll have to settle for honorary Alliance citizenship," Admiral Henrick said, handing Hughes an inscribed plaque.

"I'm happy to accept."

"Along with that I can offer you a complete refit and upgrade of *Wolf-1* at the time of your choosing."

Hughes raised his eyebrows.

The admiral passed him another engraved sheet. "This is a permanent priority clearance for Alliance space. You'll never have to worry about getting clearance again."

"Admiral, this is too much—"

"And lastly," Henrick said, overriding his objection, "my personal contact code. If you ever have a problem in the Alliance, contact me."

"I don't know what to say. Thank you."

The admiral nodded. "The pleasure is mine." He turned to Velika, who had been standing at ease. "Group Leader!"

"Sir!" she said, coming to attention.

"You also merit a commendation, but again, under the

circumstances…"

"Understood, sir."

"However, I am happy to promote you to the rank of Field Commander, effective this date."

"Thank you, sir!" Velika said as Captain Druck applied a new insignia to the collar of her uniform.

Henrick rubbed his palms together. "Now that the ceremonies are concluded, I believe that dinner is in order." He turned to Druck. "Captain, is *Defensor* ready?"

"At your command," Druck replied.

"Break orbit. Maximum speed to rendezvous."

"Aye, sir."

<Dinner? Food?>

<Soon, girl.>

<!!!>

Henrick motioned to the others. "If you'll please follow me…"

Pope Gregory cleared his throat.

"Your Holiness?"

"I believe a Mass of thanksgiving would be appropriate," Gregory said.

Henrick paused. "Of course. I believe you'll find *Defensor's* chapel adequate."

Gregory nodded. "Any of your crew who wish to attend are welcome."

Victrix barked.

Gregory started. "Ah…I'm afraid that dogs are not—"

"It's food she wants," Hughes interjected quickly.

Pope Gregory relaxed. "Let her eat. And we'll have a special blessing for the dogs after Mass."

Hughes rose, drawing Leina with him. "And then we have some catching up to do."

Her blue eyes were warm. "I can't wait," she said.

EXPERIMENTAL SUBJECTS

"She's gone." Hughes broke off in mid-conversation and stopped dead in his tracks on one of New Vegas's squalid streets.

"She's gone," he repeated, turning puzzled eyes on his companion, Javier Sumner, a former classmate.

"Who's gone?" Sumner's square face creased.

"Victrix. I can't sense her." Hughes broke into a run.

The shorter, heavier Sumner panted to keep up. "Maybe she's sleeping."

"I can always sense her, sleeping or not. But now…there's nothing."

Never, in all the years he and Victrix had been together, had contact been broken. She'd been not only a physical companion, but a mental one as well. What could have caused the link to break?

She wasn't…she couldn't be…He could hardly bear even to think the word. *Dead.*

Wouldn't he have sensed *something*? Granted, he'd been distracted, advising Javier about the mess his colleague had gotten himself into, but…

Perhaps Leina had been right to have been leery about coming to a world as disreputable and unsavory as LongShot.

After being debriefed onboard *Defensor*, she'd insisted on accompanying him on his interrupted mission to the Covenanting Worlds.

"You must have spare rooms on *Wolf-1*?" she'd asked.

"Yes. But I'm not sure how congenial you'll find the existence of a peripatetic exobiologist."

"What better way to find out?" she'd replied. "Besides, I need to get away for a while."

He could certainly understand that after what she'd been through.

"And," she'd added, "It's a perfect opportunity to get to know each other better and see…"

She hadn't finished the sentence, but she hadn't needed to.

And so he'd agreed. Victrix and Rex hadn't had any reservations at all, frisking in canine joy when she took over the guest suite on *Wolf-1*'s lower deck.

The mission to the Covenanting Worlds had ended successfully, although a more rigid, joyless, iconoclastic society he couldn't imagine. It had been miserable for both of them, although at least they'd come to appreciate even more how much they had in common.

And now they were *here,* on another pathetic excuse for a world. If she could stick with him through this…

"Javier's an old friend," he'd said when the distress call had arrived. "He sounded pretty desperate."

"What could be so urgent on a place like LongShot?" she'd wondered.

"Javier's a nice guy," he'd replied, "but not exactly top-flight material. He made the oldest mistake in the book. Seems there was a problem with the local bearrats. His solution was to import lionsnakes from another continent into the local ecosystem."

Leina had nodded understanding. "And when the lionsnakes had finished with the bearrats…"

"They turned on the human population. I gather that nobody's been killed, but enough people have been hurt that Javier's in fear of being lynched."

"And you want to bail him out."

"For old time's sake."

"I suppose you must, then," she'd conceded reluctantly.

They'd arrived at LongShot three weeks later. Hughes had encouraged Leina to remain on *Wolf-1*, a suggestion to which she'd offered no resistance.

Fortunately, the initial solution to Sumner's problem had been almost ridiculously simple: the addition of a harmless chemical into the water supply that made people unpalatable to lionsnakes.

He'd just been telling Javier that the other man now had plenty of time—given lionsnakes' slow rate of reproduction—to round them up and get rid of them, when the link with Victrix had snapped.

Maybe Leina's female intuition had been warning him…

He pounded round a corner, and there was the hotel right ahead. He burst through the hotel doors, sprinted up the emergency stairs to his room, and slapped his palm on the sensorpad.

"Victrix!" he called, not waiting for the doors to fully open. "Victrix!"

A red-faced Javier crowded in behind him.

Hughes rapidly scanned the small suite. "She's not here!" he exclaimed, not knowing whether to be relieved or succumb to the desperation rising within him. "Where can she be?"

"At least she's not lying here dead," Javier said. "Maybe she wandered off—looking for a sausage, you know. Or a cute boy dog walked past."

"I'd still be able to sense her."

"Look, Hughes, dogs do things—"

"There's something wrong!" Hughes snapped. He paced a tight circle. "Why can't I sense her?"

"Maybe she's unconscious—had an accident." Javier suggested.

"Maybe…" Hughes said slowly.

"Or been drugged."

Hughes halted. "Drugged? You mean by Animal Control?"

"No such thing, here," Javier snorted.

"Then—stolen? Kidnapped?"

"I'm running out of suggestions," Javier said.

Hughes pivoted towards the commlink. "The police!"

Javier was shaking his head. "Don't waste your breath."

"But—"

"This is LongShot," Javier explained. "The New Vegas police aren't going to care about a dog."

"She's not just a dog!"

"Maybe not to you."

Hughes bit his lip. "There's got to be a way."

"You could hire a local to look for her."

"Rex." Hughes snapped his fingers.

"Who's Rex?"

"My other dog. He's a skaggit."

"Look, I know this is a shock—"

Hughes gripped the other man's shoulders. "A skaggit is a shapeshifter. Rex only *looks* like a dog. Sometimes. But he's telepathic, with a different mode of patterning. Maybe he can sense Victrix even though I can't. He's up on *Wolf-1* with Leina."

Fumbling in his haste, Hughes entered an access code into the commlink, chafing at the delay, and when at last a woman's face flashed up on the screen, said without preamble, "Leina, Victrix is missing. I need Rex as soon as possible."

"We'll be right down," she replied.

"Javier will meet you at the shuttle port."

"On my way."

"What are you going to do?" Javier said, as he headed for the door.

"I'll be here, trying to make contact," Hughes said, sitting down on the edge of the bed and closing his eyes. "And asking for some extra help."

"What's the matter?" Leina asked, entering the suite followed by Javier Sumner and a black and tan German Shepherd that bounded over to give Hughes a slurpy kiss.

"I don't know," Hughes said, stroking Rex's head before fending him off and giving Leina a hug. "But I'm hoping Rex can help."

He turned to Javier. "I've been working with Rex for months now. Occasionally I feel as though I can connect mentally with him, but it's like trying to speak a new language without having anyone to teach you."

"Sounds like my wife and me," Javier replied dourly.

Hughes picked up a blanket that Victrix had been sleeping on, and held it to Rex's nose. "Find Victrix," he said. "Find."

Rex sat, his head cocked to one side.

"I don't think he understands," Javier said.

"He does," Hughes countered. "He's concentrating. I've seen them do this."

"What do they say to each other?"

"I have no idea," Hughes said.

"Does that mean he's sensed her?" Leina wondered.

Hughes shrugged. "I can't tell."

Rex jumped to his feet, and with his tail erect, sniffed around the room. At the door, he halted, and his hackles rose Despite his anxiety, Hughes couldn't repress a small smile at the way the skaggit had taken to adopting German Shepherd mannerisms—even down to the slightly worried expression common to the breed. Then Rex was gone, his toenails clicking on the stairs.

Hughes hurried to the window, and was just in time to see Rex emerge from the hotel entrance and disappear around a corner.

"How are you going to follow him?" Javier wondered.

"I'm not going to," Hughes replied. "We'll wait here until he returns."

He flopped down on the side of the bed.

"Let's hope it's not too long," Leina said, her nose wrinkled. "We might catch something in this place."

It was an attempt to make him feel better, Hughes knew. "Rex will come through," he said. "He *has* to."

"Quite the menagerie you have," Javier said. "How did you come to get Victrix?"

"You've never told me the whole story, either," Leina added, coming to sit beside him.

Hughes shifted uncomfortably. "It's not important—"

"Tell us anyway," Leina encouraged, resting her hand on his arm. He took it in one of his. "It will help."

"All right." Hughes took a deep breath. "Years ago," he began, "when I was a young exobiologist and desperately in need of funds to launch WOLF, I volunteered to be an experimental subject for a new procedure. The technology—if it had worked—would have enabled me to communicate telepathically with non-terrestrial species. Results with humans had failed to materialize, but the designers didn't want to give up, and since there was still a possibility, I agreed to be their guinea pig. And so I had a nanomolecular neural network implanted into my brain. But it didn't work. And it wasn't until afterwards that I was told that it would be virtually impossible to remove without causing significant brain damage. So for years I endured headaches from this useless nano-network. Useless, that was, until I met Victrix."

And the memory came flooding back, as fresh and clear as the day it had happened.

It had begun with a single word…if 'word' was even the right term….

<*Help*>

Hughes jerked to sudden attention, a muscle in his neck twinging as he did so. Around him, the monitors and displays of *Wolf-1*'s flight deck showed only routine patterns, and music—a selection of Bach's chorale preludes—played softly in the background. He was alone—a solitary voyager through space. And yet he'd heard a voice. Hadn't he?

His mind had been elsewhere, daydreaming about Earth. Sometimes, on these long journeys, he'd wonder what it would be like to be settled on Earth or another pleasant planet, to have a place other than a starship to call home. To have a companion, perhaps a wife…

He massaged the spasming muscle.

"Sofi," he said, "any incoming messages?"

"No current communications, Dr. Hughes."

Strange. A trick of his mind, no doubt. They said people could go mad in space, start hearing voices…

<*Help*>

There it was again. A voice. Or was it? A feeling, a sensation, a wordless call? He couldn't quite decide. But it was in his mind. Perhaps he'd been alone too long…

"Sofi, are you sure?"

"Positive, Dr. Hughes."

<*Help. Hungry. Cold. Hurt*>

A series of impressions flashed through his mind. But not hallucinations. Like something he'd experienced—almost—once before.

Telepathy? But from whom, or from where?

He shook his head. The failed experiments had been a long time ago. As far as he was aware, nobody had tried to repeat them. There was no logical reason why the nanonet should begin functioning now…

But if it was…

He couldn't refuse a plea for help.

<*Where are you?*> he focused the thought, not exactly sure how to project it.

<*Here. Help.*>

Tangled metal. Flickering lights. That was all he could make out.

<Help. Lonely. Scared.>

<I'll help you. Don't worry. I'll come soon.>

But to where? What was the range of telepathy?

"Sofi, are there any vessels within one lightyear?"

"Negative, Dr. Hughes."

"What's the nearest habitable location?"

"The nearest human construction is X-Con Research Facility 12. The nearest habitable world is Sheiling IV." Sofi brought up a visual schematic.

Sheiling IV was his destination—still several days away. Research Facility 12 was much closer. Remarkably close, in fact.

"Sofi, Raise X-Con Research Facility 12."

"Affirmative, Dr. Hughes."

He tapped his finger on his armrest. If his nanonet *had* suddenly begun to work, then what sort of creature was trying to communicate? Automatically, he'd assumed it was another human…but what if it wasn't?

"Facility 12 is not responding," Sofi announced.

"Why not?"

"I'm sorry, but data are not available."

He made a quick decision. "Alter course for Facility 12. Tach 9."

"Yes, Dr. Hughes. Course change programmed and initiated."

Hughes leaned back, again wondering about the source of the cry for help, for that it surely was. He sensed no hostility, no evil intent—although could such things be hidden by a telepathically advanced being? He knew so little…

<Are you there?>

<Cold. Hungry.>

<I'm coming.>

X-Con Research Facility 12 orbited a pale red star surrounded by a cloud of debris that had never condensed to form a planet, but which provided a rich source of raw materials. And as for X-Con itself—everyone knew of the giant multiworld corporation that had fingers in innumerable pies, some more legitimate than others. What couldn't legally be done on one world could often be carried on another. And if not, it could always be performed on a research facility in deep space, beyond interference from any government.

Hughes' first glimpse of RF 12 as *Wolf-1* slowed to sublight made him blink in surprise. The donut-shaped station looked as if some aggrieved celestial giant had put his fist through it, punching out a huge chunk. The shattered remnant of a personal cruiser drifted at the end of a tattered docking link.

Hughes whistled.

Either the station had been attacked—which he thought unlikely—or there'd been a massive internal explosion. Some power remained, though, as lights still twinkled here and there around the remaining rim.

"Sofi, try to access the station life-support computer," he instructed, hoping that the system was still operational.

"Here's the report, Dr. Hughes," Sofi said after a few moments.

He studied the readout. The undamaged part of the ring still had gravity and remained habitable—although just barely. Radiation levels were tolerable. Most importantly, there was a shuttle bay in the viable section.

"Sofi, ready the shuttle please," he said, throwing on a jacket.

"Caution is advised, Doctor. The station may not be structurally stable."

"I'll be careful," he said.

The corridor he entered after his shuttle had docked was chilly; his breath misted as he called, "Is anyone here?"

The illumination was fitful; cables dangled from the ceiling, and sparks cascaded from shorted-out circuits. He checked each room as he proceeded along the corridor, finding them deserted. Most appeared to be laboratories; presumably the crew quarters had been in the mainly destroyed section of the station.

In the third room he checked he found a body—a young woman wearing an X-Con Corporation uniform, her neck twisted at an unnatural angle. He checked to make sure she was lifeless. After that, he found several more bodies.

<*Are you still all right?*> he thought.

<*Come. Help*>

<*Can you speak?*> He held his breath to listen.

At first, he heard nothing beyond the hiss and crackle of destroyed circuitry. And then…

A bark?

<Speak!>

Definitely a bark, a faint one.

He raced along the corridor towards the sound, until he reached a lab with its door partly ajar. He put his hands on the panels and forced them open to reveal a jungle of shelves, tables and instruments. He plowed through them, casting them aside.

<Happy!>

A whine from the far corner attracted his attention and he made his way there, at first seeing nothing but dark shadows. He pulled aside a fallen ceiling panel and suddenly met the gaze of brown eyes.

"There you are!" he said. "Don't move. Let me get this stuff off you."

The dog was trapped in a partly crushed cage pinned under a tangle of collapsed ductwork and structural beams. Hughes lifted off the pieces one by one, clearing the crate's door. He pried it open and the dog crawled out and sat up, wagging a bushy black tail.

"Not too fast," Hughes warned, crouching down. "Let me check you over." The dog remained immobile while he ran his hands expertly over chest and limbs.

"Nothing obviously broken," he said, rocking back on his heels. The dog took the opportunity to plant a pair of paws on his shoulders and lick his face.

Hughes laughed. "You're a friendly one, aren't you?"

A flickering overhead light abruptly stabilized. In the increased illumination Hughes noticed the stumps of wires protruding from the dog's head behind a pair of erect ears.

"Let's look at you a little closer," he said. "You're a German Shepherd…female…perhaps two years old…nice teeth…a little overweight…"

She whined as he parted the fur on her head. "A scar…these wires…what have they been doing to you?"

<Hurt. Hurt.>

He glimpsed an image of distorted human faces, of instruments, of flashes of blinding pain, of long periods of confinement, of loneliness and fear…

<Pain man hurt Victrix.>

A dog, communicating in sentences?

He frowned. "Whatever they were up to, it doesn't seem very pleasant." He rose and beckoned, "Come, girl."

He made his way to the entrance of the lab, the dog following.

In the corridor, he said, "Let's get you out of here, girl. I'll take care of you."

"Not so fast."

He turned to see a man approaching. Shoulder length blonde hair framed a chiseled face, with a neatly clipped moustache perched above a straight mouth and square chin. A ragged gash on his forehead had dripped blood onto a pale blue, high-collared tunic.

Beside Hughes, the dog froze. *<Pain man!>*

"Who are you and what are you doing here?" the newcomer demanded.

Hughes straightened. "My name is Hughes. I'm an exobiologist. President of WOLF."

"I've heard of you. An animal do-gooder." The stranger's eyes were hostile. "What are you doing on a private research facility?"

"I'm en route to Sheiling IV. I received a distress call and stopped to see if I could help." From a darkening of the man's expression Hughes realized immediately that he had misspoken.

"Very kind of you," the stranger said without warmth. "But I appear to be the only survivor."

"Other than this girl."

The man's gaze shifted to the dog, his expression firming and becoming pensive. "How did you get a distress call," he asked, "when communications are out?"

Hughes hesitated, the dog's reactions preventing him from trusting this man. "Beats me," he said. "Must have been a fluke."

<Hurt. Pain man hurt Victrix>

"I don't believe in flukes," replied the other, his focus returning to Hughes.

"I told you who I am," Hughes said to change the subject. "Who are you?"

"Alessandro Flavio. Founder and CEO of X-Con."

"Bad timing for a visit," Hughes remarked.

Flavio shrugged. "I've been here for a couple of months. And I'm alive, aren't I?" He motioned towards the dog. "I'll take care of her."

"She's in pain," Hughes said. "What have your people been doing to her?"

"Nothing that concerns you."

"Judging from the facts that she's had cranial surgery and has some kind of implants inserted, I'd guess that you're working on a brain process of some sort."

"Very astute of you," Flavio said slowly. "Can you be more specific?"

Should he say more, or not? Hughes wondered. He didn't want to raise Flavio's suspicions any more than he already had, but Flavio wouldn't know about his own failed nano-net. And his curiosity had been aroused.

"There are several things I can think of that would be conducted on a remote facility," he said at last. "Studies of certain degenerative brain diseases. Evaluation of new neurologically active medications. Perhaps something to do with canine mental functioning. Possibly research on telepathy."

A slight intake of hissed breath informed Hughes that he'd struck gold.

"An interesting list," Flavio said. "And yes, you're correct about telepathy."

"It's been tried before," Hughes pointed out. "A total failure."

"But not like this." Flavio gestured toward the German Shepherd. "This is no ordinary dog. It's been genetically modified for superior intelligence, language comprehension, and extended lifespan."

"Do you have a human counterpart?"

"We did," Flavio replied sourly, with a gesture toward the destroyed section of the station.

"And?"

"Results have been disappointing," Flavio said. "And that's all I'm going to tell you. Satisfied?"

"Not quite," Hughes replied. "I think your techs have been mistreating her."

"She doesn't look harmed to me," Flavio replied. "Look—Doctor—while I love dogs as much as the next person, this one is a research subject, and that's more important to me. I've told you more than you need to know, and I'm not going to argue with you. So why don't you mosey along off my station and go and help someone's pet?"

A muzzle bumped Hughes' leg. The brown eyes looked up at him pleadingly, showing white rims at the bottom.

<*Stay. Help*>

He took a deep breath to keep from showing his amazement that the dog was apparently understanding advanced conversation. "I really think it would be best if I took the dog."

"She'll be fine with me."

"I'll buy her. Name your price."

"She's not for sale."

"Why not, if the experiments have been disappointing?"

"Because we haven't finished review of the final data," Flavio said. "And until then—"

"You want to abuse her more?" Hughes said, his patience fraying.

"There is no abuse involved," Flavio said stiffly. "I can assure you of that."

"I'd rather not have to report you for animal abuse," Hughes said. "Just because you've got a facility in the middle of nowhere—"

"Report me?" Flavio laughed and waved a hand. "To whom? Have you seen any courts out here?"

"No, but on Earth where X-Con is headquartered—"

Flavio shook his head. "Get real, Hughes. Do you think your lawyers are better than mine? Have you got the funds to take me on?" He held up a cautionary finger. "And have you got *proof* of abuse? This is no game for children, Hughes. You haven't got a leg to stand on, and you know it."

Hughes pursed his lips. He was running out of ideas. "Can you afford the negative publicity for X-Con—"

"Don't insult me with empty threats," Flavio said. "I've been threatened by bigger men than you. Let me tell you something, Hughes. I'm a businessman. I didn't build X-Con to where it is today by letting potentially valuable commodities just walk away, or by letting little people stand in my path. Do you understand? You're a little person, Hughes." He shrugged. "But if you want to go ahead and try, be my guest. Steal private property and see what happens. I'll still have the dog and you'll be in jail."

Hughes sighed. He bent over to pat the German Shepherd's head. "I'm sorry, girl, I tried. But you don't belong to me."

"Now you're being sensible," Flavio said smoothly. "Leave now, and I'll forget we ever had this little conversation. Maybe I'll even give you a donation."

"You have to stay here," Hughes continued, addressing Victrix.

<*No! Hurt! Pain man hurt Victrix!*>

"You win," Hughes said to Flavio.

"I always do. There's a supply ship due to arrive tomorrow, and the dog and I will leave this wreck."

Hughes turned, and as he did so, a wave of anger surged over him, almost making him stagger with its sudden intensity. The German Shepherd flashed past him and leaped on Flavio, sending him sprawling onto his back on the deck. She stood there, eyes blazing, jaws opened, her fangs poised above his throat.

<*No hurt Victrix any more! No hurt!*>

<*Wait. Don't bite!*> Hughes instructed, hoping she understood.

"Get it off me!" Flavio yelled.

Instinctively, Hughes had taken a step forward; now, he halted.

"What are you waiting for?" Flavio demanded.

"I guess, being of enhanced intelligence, she doesn't want to stay with you."

"Do something!" Flavio hissed.

"I'm sorry," Hughes said. "But the dog's your property. I've been warned to leave her alone, if you recall. If she was mine, I could call her off you. Pity, that…"

Flavio's eyes were wide. The German Shepherd bent lower until her fangs were touching the skin of his neck. One quick slash and it would be over. She was ready to do it, Hughes sensed.

"Help me!" Flavio whispered.

"Tough luck," Hughes said, turning away. "You're a businessman. Handle your own business."

"All right," Flavio squeaked. "You can have the dog. Just tell it to get off."

"I want an official transfer of property notice."

"I'll give it to you."

"Let go, girl," Hughes said to the dog. "You can come with me."

<*Hurt pain man!*>

<*No. Let go.*> He caught and held the gaze of the brown eyes. "Let go," he repeated out loud.

Slowly, the German Shepherd back away. Flavio scrambled to his feet, rubbing his neck, his back to the wall.

"If you breathe a word of this—" he gritted.

"I don't care about your technology," Hughes said. "Give me the transfer, and we'll be out of here."

<*Hungry!*>

<*Be patient.*>

"I'm not a man to forgive," Flavio said as he completed the transfer on a flexpad incorporated into his shirt and handed it to Hughes. "Or forget. Remember that, Hughes."

Hughes didn't relax until he and the black Shepherd were safely on *Wolf-1* and the ship was once again underway. X-Con was a big corporation. Flavio must have more important matters to deal with than the loss of a research dog. Surely.

He tried to convince himself of that.

"You really love Victrix, don't you?" Leina asked, when Hughes had finished.

"I saved her life, and she has more than repaid me," Hughes replied.

"What's it like, the bonding?"

"I can't really explain it…perhaps it's comparable to when two people have been married for so long a time that they can anticipate each other's thoughts and reactions."

"Married?" Leina asked, and Hughes realized that there was a deeper meaning—perhaps a concern—underlying the question.

"Maybe more like a higher level boy-dog thing," he clarified.

She gave him a penetrating look.

"Victrix isn't human," he said. "She's a dog. Always will be. And dogs are different. Their perception of the world is nothing like ours. They have behaviors, habits, which are unlike ours. And believe me, some of them you *wouldn't* want."

She laughed at that.

"Being telepathically bonded to a different species isn't always pleasant," he said.

"Can you really talk to the animals?" Javier inquired.

"Only to her," Hughes said. "I don't know the technology they were experimenting with—some other kind of nano-net, I suppose—but whatever they had done to her made her receptive to my thoughts and I to hers. I don't know how it works, only that it does."

Something scratched at the door. Hughes sprang up to open it. Rex barged in, his tail wagging. His eyes, almost but not quite canine, shone with eager brightness. He barked and jumped up to plant his paws on Hughes' chest—another mannerism he had copied from Victrix.

"He must have found her!" Leina exclaimed.

"Let's go," Hughes said, motioning to Javier. "Best you stay here," he added to Leina.

"No way," she said, already on her feet.

"New Vegas isn't a safe city—"

"You're wasting time." She brushed past him out the door, Rex at her side.

Hughes shook his head and followed.

Night had fallen and it was through sparsely illuminated streets that Rex loped, Hughes behind, Leina keeping pace, and Javier falling further and further back, until finally disappearing in the blackness. No matter; he lived here and could take care of himself. Hughes didn't want to lose sight of Rex.

Figures loitered in doorways and alleys, and a pair of scantily clad women beckoned to him, cursing when he didn't slow down, and shooting malignant looks at Leina.

It suddenly struck Hughes that in his eagerness to reach Victrix, he hadn't even bothered to grab so much as a neural-tranq. It wasn't safe to be out like this at night, an unarmed offworlder who probably looked like an easy mark. Rex might provide some deterrent value, however…as well as a formidable defense.

How much further did they have to go? At this pace, Leina, a marathon runner, could go for ever. He wasn't quite as fit.

From above he heard men shout, followed by a woman's scream and then the short, sharp whine of an energy weapon. A body crashed out of a lighted window and plummeted to the street, landing with a dull thud mere feet away. Leina gave a squeak of surprise and hurdled it. Hughes paused only briefly, making sure the body was lifeless, and then hurried on. They rounded a corner as renewed discharges from the building—a brothel, perhaps?—indicated the altercation hadn't ended.

Rex made a couple of quick turns, and brightly lit landing pads in the distance indicated they weren't far from the spaceport.

No reputable hotel chain had risked opening a branch on LongShot, but New Vegas held many lesser establishments. One such now faced them, its doors open to reveal a tavern crowded with occupants, music blaring. Rex skirted the building, leading them past a parked flitter to a ground floor room. The windows had been only partially darkened, and Hughes glimpsed two human figures inside. Standing near one was a black dog-like form.

"Wait here!" Hughes whispered, nudging Leina towards the cover of a disposal bin.

"Be careful," she whispered back.

"No time," he said.

The door stood ajar. Hughes flung it open. The two men inside whirled to face him.

The taller, a lithe figure dressed in black shirt and pants, had a weapon trained on him in an instant.

The other stared incredulously, until a smile spread slowly across his face.

"Hughes. What a surprise."

"Flavio. I should have guessed."

"I did try to warn you, Hughes. Too bad you didn't listen. This unpleasantness could have been avoided if you'd only been reasonable and minded your own business."

Hughes glanced to where Victrix stood, her head and tail drooping. Her eyes, dull and drugged, barely noticed him. No wonder he hadn't been able to sense her.

He said, "I want my dog back."

"Your dog?" Flavio raise his eyebrows.

"My dog. You signed her over to me."

Flavio spread his hands. "A statement made under duress. Hardly stand up in court, would it?"

The tall man with the gun spoke. "Who is this?"

Alessandro Flavio said, "The bleeding heart who appropriated my dog."

"Did you break into my room?" Hughes asked.

The man frowned. "'Break into' is such a crude phrase. Let's say that I entered it covertly on my employer's request to reclaim his property."

"Vach is a professional bounty hunter," Flavio said. "I hired him to get Victrix back for me. I'd have let you know eventually, but you seem to have forestalled me."

"So you can traumatize her with more experiments?"

Flavio cocked his head to one side. "Upon review it was determined that the experimental results were too disappointing to have commercial potential. I thought that perhaps one day we might return to them, but I considered the possibility to be remote."

"Then why come for her now? I've had her for years."

Flavio replied, "Initially my intention was to teach you a lesson and to maintain my reputation. You see, Hughes, no one crosses me or X-Con and gets away with it. No one."

"Initially?"

Flavio's voice took on a pensive tone. "I've followed your activities, Hughes. I know that there's an unusual bond between you and the dog. I've heard reports—which I believe—that the connection is telepathic."

Hughes's feelings must have shown on his face, for Flavio added, "Not very good at keeping secrets, are you?" He glanced at Victrix. "So perhaps the dog isn't worthless after all. I intend to find out."

"So you *are* going to subject her to more experiments. I thought you were a dog lover."

"Love has its limits. Other considerations sometimes take precedence," Flavio said smoothly.

Hughes clenched his teeth.

"Of course," Flavio continued, "I could use you as well. I'd even pay you."

"Not bloody likely!"

"Then perhaps another time." The blandness of Flavio's smile didn't conceal the hint of menace.

Hughes took a step forward.

Vach's weapon, which he'd allowed to droop, whipped up to train on his chest.

Rex snarled, and Vach's glance took in the dog as well.

Flavio's lips twitched. "Vach could take both of you down before you made it half-way across the room."

"You won't get away with this!" Hughes gritted, instructing Rex, with a slight motion of his fingers, to back up behind him. He didn't want the skaggit getting killed.

"I already have." Flavio turned to Vach. "You have your pay. I'm leaving with the dog. Wait until I'm gone."

Vach nodded, and resumed staring at Hughes.

Flavio held a hand just above Victrix's head. "Come, dog." He circled past Hughes toward the door, Victrix following mechanically, something she would never have done under normal circumstances.

"Goodbye, Dr. Hughes. Until we meet again."

Hughes' mind raced desperately. Leina—but what could she do? If only he could communicate with Rex as he could with Victrix! Rex! A remembered image came to him. It was far-fetched, but the only thing he could think of.

"Victrix!" Hughes hissed as the black Shepherd went by, and just for a second their eyes met. And was there a hint of connection? Was the drug beginning to wear off? Hughes sent her a mental picture, as strongly and vividly as he could. But did she receive it? He couldn't tell.

Flavio passed through the doorway, Victrix shambling along.

Hughes flicked his fingers behind his back, and, shielded as he was by Hughes's body so that Vach couldn't get a clean shot, Rex slipped out as well.

"Stay put," Vach warned Hughes.

Hughes heard a door open and close again, followed by the engine of a flitter warming up, taking off, and diminishing.

Vach motioned with his gun. "Now get lost."

Hughes blinked, too surprised to move.

Vach holstered his weapon. "Get lost, I said. I'm a bounty hunter, not an assassin. I've got Flavio's money, that's all I care about. So far as I'm concerned the pair of you can settle your disagreement on the event horizon of a black hole." He shouldered Hughes aside, and departed.

His momentary hesitation past, Hughes hurried out. Vach had already disappeared. Leina appeared from behind the disposal bin.

"Hughes—!"

"I'm fine," he said. "It was Flavio and a bounty hunter."

A soft, black muzzle pressed against him. Hughes dropped to his knees to wrap his arms around her. “Victrix! You understood!”

<*Rex look like Victrix?*>

The thought was weak, but clear.

“That’s right, girl, exactly right.”

It might not have worked in daylight, but in the darkness…

“Where’s Rex?” Leina queried.

Hughes pointed towards the departing flitter. Suddenly its lights began to wobble, then to pitch and yaw violently. It lurched towards the ground, turned, and clipped the side of a building, sending out a shower of sparks.

“Move!” Hughes shouted, yanking Leina’s arm as the flitter aimed in their direction.

But then as it entered a lighted square a block away, the flitter dropped the last few meters like a stone and slammed nose-first to the ground with a shriek of twisting metal and billow of gray smoke. The door sprang loose, and a figure pitched to the ground, then scrambled up and ran towards them.

With a glance at Leina, Hughes headed to intercept it.

“Get it away!” Flavio screamed, clawing at Hughes. “Get it away from me!”

His clothes were shredded, and bloody furrows arced across his chest. Wide, panic-stricken eyes bulged in his deathly-white face.

“It’s coming after me!” he wailed, casting a terrified look over his shoulder, before tottering away down an alley.

Hughes glimpsed motion near the downed flitter, then the craft erupted in a ball of fire and a blast of hot air that surged down the street.

“Rex!” he yelled, lunging forwards.

“Hughes, no!” Leina cried, trying to hold him back. Hughes tore free and dashed to the burning vehicle.

A few feet away, he stopped, and dropped to his knees beside a shapeless mass of singed black and tan fur, hide, and scales that looked nothing like a dog. Long talons protruded from one side, tentacles from the other, and a fuschia-colored proboscis extended from a fanged mouth somewhere in the middle. It was impossible to tell one end of the creature from the other—or even the inside from the outside. And the odor—Hughes shuddered.

He became aware of Leina standing beside him.

“The explosion must have caught Rex in mid-metamorphosis,” he said dully. "I never thought this would happen. I didn't expect to lose Rex." His voice broke off in a choke.

Leina laid her hand on his shoulder. "It wasn't your fault," she said. "You didn't know what Rex was going to do."

He looked up at her through misty eyes, and saw that hers were moist as well. "I thought…I thought he'd just shapeshift and slip away."

"Animals are unpredictable."

"He was the last of his species. Did you know that?"

Victrix lay down and nuzzled the inert form. She whined.

"I know, girl," Hughes said. "You loved him too."

The black Shepherd raised her head and stared at him.

<Help Rex.>

"I'd love to, girl, but there's nothing I can do."

<Help Rex!>

"Victrix, I—"

<HELP REX!!>

And then he detected it, as if from a great distance, a mere flicker of an alien consciousness—

"He's still alive!" he exclaimed, jumping to his feet. "Victrix is sensing him!" He scooped up the tangled mass, thankful that Rex wasn't as big and heavy as Victrix. "Let's get him to the shuttle and up to *Wolf-1*—and pray that I've learned enough about skaggit physiology to help him."

<Help Rex, too,> he sent the thought to Victrix. *<Help Rex to hang on.>*

"Did you hear the news?" Leina asked.

Hughes was sprawled on a lounger on board *Wolf-1*, with Victrix stretched out on one side of him chewing on a mock rawhide, and Rex on the other, napping with his head on Hughes's shoulder. Two weeks had passed—two weeks in which he'd used every skill and every scrap of knowledge at his disposal—and more than a little prayer—in an effort to save the skaggit. Rex's life had hung in the balance for days. Hughes had been almost at the point of despair, when Rex finally began to turn the corner—also helped, he was sure, by Victrix's constant presence and mental encouragement.

Once that corner had been turned, though, Rex's progress had been rapid. He looked like a badly frayed and worn child's stuffed toy. But he was out of danger, though he still had a long ways to go. The skaggit was, Hughes had learned, a very tough creature.

LongShot lay lightyears distant, but not Hughes' worries. What if Flavio carried through on his implied threat and came after *him* as well as Victrix? How long would he have to be looking over his shoulder, always on the alert?

"What news?" he asked, too exhausted to raise more than marginal interest.

"Apparently Alessandro Flavio has been removed from his position by X-Con's board of directors."

"Come again?" Hughes exclaimed.

"He was found wandering, half-naked on LongShot," Leina continued, "raving that he was being chased by monsters. He's been admitted to a mental institution on Earth for treatment of an acute psychotic break. A company spokesman said that it's not known why Flavio was on LongShot as X-Con has no interests on the planet."

"Whom the gods destroy, they first make mad," Hughes quoted, a surge of relief washing over him. "Unfortunately, there are all too many people willing to abuse animals—or other people—for their own gain."

"But at least there's now one less," Leina said.

"One. Out of how many? On how many worlds?"

<*Pain man gone?*> Victrix's query broke into his thoughts. He hadn't realized she'd been listening in—and understanding.

"He's gone," Hughes said, reaching down with his free hand to stroke the top of her muzzle. "And this time, I don't think we'll have to worry about him again."

THE BELLY OF THE BEAST

"There's nothing here!" Leina exclaimed, slumping to the ground.

Hughes stared in near-disbelief at the featureless forty-foot tall wall in front of him. He reached out a hand to touch its slippery smoothness, to assure himself that it was real. Then he studied a mark in the sand, a mark that he himself had made.

"Not again!" He looked down at Victrix. "Take us back, girl."

<Here!>

<No, it's not.>

<Here!!>

"She says the entrance is here," Hughes said heavily. "Just like she did before."

"Then she's wrong!"

"She's never wrong."

"She must be. This is the fourth time we've been in this spot, and there's no sign of an opening!"

Hughes couldn't argue with that.

"Why can't we find our way out?" Leina pounded a fist in frustration. "It shouldn't be this hard."

He couldn't argue with that, either.

"Let's try again," Hughes said, giving her a hand to her feet.

"You think it will help?"

"Maybe we'll see something we missed."

"I doubt it."

"Do you have a better idea?"

She pushed the bangs of her long, reddish-blond hair back from her forehead. "No."

They began to retrace their steps through the labyrinth of endless walls that imprisoned them.

Some honeymoon this had turned out to be, Hughes thought. The honeymoon from hell.

Winfryd, the capital planet of the Alliance was, Hughes had rapidly decided, an exceptionally pleasing world—a very welcome change from the Covenanting Worlds and LongShot. Hughes hadn't raised any objection when Leina expressed her desire to return to her homeworld; rather, he embraced the idea enthusiastically.

Hughes had taken to Winfryd immediately, falling in love with its verdant, gently rolling hills, the translucent blue of the sky and seas, the softness of the scented air—all of which brought back memories of his childhood.

Leina had delighted in showing him the sights of Winfryd, from the site of First Landing to the magnificent Glindan Falls to the mysterious, seemingly endless Borrowman Cavern with its underground river.

"In Xanadu did Kublai Khan a stately pleasure dome decree, where Alph the sacred river ran through caverns measureless to man, down to a sunless sea," he recited as they stood on an overlook watching the river plummet into an abyss.

And he met Leina's family who welcomed him warmly.

"She must have run really fast to catch up with someone traveling as many lightyears as you do," laughed her father, a university professor.

"At least he's not *too* old!" a younger sister chimed in, while Leina's mother served a meal of local specialties—pastries stuffed with cinil fruit that reminded him vaguely of plum, a fluffy soufflé of herbs and spices, a dish of nisfa rice sprinkled with nuts that sparkled like opals…

The days were magical.

One day was especially so.

They were having a picnic in a forest glade carpeted with tiny flowers reminiscent of bluebells. Mellow sunshine filtered between leafy trees close enough in appearance to those of Earth that it would have taken a botanist to tell the difference.

They'd spread a blanket on the ground, opened a bottle of wine…

Leina was leaning against him, Victrix sprawled in a patch of sunshine, almost but not quite dozing.

"It's almost like a fairy tale," Hughes said dreamily.

"It is," Leina replied.

"I could imagine a unicorn walking out of the woods…"

She chuckled. "Sorry, wrong planet."

"You sure?" Hughes said, pointing.

Leina gasped and sat up straight. "I don't believe it!"

From the trees emerged a snow-white horse-like creature, perhaps two feet tall, with a single horn on its forehead. It cantered casually towards them.

"Sometimes fairy tales come true," Hughes remarked.

"But it's so—small –" She broke off and punched him playfully on the shoulder. "It's Rex, isn't it?"

"Had you going for a moment," Hughes laughed. "Look, he has something for you."

Leina reached out to remove a diamond ring that dangled from the tip of the horn. "Hughes, it's beautiful!"

"Leina Dickson, how'd you like to become the wife of a space-faring exobiologist?" he asked.

She planted a kiss on his lips. "Dog, shapeshifter, and all," she replied.

Their marriage some months later had taken place in a stone-built church that had stood for nearly three hundred years—a rarity on all but the oldest colony worlds. The priest, a cheerfully chunky man who'd known Leina since she was a girl, had performed a traditional wedding Mass, complete with choir, organ, incense, most of Leina's relatives, and the handful of Hughes' as had the time and means to make the journey from Earth and a smattering of other worlds.

Hughes had taken up Admiral Henrick's offer of a complete refit for

Wolf-1, and while that was in progress had made the fateful decision to rent a yacht at Leina's urging.

"I've always wanted to see the Dancing Moons of Tahki," she confided when he asked about potential honeymoon destinations.

"Then let's do it," Hughes replied instantly, having no idea what the Dancing Moons of Tahki might be, or where they were located.

Had he known that they lay in a poorly charted, dangerous region on the fringes of Alliance space and, more importantly, that the yacht rental company had a reason—and a poor reputation—behind its ridiculously good honeymoon deal, he'd have urged Leina to select an alternative destination.

They set off full of excitement…

But passage through an area of warped space subjected to intense gravitational anomalies and energy surges far beyond the yacht's capabilities to handle had deposited them, shaken but unharmed, near a rather peculiar star and its equally peculiar planet.

The sphere in question was approximately the size of Mars, but considerably denser, enabling it to maintain a breathable if not fragrant atmosphere. The surface was mostly desert, broken by patches of scrubby vegetation and the desiccated remains of what had probably once been larger plants.

So far, so boring. But what had caught their attention as they studied visuals from orbit, were spherical structures of concentric rings.

"Ruins, do you suppose?" Leina wondered. "Let's go and see."

Hughes, who'd been attracted to ruins ever since he was a young boy exploring England's many ancient castles, needed little urging.

"We might as well, while we wait for this piece of junk to repair itself," he said, slapping a bulkhead.

"That's the spirit!"

And so they'd taken the shuttle down, accompanied by Victrix and Rex, landing not far from what appeared to be the largest set of rings. The fiery little sun blazed down from a sky that veered from blue to violet, and the desert shimmered with heat haze.

"I don't think I want to stay here too long," Hughes said, squinting as sweat dripped into his eyes. Even with heat-repellent suits, the temperature was scorching.

"You brought water," Leina reminded.

He patted the pack slung over one shoulder, which contained the basic emergency gear he always carried when visiting a strange world. "Yes, but four of us will go through it quickly."

His voice felt hoarse from dryness almost immediately. The humidity had to be near zero—so dry that even the air seemed as though it would crack.

He scuffed through the sand; his foot struck something, and he turned it over.

"It looks like a bone!" Leina exclaimed.

Hughes picked up a bleached white object as long as his leg. "It is. And very dense, too," he said, hefting it.

"There's another one!" Leina lifted a second curiously shaped object.

"I've never seen anything quite like this," Hughes said, examining it from different angles. "Not that I'm an expert on bones."

Victrix gave the bone a cursory sniff then dealt Hughes a bored look.

<Old.>

"Not good enough to gnaw on, eh girl?" Hughes chuckled.

Leina was rooting in the sand, uncovering more bones. "It's like a graveyard." She looked up, her blue eyes twinkling mischievously. "Maybe you can have some new species named after you."

He snorted. "Extinct ones. Scan showed no large animal life on this planet."

"The first extinct Hughesasaurus discovered on Leina's World."

He grinned at that. "You take the planet and give me the old bones, huh?"

"If this is a previously unknown world, then we're entitled to naming rights."

He set the bone down again. "We'll document this and take a few specimens with us. I'll collect them on the way back so I don't have to carry them now."

<Play!>

Victrix's thought was directed at Rex. She gave the skaggit a playful bite on the shoulder, and they raced off in an exuberant game of chase. Victrix leaped over a low mound, and as he approached it, Hughes noticed that it was another pile of thinly covered bones.

"Curiouser and curiouser," Leina commented. "What do you suppose killed them?"

"Climate change?" Hughes shrugged. "There's not enough vegetation here to support much of anything, let alone creatures with this size bone structure." He glanced towards the hot little star. "Perhaps the sun's output increased. I doubt that it's always been this intense."

They crested a dune, and the ruins lay before them, sheer inward-sloping walls of bluish-gray. The dogs raced down the dune, skidding to a halt before the structure.

"Pretty odd," Hughes said. "No windows, no carvings, nothing."

"I can't tell what they're made of," Leina added, running her fingertips over the surface. "The texture is strange."

Hughes rested a hand beside hers. "Smooth as silk. You'd think they'd be pitted by sandstorms." He scratched the wall with a fingernail. It left no mark.

Leina was walking around the curve. "There's an opening here," she called.

"Wait for me!" Hughes hurried to join her, followed by the dogs.

She stood in front of a ten foot wide section where the wall was only about three feet high. Through the opening, an inner wall was visible.

"Let's check it out!" she said, swinging one leg over the obstruction, but then Victrix was jamming herself in the way, pulling Leina back.

Hughes hadn't been paying attention to the dog's thoughts. Now he did.

<*No go in!*>

He frowned. <*Why not?*>

<*Not right.*>

All he could sense from her was a vague unease. From Rex, nothing.

"What's the matter?" Leina asked.

"Victrix thinks there's something wrong."

"There's nothing alive here bigger than a bug. Come on." She nudged Victrix aside and vaulted over the wall. Then she reached for Hughes' hand. "Need help, old man?" she teased as he clambered inside.

Victrix and Rex bounded over.

"See?" Leina said. "Nothing bad happened." They began to follow the curving wall. "Let's see if there's an opening in the next one, too."

There was. And in the next ring as well, and the one after that. It had been fun to explore, at first. Until they reached the center.

"It's weird," Leina said, gripping his arm, her prior excitement having vanished. "Hughes, I don't like it."

"It gives me the willies, too," Hughes replied, looking around.

A ring of tapering pylons—some tautly erect, others slumped or wilted—towered a hundred feet or so into the sky, like frozen tentacles. And in the center of that bizarre ring, triangular slabs as high as the walls jutted like teeth from the sand, coming together at the apex to form a massive cone. But the fit wasn't quite perfect; some of the slabs not extending high enough, leaving gaps between them.

He peered between two of them, seeing only a circular expanse of sand with a hollow in the center.

"Let's not stay here," Leina urged.

Hughes sought for Victrix's emotions. The dog wasn't afraid, but neither was she completely calm, either.

Perhaps that was because Rex had developed paws that could gain traction on the sleek surface of the stones and climbed half-way up one of the tilted slabs, while Victrix could only bark in frustration, slipping back every time she tried.

<*Enough!*> Hughes commanded, breaking into a train of canine cussing. He beckoned to Rex to return to earth.

And so they'd retraced their steps—as well as they could remember them—searching for the exit. An exit which inexplicably eluded them.

That had been eight exhausting hours ago.

"Looks the same to me," Leina commented in an 'I told you so' tone as they reached the center again.

"It's like a Neolithic monument gone mad," Hughes remarked. "I can't think of any purpose for it."

"How about as a trap for accidental tourists?" Leina sighed. She leaned her back against a wall, and slid down into the scanty patch of shade it created. "I can't go any further, Hughes. I'm not used to this kind of heat."

Winfryd was, Hughes had learned, a very temperate world, not given to extremes of either heat or cold. Hughes had spent time on Earth and sundry other planets with wider temperature ranges. Leina, with her more limited experience of alien worlds, hadn't.

"What happened to the marathon runner?"

The whites of her eyes were bloodshot. "She's not in race shape," she replied tartly. "Something about falling in love and being busy with other things."

He sat down beside her, conscious that his shirt was sweat-drenched. Panting, Victrix did likewise. Rex had shapeshifted into something with a silvery, lizard-like hide to conserve water. Hughes wished that they all possessed the ability. "Maybe we should rest until morning."

He handed her the water, and she sipped it before giving a mouthful to an eager Victrix.

"We can't endure much more of this," Leina said. "We'll be dead of thirst in a couple of days. We can't wait for the emergency beacon to be received."

"Agreed."

He'd activated the yacht's emergency beacon as soon as they'd dropped unexpectedly out of QV-space, but the chances of another ship being within range, or being able to detect it in this area of weird space, were remote.

"Let's consider this logically," Hughes said, as much to benefit his own thought processes as for Leina. "Let's assume that Victrix is correct, and that the way we came in no longer exists."

"It's not an assumption. It's gone. We don't know how, but it's not there any more."

Hughes steepled his hands beneath his chin. "I don't think there's any reason to waste more time and energy looking for it."

"No argument here."

"We therefore have to find another way out."

"And how do you propose we do that? The walls are too high and slick to climb—and lean inwards, for good measure. Do you have any kind of climbing equipment in your pack?"

"No."

"What about Rex?"

"Rex could easily shapeshift and fly over the walls. He could get into the shuttle. But then what?" Hughes shook his head. The skaggit couldn't fly it. Such a task was far beyond Hughes' ability to communicate via Victrix. And even if Rex was able to make passable human vocal cords, Hughes couldn't transmit language to him—or get him to imitate his or Leina's voiceprints. Some things were simply beyond a dog's—or skaggit's—comprehension and abilities.

"It's too bad you can't contact the yacht's computer."

"There's something about this planet or the space surrounding it that's interfering with communications," Hughes said. "But it wouldn't help anyway, because there's nowhere inside the rings big enough for the shuttle to land. And it's not equipped with a flitter."

"We're really in a mess, aren't we?" Leina said.

"There must be a way to escape. We just haven't hit upon it yet."

"Makes you wish that teleportation was a reality, doesn't it?"

"A fantasy, my dear. A perpetually elusive fantasy."

He stretched out his legs, and his foot hit something hard. He leaned forward and picked up a skull.

"Great," Leina said wearily. "Something else that didn't make it out of here."

"Three eye sockets," Hughes remarked absently. "Small cranial capacity."

"Is that supposed to make me feel better?"

He pitched the skull away. Rex and Victrix made no move towards it. "The answer's here," he said, "in the center."

"Why's that?"

"Just a hunch."

"That's all?"

"There's something about this place…I can't put my finger on it…although I feel like I ought to."

She nodded. "Why are there so many of these things, all over the planet? And why are there no other buildings?"

"That's it," Hughes replied. "That's the question, exactly."

Night gave only marginal respite from the heat, and became an eternity of sweating and scratching as fine sand penetrated every portion of their clothing. Only Rex in his new form as a desert lizard was unaffected. Hughes had visited the Australian Outback once; it was nothing compared to this nameless world. His stomach rumbled incessantly; the energy rations they'd shared in silence not alleviating hunger.

Morning arrived with an eerie rainbow of colors coruscating across the pylons and walls. Hughes, emerging from what had finally become a troubled half sleep, jerked to awareness.

Leina was already awake, sitting with her arms wrapped around her legs.

"What are you doing?" Hughes asked.

"Praying," she replied. "Do you wonder if God gets tired of hearing prayers for help? We can hardly bother to pray when everything's OK, but when we're in trouble, we want Him to bail us out."

"It's an easy attitude to fall into," Hughes replied.

"Do you ever wonder why He bothers with us?"

"Frequently. But we'd be sunk if He didn't."

"One of things involved in being God, I suppose." She puffed out her cheeks. "I've petitioned every saint I can think of."

"Good. And one of them may have given me an idea." He rose stiffly and stretched. "Come on, my dear."

"We're not going to be walking around in circles again, I hope."

He shook his head. "No. It has to do with the center."

"The mysterious center." She followed him over to the conical array of slabs. "What about it?"

"I'm guessing that it's our way out of here."

She gave him a skeptical look. "And I thought I was the one suffering from the heat."

"Maybe. Victrix and Rex will determine whether or not I'm right."

He motioned to the dog and skaggit, then bent over to make eye contact with Victrix.

<Dig. In there. With Rex.>

<*Dig?*>

He could sense the tiredness in her thought. Usually she loved to dig.

<*Yes.*> He straightened and motioned. <*Go ahead.*>

Victrix squeezed through a space between two of the slabs and wandered out about half-way to the hollow. Rex joined her, and sand began to fly. Hughes found a slab that was only five feet tall and peered over it.

"Wouldn't they do better digging under the outside wall?" Leina asked, coming to stand beside him.

"You'd expect so," Hughes said, "but I don't think that would work."

"Then why should this? It's a long ways to the other side of the planet."

"Digging a hole to China is what we used to say on Earth," Hughes replied. "That's not my idea."

"Then what—? Oh." She nodded. "Since there are no different structures above ground, perhaps they're underground."

"Exactly."

The spray of sand halted.

<*Look!*>

"I think Victrix has found something," Hughes said. "Help me over."

Leina boosted him up, and he wrenched himself across the slab. Once over, he crossed to the hole Victrix and Rex had made and knelt down.

"Curious."

"What is it?" Leina called.

For answer, Hughes helped her scramble over the slab, and led her to what the dogs had exposed. He crouched down and ran his hand over a layer of some gray material. It felt like parchment.

"It's flexible," he said. "There's some give in it."

He visualized a thought for Victrix.

<*Rex cut.*>

Obligingly, the skaggit grew claws on his forepaws and drew them across the wrinkled surface.

<*Harder.*>

Rex leaned his body into the attempt. A crack opened in the surface.

"Tough stuff," Leina commented, "if it can bear our weight."

<*Make a circle,*> Hughes pictured for Victrix to relay to Rex, and gradually the skaggit carved a four foot opening. Sand cascaded down into a black void beneath.

Hughes rummaged in his pack for a flashlight, lay on his stomach and shone the beam through the aperture. The light reflected off long bands of gray material that angled away into the distance. It was like looking into a tunnel whose walls were made of irregular, crisscrossing strands.

He looked up to see that Leina had joined him.

"What *is* this place?" she whispered, her eyes wide.

"Let's find out," he said, rising.

"You can't—it's too deep!"

"Look there," he said, pointing to an immense cone of sand that was situated directly beneath and extended upwards to the hollow on the surface, which from underneath was fringed by strands and flaps of the surface material. "If I can hit that slope, then it's a slide down to the floor of the tunnel."

"You're not serious!"

"Perfectly. But if it will make you happy, Victrix or Rex could go first."

"And then what? Once we're down there, there's no way back up again."

"We don't know that."

"We could be trapped underground."

"At least we'll be out of the sun."

"It's not a joke!"

"No, but since there's no escape up here…"

Finally, she sighed. "All right then."

Hughes motioned to Rex. "Jump, boy." If it was more dangerous than it appeared, the skaggit could always shapeshift to avoid harm.

Rex paused on the lip of the hole, then launched himself into space, morphing as he did so into something vaguely like a flying squirrel. He made a pinpoint landing on the slope and slid gently down.

"See?" Hughes said. "It's doable."

"Fine. Let me see you shapeshift into a winged quadruped."

Hughes flashed her a smile. He jumped up and down. "The surface should hold. If I swing from the edge—"

"Just do it!"

He lowered himself, gripped the edges of the hole, the rough material of which gave much more purchase than the exterior walls had, and let his legs fall through, so that he was dangling by his hands.

"Here goes."

He swung himself back and forth a couple of times, and at the top of his arc, released his grip. The drop was further than it seemed, and he hit the incline awkwardly, falling onto his side, and tumbling down.

"Are you all right?" Leina called anxiously.

Hughes rose gingerly to his feet and looked up to where she was silhouetted against the sky.

"I might be bruised tomorrow, but otherwise unharmed."

A black figure shot past Leina and through the hole. In a moment, Victrix was beside him.

<*Victrix too!*>

Hughes rubbed the top of her head. <*Good girl!*>

"You can do it," he called up to Leina. "I'll cushion you."

"Not the cushions I had in mind for a honeymoon," she replied, lowering herself into position as he had done, and beginning to swing.

"A little more…" Hughes urged, climbing up part-way. "Now let go!"

Her landing was better than his, and he caught her before she fell, and together they staggered down the slope.

"Under other circumstances, that might have been fun," she said. "But are we any better off?"

He shone the light around a cavernous enclosure. It appeared even stranger from floor level, the lattice-work of gray material distributed haphazardly, cocooning the bases of the triangular slabs. In places, the walls of the cavern had collapsed, while above them, strands of the roof material hung down.

Other tunnels stretched off into darkness, and the floor was strewn with piles of some shapeless substance. The air was stale, but breathable.

"More bones," Leina said, studying the floor. "This place is a regular graveyard." She turned a circle. "Now which way?"

"I vote for the largest passageway," Hughes said, pointing. "Victrix and Rex can scout."

<*Search,*> he thought, and the two animals disappeared into the gloom, Rex having resumed a roughly dog-like shape but with larger eyes.

He held Leina's hand as they began to walk, their footsteps echoing hollowly. Other chambers, some choked with rubble, opened off the passageway they traversed. Black holes were the orifices of smaller tunnels, and everything was veined with the gray strands. Victrix and Rex checked in from time to time.

After perhaps ten minutes of walking, the chamber narrowed, and then ended. The flashlight reflected off a circular gray wall.

"Dead end," Leina said.

"Not quite," Hughes replied, inspecting the wall. "Look—it's made of panels, almost like petals. Grab a hold and let's see if it will open."

Together, they pulled on one of the leaves. For a moment, nothing happened, then the leaf began to retract. It stopped.

"Another," Hughes exclaimed.

"It's hard," Leina said, wiping sweat from her forehead and leaving dust in its wake.

A second petal yielded, and a third. The hole wasn't big, but enough for them to crawl through into a narrower passageway. Victrix and Rex jumped through easily.

Hughes whirled, as without warning, the panels snapped shut behind them.

"Bet you that's what happened to the opening in the wall that we entered," he said. "It might have been stuck open, and our crossing it loosened it enough that it closed behind us."

"Maybe I owe Victrix an apology," Leina said.

"She'd probably prefer a treat."

"If we make it out of here, she can have a case of them."

Victrix and Rex scurried ahead into the darkness.

Leina stumbled, and Hughes caught her. "More bones," she said ruefully.

The passageway meandered aimlessly, making them feel as if they were walking in circles. But at least it angled slightly upwards.

"I hope this goes somewhere," Leina said.

"Me too," Hughes said, as the passageway was now barely above his head, and just wide enough for them to walk side by side. The veins of gray material in the walls were clustered closer together, at times forming rings. They rounded a curve, and found Victrix and Rex waiting for them. The tunnel dead-ended in a mound of sand.

Leina puffed out her cheeks. "Well."

"Time for more digging," Hughes said, sending a thought to Victrix and receiving a grumble in return. Rex obligingly developed enlarged forepaws.

He and Leina moved to the side as the animals dug in. For a while, fresh sand cascaded down as quickly as they moved it aside, but finally, the hole began to deepen.

"Let's help," Hughes said, using a plate of bone as a shovel.

"Kids have suffocated digging sand caves," Leina cautioned.

"This is for survival," Hughes replied.

The stale air in the passageway made the work even harder. Hughes' arm muscles began to ache. And then suddenly, a golden shaft speared across the sand.

"Daylight!" Leina exclaimed. "Hughes, it's daylight!"

With the light came fresh—though hot—air.

They clawed at the sand, enlarging the hole until first Victrix and then Rex wriggled through and began tunnelling from the other side. Finally, the opening was big enough for a human.

"Ladies first," Hughes said, and Leina crawled through. Hughes followed.

And then they were standing on the bone-strewn desert, blinking in the fierce sunshine. Leina wrapped her arms around him, and he returned her embrace.

"I've never been so glad to see the end of a creature," he said.

Frowning, she held him at arm's length.

He turned her so that they were facing the distant walls, which instead of seeming enticing as they had at first, somehow struck him as sinister.

"You don't think they're still ruins, do you?" he asked.

Her frown deepened. "What else could they be?"

He grinned. "A skeleton."

"No way!"

"The exoskeleton of a long deceased, incredible predator," he said. "Can you imagine this world green, with dinosaur-sized herbivores grazing? Some of them enter an opening in those walls, which closes behind them, as it did us. Then those pylons—tentacles, really—direct them towards the center. The mouth."

"You mean…we came out through its gut?"

"Exactly. The softer parts have long since decayed away. The piles of bones both inside and on the surface are what's left of its final meal and its excrement."

As if with one mind, they turned away from the walls.

<*Take us back,*> Hughes directed Victrix. Proudly, her head and tail

erect, the black dog headed across the desert, Rex, fully dog-like again, at her shoulder.

Hughes continued to muse as they walked. "I suspect they're not native to the planet. There are too many. They might have denuded the planet of native animal life so much that they starved to death. Climate change did the rest."

"Then where did they come from?"

Hughes shrugged. "Who knows? I've never seen organic material like that before. Perhaps even from another galaxy…another universe."

Leina shivered.

Hughes regarded her slyly. "Still want to see the Dancing Moons of Tahki?"

"No way! I want to go home. Get away from this godforsaken sector."

The shuttle came into view over a low rise.

Leina strode ahead. "All I asked for was a nice honeymoon, and I get treated like poop."

"It's not that bad, surely," Hughes protested, closing the gap. "I'll make it up to you."

She swung around and planted her lips on his. "I'm going to hold you to that."

Victrix barked, ran ahead to the shuttle, and pawed at the access panel.

"See," Leina said, "she wants a second chance, too."

What she really wanted, Hughes knew, was a drink of water.

But he didn't say.

AZRAEL

Anya sat Indian-style in the shallows, enjoying the cool caress of the gentle waves and the warmth of the sand beneath her. The sun, low in the afternoon sky, cast a golden radiance, and a breeze rustled the fern-like trees that flourished just above the tide line.

In the distance, a pod of sea-skimmers broke the azure surface, flew above the waves, then dived beneath again. She watched them vanish, wishing that her life was as uncomplicated as theirs.

She inhaled deeply of the sea air, as if it were a tranquilizer; which, in a way, perhaps it was. She could spend all day at the beach. It had been her second home for as long as she could remember. One day, though—all too soon—she'd be forced off-world; but for now she was one of the few planet-born natives of this retreat world for the super-wealthy who had never left. Except for her studies, her eighteen standard years of life had been a permanent holiday in paradise.

She wiggled her toes in the water and half closed her eyes. She never wanted to leave. But her parents…!

There was no need for her to work, to follow a profession. Ever. Why couldn't they understand?

"You need to see the colonized galaxy," they'd said this morning.

"But I never want to leave Bluepoint!" she'd protested.

"You can't stay here forever."

"Why not?"

"Because a young woman needs an education. To experience life."

"But I've got money!"

"After this summer, we're sending you to Mingtang to stay with your cousins."

"I'll hate it. I know I will."

But her parents were adamant, and her arguments fruitless. And so she'd retired to the beach to let the sun and the sand and the waves take the edge off her anger and disappointment.

If only she could run away. But on a world of small islands, where was there to run to?

Her mind occupied and senses dulled, she watched in a bemused haze as a dark shadow sped across the glistening waves and the pink-silver beach, heading right towards her.

It took a moment for her mind to recollect that it was a cloudless day. And no flying creature was that big.

But by then it was too late.

"You need *my* help?" Hughes said, staring in disbelief at the man who addressed him as he leaned against the balustrade of Kingsfold's famed CliffTop Garden, perched above a seemingly bottomless chasm.

Towering over Hughes, his muscular physique making the exobiologist feel like the runt of a litter, the shaggy giant looked as though he should be holding a blaster in one of his immense hands and a battle-axe in the other. With his fiercely tinted blue eyes and off-blonde hair, he could have posed as Thor in a Norse epic. He was young—in his mid-twenties, Hughes guessed.

Hughes would have feared for his life but for the fact that the man wore a charcoal-gray habit and a pectoral cross in the form of a silver crucifix surrounded by a ring of stars and the letters IMC—Interstellar Missionaries of the Cross. He therefore belonged to one of the several Vatican-approved orders popularly, if irreverently, known as 'space priests'.

His accent, as rugged as his features, branded him as a native of Auduna, a world of rough-hewn Scandinavian descendants regarded as barbarians by the residents of more cultured societies. Auduna's colonists had shunned contact with other worlds for centuries, and gone their own unique way. It was rare to meet one offworld.

"That is so," the man replied.

"I don't understand, Father—"

"DeSmet Hawksclaw."

Hughes gave a respectful nod. "I've never been asked for help by a space—uh, missionary priest."

"I need transportation to Bluepoint," Hawksclaw replied. "For the life of me I can't find any commercial ship going there, and I don't have the funds to hire a private vessel."

"So how did I come across your navigational screen?" Hughes wondered.

A voice spoke from behind Hughes. "It was my idea."

He turned to see Leina, pretty in a flowered sun dress, coming towards him, followed by Victrix and Rex. The two dogs slowed when they saw the priest, approached cautiously, then sniffed him politely before sitting down to observe him.

"I might have guessed," Hughes said, putting an arm around her shoulder and receiving a smile in return.

"What are these creatures?" Hawksclaw asked, standing rigidly.

"The dogs?" Hughes asked. "They're German Shepherds. The all-black one is Victrix, and the black and tan is Rex."

The priest regarded them warily. Victrix's posture was relaxed, but Rex had his lips pulled back in a fang-baring canine grin. While the skaggit could easily impersonate a German Shepherd's appearance, imitating the nuances of a real dog's behavior was something he hadn't yet fully mastered.

"I've heard of dogs," Hawksclaw said, "but we don't have them on Auduna."

"That's a shame," Leina sad. "Dogs have gone almost everywhere with humans."

"I believe that our native wildlife ate the ones that came with our first colonists."

Leina made a face.

"They're harmless," Hughes said, reassuringly. "Both good Catholic dogs."

Seeing the priest's doubtful look, Leina cut in. "I overheard Father making inquiries, and, well, it seemed as though it might be a good idea to give him a lift," she explained.

"Bluepoint isn't on the way to anywhere," Hughes mused. "Though I'd have to ask Sofi to be sure."

"If it's not convenient, then I withdraw the request," the giant said, beginning to turn aside.

"I suppose the matter is important?"

"If you consider the salvation of souls to be important. The Church has no presence on Bluepoint."

Hughes nodded slowly. "In that case, I would be pleased to be of service."

Hawksclaw gave a big grin. "I'll be eternally grateful."

"I might hold you to that, Father," Hughes replied, returning the grin.

Hawksclaw extended a massive hand, and Hughes braced himself for a crushing handclasp.

"When do we leave?" the priest asked.

"Are you ready?" Hughes asked Leina. Since she'd joined him, he'd learned that *Wolf-1* lacked many essential items that he'd never realized he'd needed. Hence this layover on Kingsfold so Leina could shop—or "resupply"—to use her terminology.

"Pretty much," she said.

"All right then. I'm waiting for a component for one of the analyzers"—he'd figured he might as well improve his starship's medical systems while he had the opportunity—"which should arrive tomorrow. Let's say in two days time."

"I'll be ready," Hawksclaw said, taking his leave. "And I promise you I won't get in your way."

Hughes waited until the priest had disappeared before turning to Leina and laughing.

"What's so funny?" she demanded.

"I'm quite happy to transport a priest," Hughes said, "But did you have to find one who's so big? How's he *not* going to get in our way?"

"Well, when you put it like that…" She took his hand. "Come and see what I bought."

"I didn't know you had so many needs," he teased.

She looked at him with mock severity. "Not for me, silly," she replied. "Some is for the dogs—why they haven't gone crazy from boredom while in space is beyond me. And the rest is for your patients. Your recovery wards needed some serious upgrading."

Hughes grimaced. The feminine touch. He should have expected it.

Night was Rayne's favorite time, when he could leave behind his thankless job in city maintenance and be comforted by the cold twinkling of the distant stars he might one day visit.

He scuffed along the deserted streets of what passed for Bluepoint's major settlement. On any other world it would barely classify as a small village. Bluepoint didn't need a city; the settlement's only function was to serve as a hub for the small spaceport, a distribution center for arriving off-world goods, and a gathering place for the few residents of Bluepoint who actually wanted to meet other people.

For him, it was a dead-end.

What did the wealthy snobs who came to the planet only to relax and party care for those who upheld the minimal necessary infrastructure?

Nothing. Never had and never would.

He rounded a corner, not caring where his feet took him. It wasn't possible to get lost here.

He'd arrived as a teenage stowaway on a tramp freighter, thinking he'd find adventure and a better life. Instead, after a spell in Reformation as a result of his improper mode of immigration, he'd been mired for a decade in a job that offered him only minimal prospects for advancement.

He looked up at the stars, finding no solace, this night. He shifted his gaze to where one of the trio of Bluepoint's small moons hurtled through the starfield.

Most nights, the sky gave him hope, that there was life elsewhere, even though he couldn't as yet grasp it. But tonight—all he wanted to do was curse the stars.

He returned his gaze to where he knew the stars were brightest, more densely clustered.

They were gone.

He stood in shock, unable for a moment to comprehend what had happened, until with a start he realized they were being blotted out by something immense and dark.

He turned to run, but before he'd taken a pair of steps, the falling blackness enveloped him.

Despite Hughes's fears, the voyage to Bluepoint passed uneventfully. Father Hawksclaw said Mass daily in *Wolf-1's* small chapel, and otherwise generally passed his time in prayer and study—that was, when he wasn't being pestered by Rex, who seemed to have taken a liking to him. He ate surprisingly little for a man of his size. And, when he joined Hughes and Leina for meals, he proved to be a convivial companion, regaling them with the legends and stories of Auduna which had developed a detailed and extensive mythology during the centuries of its isolation.

Only one awkward moment occurred, and that was when Hughes wondered why the priest had been stranded on Kingsfold. The big man had blushed and hesitated.

"I'm sorry," Hughes said quickly. "I didn't mean to embarrass you."

Hawksclaw looked down at the remains of the food on his plate. "I'll tell you," he said. "It's part of my penance."

Hughes met Leina's concerned glance.

"You see," Hawksclaw said, "I failed."

"You really don't have to dig up the past for us," Leina said.

The priest raised his eyes. "We Audunans are a clannish people," he said. "Family ties are immensely strong. My clan objected strongly when I joined an interstellar order, rather than one based on Auduna. They were even more displeased when I was instructed to join a mission on White's Freehold."

"Never heard of it," Hughes said.

"An unaffiliated world," Leina supplied. "Very remote. Primitive, too."

Hawksclaw nodded agreement and took a deep breath. "I thought it was my calling. But I never realized it would be so hard…it was as if I had suddenly become an outcast from my people. I made it as far as Zion's Gate. And then…" his voice dropped. "I turned tail and went home."

"A man like you?" Hughes exclaimed, belatedly thinking that bravery and size didn't necessarily go together. Was Hawksclaw a gentle giant at heart?

"I'm not a coward!" Hawksclaw flashed. Then the fire faded as suddenly as it had come. "But I was too homesick to go on. I returned to Auduna in disgrace." He raised a hand. "There is nothing worse for an Audunan than disgrace. There is nothing worse for a Christian, either. I had put my hand to the plough and turned back. I had valued my family ties more than Our Lord."

His eyes were hollow. "But my return was even worse. My family would have nothing to do with me. Fellow priests shunned me. My life fell apart. Quite literally, I didn't know what to do -" He clenched his fists. "I wanted to die."

"You didn't try to—" Leina began.

He shook his head. "You can't avoid death, but you must be prepared for it. I wasn't."

"What happened, then?" Leina asked softly.

"My superior informed the Secretary for Interstellar Missions of my failure. I received a summons from Rome. Needless to say, I went, expecting the worst. I was astonished when the secretary—Cardinal Yassi—greeted me warmly. He offered me a second chance."

"'We need good men,' he said. 'I am not a good man,' I replied, 'I am unworthy.' 'St. Peter failed at first,' he said. 'As did St. Mark. And there are others.' I thought about it, then said, 'Send me somewhere where the Church has no witness. Where no witness is wanted.' He agreed."

"But Bluepoint?" Leina inquired. "How can you start a mission on a planet where people avoid each other like the plague?"

Hawksclaw folded his giant hands. "The cardinal explained that I'd have my work cut out for me."

"To put it mildly."

"I said that I would make my own way, that I would not be a burden upon my order." Hawksclaw gave a wry smile. "I thought I was proceeding well until the captain of the freighter I was on came to the conclusion that carrying a priest was bad luck and dumped me on Kingsfold where I found I could go no further. And then the Lord sent you to my rescue."

"It takes a strong man to pick himself up after failure and go on," Hughes said.

Hawksclaw shook his head. "It takes grace," he replied, "and the willingness to accept that grace."

"We'll get you to Bluepoint," Leina said.

"That's all I ask," Hawksclaw replied. "As for what awaits me there…it's in God's hands."

"Anyone home?" Russel Slotzve called as he entered the land-side door of his house, his previously existing irritation already increasing at the lack of an answer. He'd flown to one of the neighboring islands at the invitation of an old business partner—"Let's play chess and discuss a new venture"—only to find her estate deserted. He'd left an angry note, and headed home.

Now it was dusk, he'd wasted a perfectly good afternoon, and his partner and their children were missing.

"Lorli! Where are you?"

He went from room to room. They weren't inside. Perhaps down on the beach or in the gardens. He walked out onto the terrace, and scanned the strip of sand.

Nothing. The waves beat a lonely nocturne that he was in no mood to enjoy.

He cut around the house to the gardens.

"Lorli! Lorli!"

And there he paused. Normally, the gardenbots kept the shrubs and flowering plants in immaculate condition. But now…broken stems and trampled blossoms lay strewn everywhere. It looked as if something—or someone—perhaps several someones—had run heedlessly through the gardens.

His chest tightened.

What had happened?

Nothing happened on Bluepoint. Nothing. Ever.

The dropping sun had cast his elongated shadow before him.

As he stared, bewildered and anxious, something larger, darker, blotted it out.

He spun on his heel—

But there was no one to hear him scream.

Hughes wondered what awaited any of them when, after *Wolf-1* had entered orbit around Bluepoint, repeated hails went unanswered. Sofi could provide no explanation for the silence.

"The systems are active, Dr. Hughes."

"The lights are on but nobody's home," he said to himself. "There's nothing for it but to go down and see for ourselves," he added, studying the image of the watery planet which looked like a blue droplet against the black background of space.

"I'll come too," Hawksclaw said.

"As will I," Leina added.

"You'd best stay here," Hughes countered. "It might be dangerous."

"Since when am I a stranger to danger?" she said. "I'd bet I've been in more dangerous places than you have."

Hughes conceded the point. "Father—" he began, but broke off at the determined expression on the missionary's face. "I can see that I'm outnumbered," he said. "Very well."

He indicated a schematic of Bluepoint. "There's nothing that really constitutes a continent, merely an assortment of islands, the majority in the southern hemisphere. The largest is here, unimaginatively called the Big Island. The population's only a few hundred." He glanced at Hawksclaw. "Not much of a mission field, Father."

The Audunan shrugged. "All are valuable in God's eyes."

"Let's go, then."

It was a deserted landing pad that awaited them when they stepped out of the shuttle into an eerie silence that enveloped them when the whine of the shuttle's engines had died away. Even the dogs seemed affected, scanning the surroundings with ears erect. A pair of other shuttles stood parked nearby, in the vicinity of several service vehicles. The modest spaceport buildings turned blank windows to the world. A few creatures that resembled flying reptiles of some sort perched on the roof.

The humid air was redolent with the scent of the not far distant sea; Victrix turned hopeful eyes on Hughes.

<*Swim?*>

"Not at the moment, girl," he said absently.

"There's something very wrong here," Hawksclaw said.

"I can feel it too," Leina added.

<*SWIM!!*> Victrix pawed at the ground.

<*Later!*>

"Let's check out the spaceport first," Hughes said, leading the way to what appeared to be the control center. The door wasn't secured.

Leina ran a finger across a console, wiping away a thin layer of dust that covered the screens.

"Nobody's been here in a while," she commented.

"But the systems are active," Hughes said as he wandered from one empty room to another. "Just as Sofi said."

"Maybe everyone's in the settlement," Leina suggested, indicating a slideway access.

"All aboard," Hughes said.

"A ghost town," Hawksclaw observed, as a huddle of utilitarian buildings came into view.

The slideway came to an end, and they stepped off.

"You'd expect to see *somebody*," Leina said, looking around.

Hughes glanced at Victrix. <*People?*>

<*No smell.*>

"Victrix doesn't scent anyone," he said.

"So they've been gone long enough for their scent to disappear," Leina said.

"Search," Hughes told the dogs, and Victrix and Rex trotted on ahead, separating to go in different directions.

Victrix reached one of the houses, entered through an open door, then stuck her head back out and barked. Hughes hurried over, and stared at several dark, reddish-black streaks on the floor.

"Blood," he commented.

"But where are the bodies?" Hawksclaw wondered, gazing over his shoulder.

"And who did this?" Leina asked.

The sea breeze brought a distant bark, followed by a thought from Victrix:

<*Rex find!*>

<*Take us*,> Hughes instructed.

She led them along a street toward the center of the settlement, to a building that was probably some sort of administrative center. Rex peered out from a partially open second storey window.

"How did he get up there?" Hawksclaw asked.

"He's talented," Hughes replied. He placed a palm on the sensorpad. Nothing happened. "Can you force the doors?"

"Easy," the priest replied, aiming a handweapon at the sensorpad and firing.

"Where did *that* come from?" Hughes demanded.

"I picked it up from the last house," Hawksclaw replied. "It was lying on the floor. I thought it might come in handy."

"You Audunans are certainly direct."

The door slid open and they eased inside. Victrix bounded up a set of steps, the humans following.

The room at the top was an office; a woman lay on the floor, Rex standing over her. A huge gash stretched across her chest, and she lay in an ominously large puddle of blood.

Hughes dropped to his knees, felt the woman's neck.

"She's alive, but barely."

Victrix licked the woman's face; she stirred and her eyes opened. "No! Get away from me!"

"We're friends," Leina said, taking one of her dreadfully cool hands.

Her eyes struggled to focus. "The children…where are the children?"

"We haven't seen any children," Leina said.

"Gone…gone…," she moaned. "You must…get away from here…"

"What happened?" Hughes asked.

"Took us…one by one…didn't know what was happening until…until it was too late…"

The woman gasped for breath.

"Can't…can't fight it…"

"Fight what? What did this to you?" Hughes persisted.

The woman's voice dropped to a nearly inaudible whisper. "Azrael…Azrael…"

Her breath rattled in her throat. Hughes laid her back and closed her eyes.

Hawksclaw made the sign of the cross and said a prayer over the inert form.

"What was that she said," Leina wondered. "Azrael?"

"I have no idea," Hughes replied.

"The angel of death has been abroad throughout the land," Hawksclaw intoned, his deep, resonant voice making the words even more ominous. "You may almost hear the beating of his wings. There is no one as of old to sprinkle with blood the lintel and the two side-posts of our doors, that he may spare and pass on."

"Angel of death?" Leina asked.

"In various mythologies," Hawksclaw explained, "including Hebrew and Islamic, Azrael—the name means, 'Whom God Helps'—was the angel of death. He was said to have four faces and four thousand wings, and a body made of eyes and tongues, one for each person on earth."

“Ghastly.”

“Mythology, you said,” Hughes replied. “But there’s a very real dead woman over there.”

The priest raised his shoulders. “Perhaps this is a world under judgment.”

“Not that it doesn’t necessarily deserve it,” Hughes said, “but there are planets much more decadent than Bluepoint.”

“Who knows how much is too much?”

“But then why call you here if judgment was in the offing?”

“If it hadn’t been for my disobedience, I might have arrived in time.”

“If you hadn’t been disobedient, you’d be on White’s Freehold now, not Bluepoint.”

Leina cleared her throat. “As fascinating as this discussion is, gentlemen, don’t you think a natural explanation is more likely?” Then, when the two men stared at her, added, “That’s a very nasty wound the woman has. You think the angel of death took a casual swipe and then just left her there?”

“Leina’s right,” Hughes said. “There’s no need for you to blame yourself, Father, until we know for certain what’s going on. And a natural explanation is a definite possibility.”

“Perhaps if we find the children…” Leina said.

“The children!” Hughes slapped a hand to his forehead. “Of course! Tell you what. Why don’t you and Father take Victrix and look for the children. I’ll take Rex and do a flyover in the flitter.”

“I don’t want to separate the two of you,” Hawksclaw said. “Why don’t I do the flyover?”

Hughes was shaking his head. “Because I’m a trained exobiologist. If there’s a natural phenomenon to account for the disappearance of the population, I’m more likely to spot clues.”

“Be careful,” Leina urged.

Hughes gave her a quick kiss. “I’ll keep in touch.” He crouched down to face Victrix.

<*Stay with Leina.*>

<*Not you?*> Her disappointment was almost palpable.

<*Not this time. With Leina.*>

<*“$%^##!!*> Victrix’s’s annoyance expressed itself in a series of high-pitched frustrated barks. She reared up and down on her hind legs.

Leina laughed. "A true hissy fit!"

"Maybe we should take Rex instead?" Hawksclaw suggested, glancing down at his new-found friend. For a man who'd never known dogs, he was certainly hitting it off with this imitation one.

"Rex is a work in progress," Hughes said. "Victrix understands humans and their behavior much better. She can communicate with you even without telepathy. Just follow her lead."

He caught Victrix's gaze again.

<*Victrix work.*> Hughes formed a mental image of children. <*Find children. Find for Leina.*>

The dog's mood changed abruptly. <*Victrix search!*>

Hughes straightened. "Rex and I will be off." He held a hand for Victrix to give him a high-five. "Don't be afraid to trust her," he said to Leina and the priest.

"Don't take any chances," Leina said.

"You either." He turned towards the door, motioning to the skaggit as he did so. "Come, Rex."

There was, Marli Childers thought, nothing better than sailing on a pristine ocean where the chances of encountering another human being were almost nil.

Humans.

She needed them—because, after all, humans were the source of her income—but she preferred not to encounter them in person. On Bluepoint she'd discovered the perfect place. She could run her business ventures via a chain of intermediaries, none of whom ever met her in person, and, unlike on other, more densely populated worlds, she could indulge her passion for sailing and almost never see another sail disrupt the contours of the sky and sea.

Right now, her boat drifted past an island—its name she didn't know, nor bothered to determine. A couple of mansions—nearly invisible, they blended in so well with the rocks and foliage—clung to the tops of a series of cliffs that ringed a shallow bay.

But even this evidence of humanity was too much for her, and she directed the sailboat's autocaptain to continue on, to another, smaller bay where she could anchor for the night.

Humans.

There were so many.

Soon, there would be one less.

One that posed difficulties for her business dealings.

She'd sent out the order earlier today. And the problem would be removed, as other problems had been removed in the past. There were no second thoughts, no regrets, no worries. She would lose no sleep—in fact, she'd sleep even better tonight.

The sun dipped towards the horizon; the boat reached the bay and dropped anchor, rocking gently. The cliffs shone mellow in the fading light, only to darken as dusk overtook them.

Marli stretched out on a deckchair, watching the interplay of light and shadow.

As she watched, the shadows on the cliffs shifted. She squinted. Were her eyes playing tricks on her? A section of cliff face seemed to detach and flow towards her, undulating above the surface of the sea. Impossible, surely.

But what was it?

She stood up.

The boat lurched, and it was as if the sea itself rose up to swallow it.

But it wasn't sea. Neither was it shadow.

For a brief moment, before terror overwhelmed her, her mind unable to comprehend the incomprehensible, she wished for the presence of another human being.

But she was all alone.

Solitude was fine, at times, Hughes mused as his flitter circled the main island, even desirable. But there was something abnormal about Bluepoint, a world of misanthropes who shunned the company of their fellows. Below him, the island was dotted with the estates of the super-rich and super-reclusive. Whereas once people on Earth had gone to the mountains, the deserts, or sea-side retreats to escape the bustle of daily life, now those with the means to do so sought isolated worlds inaccessible to the mass of common humanity.

He dropped down to check several estates. Most were simply unoccupied—their owners offworld, their security systems active. Others showed signs of recent habitation—parked flitters, open doors, clothing laid out—but no residents. Had he been a thief, Hughes could have made the haul of a lifetime.

On one estate, though, he found definite signs of something more sinister. The nape of his neck prickled as he entered what had once been a well-tended garden, but was now a trampled, flattened mass of vegetation. Beside him, Rex's hackles rose.

"What is it, boy?" Hughes asked, trying to tune in to the skaggit-cum-dog's emotions, but found only a vague dread and a sense of something foreign to Rex's experience.

Victrix, on the other hand, as he made a connection with the black Shepherd, was pursuing her task eagerly.

Which reminded him that it was time to check in with Leina.

"She's doing her best," Leina reported. "It's weird here, Hughes."

Hughes summarized what he'd found, then said, "I'm going to check a couple of the nearby islands."

"Don't go too far," Leina said. "Hughes, I'm worried."

"I'll be back before dark," he said, aiming the flitter out to sea.

He found the same pattern on the outlying islands as on the Big Island—either vacant homes or residences whose occupants had simply vanished. He saw not a person, not a flitter in the air, not a boat on the sea, not an animal on the hillsides.

It was eerie, and Rex sensed it as well.

If there had been an epidemic, there'd be bodies. If an assault, damage from weapons. Ditto for mass abductions. There was no evidence of natural disaster—which again, should have left bodies.

He noticed something else curious: All the islands were strangely similar, roughly circular, rising to barren, flat-topped conical centers ringed by vegetation which in turn yielded to either beaches or cliffs on the peripheries. It was odd. He was no geologist, and at first glance thought they might be volcanoes, but the rocks at the summits appeared to be sedimentary, eliminating that possibility.

Rex, peering out of the windows, growled as they flew over the center of one island.

"What is it, boy?" Hughes asked, studying the ground below. He saw nothing beyond another vegetation-fringed cone no different from any of the others, and wished he could touch the skaggit's mind as he could that of Victrix.

He set course to return to the Big Island, passing over one more smaller island. Something near a pristine beach caught his eye, and he circled low. It was a boat, lying on its side, half-submerged on a sandbar. He doubted there was anyone on board.

"But best take a look, eh, Rex?"

There was just room to land the flitter beside it. He jumped out into the ankle-deep water, followed by Rex, and splashed over to the boat.

"Is there anyone here?" he called, hearing nothing but the lap of water.

Rex sniffed around the boat, then barked. Hughes hurried over to where Rex was standing on his rear legs, his front paws on the boat's deck-rail.

"What did you find?" Hughes asked.

A strip of torn fabric fluttered from the rail. Hughes reached up to grab it. It was soft, almost translucent, and undoubtedly expensive. Probably a woman's, he guessed, from a faint odor of perfume.

It was a clue that told him exactly nothing.

He returned to the flitter and resumed course towards the Big Island.

And then he realized that there was something else strange about Bluepoint. He hadn't expected to see many signs of life—but certainly some. Instead, he hadn't seen any. Not only were there no people, he hadn't spotted any sizeable animal life, either, the few flying creatures they'd noticed on their arrival excepted.

He accessed *Wolf-1's* data banks, and learned that Bluepoint was home to several species of land herbivores, some small carnivores, and flightless birdlike creatures vaguely resembling the long-extinct dodo. Some of them—except perhaps the carnivores—he should have spotted from the air. But he hadn't.

Nothing moved on the surface of Bluepoint.

It wasn't only the humans that had disappeared.

The woman's name was Donia, Nyle recalled, pivoting at the sound of a voice to see a frightened-looking woman accompanied by a gaggle of children following him.

"What do you want?" he demanded.

"Help us," she pleaded, running a hand across her forehead to brush back a straying lock of brown hair. "I think…I think everyone else has vanished."

"Yeah," he said. "And I'm going to vanish as well, as soon as I reach the spaceport." He began to turn away.

"Let us come with you, please."

He studied the group. Two of the children were Donia's, he recalled, a girl named Mora, about twelve years old and a slightly younger boy whose name escaped him if he'd ever known it.

"Where'd they come from?" he asked, indicating the other children, a girl about Mora's age, and a pair that looked to be about two or three.

"I found them in an empty house," Donia said.

"Look, I can't wait for children," Nyle said. "It's getting late. It's creepy enough in the daytime; I'm not going to get caught outdoors after nightfall."

Even though he'd walked down this road countless times, today it was strangely unfamiliar. The clouds, whose lacy streaks formed vaguely threatening patterns, glowed with eerie, disquieting colors.

Nonsense. Clouds formed many patterns. And colors were colors. A trick of his imagination.

"Please wait for us," the girl, Mora, asked.

"I don't have time," Nyle replied. "But if I'm still there when you arrive, I'll take you up."

"Getting offworld is our only chance," Donia said, her voice sounding shrill.

"Then you'd better make the brats walk quickly," he replied, turning on his heel.

Mora said, "But what if there's not a shuttle?"

"Then we're dead," he answered harshly, beginning to walk.

Behind him, one of the younger children began to cry. Screaming children. The last thing he wanted to deal with.

His nerves on edge, every shifting shadow seemed alive; every dark patch concealed an unimaginable horror. One by one it had taken them, and their very isolation had made them vulnerable. They hadn't realized what was happening until it was too late. Nyle's first glimmer of insight only came because of his position as supply chief for the storage depot. People weren't placing orders. Goods weren't leaving. Customers didn't respond to queries. It dawned on him that Bluepoint was being slowly, inexorably depopulated.

The sky had faded to a dull gray. The deepening dusk was preternaturally quiet; the childrens' wails reverberated off the walls of empty buildings.

"Can't you shut them up?" he snapped, whirling about.

"They're scared," Donia replied.

"We're all *scared." He turned away again, picked up his pace, and reached an intersection.*

Nyle leaned forward to check around the angle of the building, then glanced back at Donia struggling with her entourage.

And then, out of nowhere, it was upon them—an immense, writhing something *that plummeted from the sky—a something full of mouths and fangs—*

Donia reeled backwards, blood spurting from her chest, her high-pitched scream joining those of the children.

"Mother!" Mora shrieked, before her brother hauled her down a narrow passageway between a pair of buildings, followed by the other girl yanking the two toddlers.

It was the last thing Nyle saw before the creature blotted them from sight.

A fan of horror, Nyle had enjoyed multisensory entertainment programs in which people had been eaten alive by a variety of imaginary alien creatures.

Now, he experienced it for real.

"Do you think this is going to work? "Father DeSmet Hawksclaw asked as he and Leina followed Victrix down one deserted street after another.

"Hughes has faith in her," Leina said.

"I researched dogs on the way here," the priest said. "They have some impressive abilities."

"And Victrix is no ordinary dog," Leina replied. "Neither is Rex."

"I wish I'd had one as a boy."

They'd left the building where the injured woman had died, Victrix sniffing the ground with the utmost seriousness, leading the way but never getting too far ahead.

She halted, nose to the ground. The two humans hurried over, and studied a dull, reddish-brown splotch on the ground.

"Blood," the priest said, crouching down to scratch the stain with his fingernail. "This may be where the woman was injured."

"Good work, girl," Leina said to Victrix. "Now where did she come from? Keep searching."

The German Shepherd trotted off.

"Since we don't have any scent items from the children, maybe backtracking the woman's trail will help," Leina said in response to raised eyebrows from Hawksclaw.

"Worth a try," he said.

This time, Victrix ranged further ahead, and soon summoned them by excited barking.

"More blood," Hawksclaw said as they reached the dog. He looked around the street. "I don't see any other signs of a struggle, do you?"

Victrix was sniffing in circles. Another yip directed Leina to an object lying on the ground. She bent over to pick it up.

"What's that?" Hawksclaw wondered.

"A teddy bear," she said. "Children have played with these for centuries. They must have been here. Sniff, Victrix." She held the dirty, frayed bear to the dog's nose. "Now search, Victrix, search."

"The children came and then left," Hawksclaw said, "possibly from different directions. What if she chooses the wrong way?"

"She'll likely follow the stronger, fresher scent," Leina replied. "Hopefully that will lead us to them."

They hurried to keep Victrix in sight, as the dog moved swiftly, eventually pausing outside a large, featureless building. She sat and looked expectantly at the two humans. Leina wondered what she was thinking, what telepathic communication with a dog was like.

"*Bluepoint Storage Depot.*" Leina read the wording beside the door.

"Not a bad choice," Hawksclaw said. "Probably plenty of food in there."

"It's locked," Leina said, as the door refused to open at her approach.

"Allow me." As he had earlier, Hawksclaw disabled the lock with a well-placed shot and pushed the panels open as alarms sounded. Victrix padded inside, and Leina followed.

Leina studied the rows of stacked containers. "Is anybody here?" she called. "We're friends."

After a moment, the figure of a girl appeared in one of the rows. Four other children stood behind her.

"I'm Mora," she said. "Did my mother send you?"

Leina was waiting to meet him as he set the flitter down in an empty street.

"I think I know what's going on!" Hughes exclaimed.

"We found the children!" she said at the same time, giving him a hug.

"It's some kind of—"

"Their parents were attacked by—"

Both of them broke off.

"Let's go inside and talk," Hughes said. "It's getting dark."

"We'd do better to get out of this place entirely," Leina said. "Hightail it up to *Wolf-1*. I don't want to spend another minute on this planet."

Hughes nodded. "Right you are. Where's Father DeSmet?"

"Inside with the children and Victrix," she said, opening the door.

"Did Leina tell you?" the priest asked as Hughes entered the building and eyed the assembled children. Victrix bounded over to lick his hand, then turned her attention to Rex.

"Explanations can wait," Hughes replied. "Let's get off Bluepoint, first."

Mora said, "I went to the spaceport, but I couldn't get into any of the shuttles."

"Don't worry," Hughes said. "We have our own."

"Lead on," Hawksclaw said, motioning to Hughes. "Children, stay near me."

He carried a long metal pole as well as the laser pistol.

"What's that for?" Hughes asked.

Hawksclaw hefted it. "Backup," he replied shortly.

A light breeze gusted mournfully along the street. Hughes cast a regretful look at the flitter. "Too bad it won't hold everyone."

"Don't worry about it," Leina urged, and directed her steps toward the spaceport.

They'd gone only a few blocks when Hughes halted. "Did you hear that?"

Leina shook her head. "Nothing."

<Something coming.>

<*What?*>

<*Something bad.*>

"Victrix is alarmed," Hughes said. He received a sense of foreboding, and realized it came from the skaggit. "Rex is, too."

One of the children began to cry. Leina picked her up.

"Come on, then," Hawksclaw said. "Let's move."

Victrix growled, a deep, menacing rumble, and her hackles rose.

<*What is it?*>

<*Hungry. It hunts.*>

"I don't want to die," Mora cried.

And then Hughes heard the noise again. It was faint, like the distant twitter of birds rustling among the skeletal leaves of fall, but somehow threatening, like the far-off rumble of an approaching thunderstorm, barely disturbing the unnatural silence that preceded it.

The shadows lengthened.

*The angel of death has been abroad in the land…*he could almost hear the priest's resonant voice intoning the words again. He grabbed the hand of one of the children and broke into a jog.

"It's not too much farther—" he began.

Victrix spun around and barked, her teeth bared, flashing white against the black of her muzzle.

And then it was upon them, flowing over the top of the buildings like a tidal wave of death. The children screamed. "Azrael!" Hawksclaw exclaimed. Leina gripped Hughes's arm, her nails digging into his flesh.

What he glimpsed in that fraction of a second surely couldn't exist on any rational world. It had to be physically impossible. His mind balked at the impression of night-black wings, tentacles, burning red eyes and gaping mouths in multiple heads, all in an ever-changing, churning, writhing mass that somehow, he supposed, was a single, unimaginable, nightmarish entity. Yet as it dropped towards them there was no mistaking the glint of fangs or the stench of decay that accompanied it.

Rex's furious barking rose to a frenzied crescendo, but Victrix fell silent. With her fully erect hackles, raised tail, and tensed muscles, Hughes realized she was about to spring.

"No!" Hughes yelled, following it with a strong mental command. <*Victrix, NO!*>

Rex was faster. In seconds, the skaggit had mutated into an avian-like creature with a wicked beak that Hughes didn't recognize—perhaps an animal that had once existed on the metamorph's homeworld of Sultan—and launched himself at the creature, harrying it like a small bird harassing a much larger bird of prey. Hughes experienced a moment of amazement as the skaggit somehow avoided the creature's mouths and tentacles.

Hawksclaw aimed his weapon and loosed a barrage of shots at the thing. "Run, Hughes!"

Hughes scooped up a pair of the children, shouted to the dogs to follow, and broke into a sprint, Leina by his side with another child in her arms, and the two eldest keeping pace.

"Hawksclaw!" he yelled, as the priest made no move to follow.

"Save the children!" Hawksclaw shouted back as the thing flowed towards him. "I'll distract it!" But if he hit an eye, a mouth, or wing, there was another taking its place. His shots had no effect.

"Don't be a fool!" Hughes called, pausing at the street corner, Victrix beside him. "Come along!"

Rex was still harassing the creature, snapping, and snipping the tips off tentacles.

Hawksclaw thrust the pistol into a pocket of his habit, transferred the pole to his other hand, took aim, and launched it towards one of the creature's heads. It flew straight, and the thing screamed as the pole pierced the face from front to back.

A thick, puce-colored ichor spewed from the wound. The pole came free as the creature thrashed, and clanged to the ground.

"Rex, COME!" Hughes bellowed, and the skaggit swooped towards him, changing back into a German Shepherd even as he hit the ground with his paws.

"Hawksclaw!"

The priest dove, rolled, and came up running the opposite direction, slipping on gobs of fallen ichor, and even so moving faster than Hughes would have guessed for such a big man. The enraged, wounded creature surged after him.

Hawksclaw pulled out the pistol and loosed off a few more shots; then he was out of sight, and Hughes was pounding along a clear street, the dogs with him. Leina was running easily, the marathoner in her coming to the fore. Hughes began to labor under the weight of the children. Hawksclaw could have carried them easily, but they were too much for him.

"Give one to the dogs," Leina said, seeing his distress.

He visualized an image for Victrix, then set the smaller of the children down.

<*Carry it.*>

Victrix gripped its collar, Rex the seat of its pants, and together they bore the child at a trot. Relieved of the weight, Hughes picked up his pace.

The whine of Hawksclaw's weapon ceased.

He met Leina's frightened but controlled gaze. They shared an unspoken thought—the creature would be after them once it had finished with the priest.

How much time had Hawksclaw bought them with his sacrifice?

Not enough.

A shadow fled across the ground, gaining on them, but then they were at the spaceport, and the shuttle was just ahead.

<*Open it!*> He sent the thought to Victrix, and scooped up the child the dogs had been carrying. She raced ahead, jumped up, and slapped her paw against the shuttle's sensorpad—probably the only one in existence configured for a dog's pawprint, he thought. The port slid open. The dogs bounded inside, followed by Leina.

"Hughes!" Leina screamed.

Gasping for breath, Hughes was almost there when the thing swooped at him. He ducked, as teeth and talons raked across his head and back, lost his balance and fell. He tried to roll, to cushion the children, and came down hard on his left shoulder. Something popped, and pain seared through the joint, taking his breath away and graying his vision.

The thing was coming back for him. He didn't have to look to know that.

Something jerked on his shirt.

Victrix, paws planted, tugging with all her might…

"Victrix. Get away, girl…"

The dog tugged harder, dragging him across the ground.

Something crackled past him, and he dimly recognized the sound of a neuraltranq. He looked up to see Leina leap from the shuttle, tranq-rifle in hand.

He groaned. Were they all to die here, like everyone else? Azrael spared no one…no one…

Rex appeared, lifted one of the children in his jaws, and headed back to the shuttle.

Leina bent over and took the other one. "Come on, Hughes!"

"I can't—"

Victrix pulled him harder.

"You can!" She fired again at the creature. Did it pause, perhaps slow a fraction? Maybe the wound Hawksclaw had inflicted was beginning to take a toll. It was still leaking purplish-brown ichor from a shattered face…it was a real creature, a creature of flesh, no matter how repulsive…

With a sudden burst, he was on his feet, stumbling toward the shuttle. He wrapped his usable hand in Victrix's fur for support.

"I'll cover you," Leina said.

"Don't risk—"

"Move it, Hughes!"

Victrix pulled him forwards, and then he was at the hatch, scrambling in.

Another shot, and Leina bundled in beside him. The hatch slid shut. The shuttle rocked.

"Can you—?" she asked.

He nodded, already reaching for his restraints with his right hand. "Sofi, emergency lift-off sequence. Initiate." He turned his head to Leina. "Secure the children. The dogs know the routine."

The engines powered up.

The shuttle rocked again, and bounced, as if a heavy weight had landed on top of it.

Could the thing eat through a spaceship's skin, Hughes wondered?

Leina dropped into the seat beside him. "Go."

"It'll be rough," Hughes said. "I've never used emergency lift-off before. Sofi: Launch!"

The shuttle lurched, hesitated, and then burned skyward. Something shrieked, and Hughes had a last glimpse of an unspeakably horrid creature trailing strands of puce-colored slime flash past the viewport before g-forces crushed him into his seat and forced him into unconsciousness.

"Are you all right?" Leina's voice came to him through a haze, and he opened his eyes. It took a moment for his senses to register that he was lying on his bed in his cabin on *Wolf-1*, and that Victrix and Rex lay beside him. He struggled to sit up, realizing that his left shoulder was immobilized in a sling. Leina helped him up.

"Easy does it."

He grimaced. "This is awkward."

"At least it was only dislocated, not broken," she said. "The robodoc reduced it."

He nodded. "The children?"

"Fine. Mora is keeping an eye on them. I let them play in a storeroom."

"Where are we?"

"Still in orbit," she replied.

"Let me see."

With her support, he walked slowly to the flight deck. The shimmering expanse of Bluepoint lay far beneath. That such tranquility could conceal such horror…

"He was a brave man, no matter what he said," Hughes murmured.

"Are you certain that…that he's dead?"

Hughes exhaled. "He would have delayed that thing as long as was humanly possible—bought us all the time he could."

Leina gave a sad smile. "I don't think he would have minded the outcome."

"If it hadn't been for him, that thing would have eaten all of us," Hughes said.

"Eaten—?" Leina shivered.

"Oh yes. It was hungry. Victrix told me."

"What was it? Was it really the angel of death?"

"Look at this," Hughes said, activating a computer screen and accessing a file. "I was working on this while doing my flyover of the islands, and saved it to *Wolf-1's* data banks."

Leina studied the graphics. "What do they mean?"

"I'll explain. Bluepoint has been surveyed several times, and settled once before."

"I didn't know that."

"Neither did I. But look here. On the initial survey, ninety-five years ago, there were very few surface animals noted. A subsequent survey seventy years ago found abundant populations, but sixty years ago when the first colony was established, there were very few again. Forty-eight years ago the first colony disappeared, without a trace."

"None?"

"None," Hughes said. "The people just vanished. Twenty-five years ago, a survey found an abundance of animals, but when the new colony was founded twenty years ago, there were very few. Checking the colony data banks, I found that animal populations had been increasing. Yet now, as I noticed, the animal life has disappeared again."

"Some kind of cycle?" Leina guessed.

"And if you look at the islands," Hughes said, bringing up an image of Bluepoint's archipelago, "what do they remind you of?"

Leina furrowed her brow. "I'm not sure."

"They almost look to me like nests."

"Nests?" Leina echoed. "Surely that's not possible!"

"I've learned never to say never, and to eliminate the word "impossible" from my vocabulary," Hughes replied.

"So what are you getting at?" Leina asked.

"I think," Hughes replied, "that that thing—Azrael for lack of a better name—is the top predator on Bluepoint. The cycle of animal disappearance and reappearance appears to be every twenty-four years. My guess is that the creatures—possibly one for each island—lie dormant, or hibernating, and every twenty-four years awaken and go on a feeding frenzy."

"So it *is* the angel of death," Leina said.

Hughes nodded. "They must leave a few animals behind, so the prey population can build up again." He placed his hand on his chest. "It saw humans as just another food item on the menu."

He regarded her steadily. "Bluepoint must never be colonized again."

"Or if it is, evacuated every twenty-four years," Leina countered.

"Regardless, Father DeSmet must be its last victim."

"He wasn't a victim," Leina said, shaking her head. "He saved us, and he saved the children. He denied Azrael its final meal. In a sense, he won."

"Perhaps you're right." Hughes exhaled. "He wanted another opportunity—but what a price he paid!"

"Heroism never comes cheaply," Leina said.

"And he was certainly a hero in my books," Hughes said. "I'll make certain his order knows that."

"And his family."

"Definitely." He tapped the control panel. "Let's get these children back to civilization. They've been through enough. The appropriate authorities can search out their relatives."

Victrix whined, and nuzzled against Hughes.

<Go play ball?>

Hughes laughed. *<All right, girl. I'll try.>*

"What does she want?" Leina asked.

"It's a dog thing," Hughes said.

DRAGON RUN

"Push it, dear!"

Hughes responded to Leina's grinning encouragement with a mock glare.

"This," he gasped, eyeing the slope rising up before them, "is as fast as I go uphill."

"A hill is only a flat stretch on an angle," she replied cheerfully. "Besides, it's not *that* steep."

Hughes turned his attention to his other jogging companion, a young man all elbows and knees, his equally bony head surmounted by short-cropped black hair. "Any chance of making the mountains and hills low, Father?"

"The crooked straight and the rough places plain?" The priest shook his head. "Sorry, Hughes. Hills are part of the experience."

"Just like the thin air, eh?"

"Comes with the scenery, doc."

Hughes gritted his teeth and pressed onwards, pretending to ignore Leina's chuckle.

It was fine for them—Leina was a good eight years younger than himself, and Father Stefan Tomislaw younger than that, in his late twenties, and thin as a rail to boot. They were in a totally different class than he—a newcomer to the world of distance running.

<*Look!*>

Victrix's thought broke into Hughes' grim concentration, and he slowed to a halt halfway to the crest of the low rise. Ahead of him, Victrix was silhouetted against a pastel sky.

His two companions—and Rex, who'd been lagging behind to sniff at something—didn't break stride.

"Don't stop now," Leina exhorted, glancing back at him. "Make it to the top!"

"It's only a training run."

"Fortitude and stamina, darling!"

Hughes muttered under his breath, then said, "Victrix is sensing something." He resumed motion and arrived panting at the crest of the rise to join the black shepherd.

She was staring into the distance, a jumble of weathered hills, hoodoos, and bluffs, separated by shallow streams and oddly-colored ponds, and punctuated by scattered patches of olive-green vegetation. It was a weird, almost prehistoric landscape.

Hughes found it fascinating.

<*Where?*>

<*Out there.*> Her nose twitched as she scented.

<*What is it?*>

<*Hurt.*>

He couldn't make sense of the confusing sensations he received from her.

"There's someone out there," he said. "In distress."

"Another runner?" Leina asked.

Hughes shook his head. "Victrix can't tell. I'm not even sure…she isn't sure…"

"Sure of what?"

He pursed his lips. "Let's go see."

"Why not?" Leina agreed. "On a training run, we can go wherever we want. But let's not overdo it, OK? This is your first marathon—you don't want to be sore before the start."

"Quite right," Hughes agreed. Taking on his first marathon would be enough of a challenge as it was. He wasn't quite certain how Leina had talked him into it.

"Why do I need to run a marathon?" he'd asked when she'd broached the subject.

"Because I have," she'd replied, somehow making it sound obvious.

"You're a born runner," he'd protested. "I'm not."

"Think of the accomplishment," she'd said.

"Think of the pain," he'd countered.

But all his arguments had fallen on unsympathetic ears, and so he'd begun preparing nearly six months ago. Training onboard *Wolf-1*, though, was hardly an exciting affair, so he'd taken to running with Leina on whatever planet business had brought him to next. He had to admit that he was feeling physically better than at any previous time in his life—even when he'd supposedly been young and fit.

Leina, too, had never looked better in the time he'd known her. While he'd been attending to patients, she'd been racking up the miles. He thought she looked fantastic in her running outfit, and wondered what he'd done to deserve her.

And now here they were, on the uninhabited, ringed world Kalara, readying themselves for the Dragon Run in a few day's time.

It was a marathon, Leina said, that she'd longed to run, but, since it was located far from her homeworld, had never really thought she'd accomplish it.

It wasn't until well after their marriage that Hughes had learned of her goal to join the 100 Worlds Marathon Club. Well, that didn't mean that *he'd* have to run a hundred marathons…

He brought his mind back to the task at hand.

<*Show me,*> Hughes instructed Victrix.

"Would you mind telling me what's going on?" Stefan Tomislaw asked.

"Sorry, Father," Hughes said. They'd met the young priest some weeks ago during a layover on Mandek. He was on leave from his bishop; having doubts about his call to the priesthood, he'd been given time for spiritual discernment. He was also a runner—something Leina had learned quickly. Tomislaw had eagerly accepted their offer to join them on Kalara. Hughes just hoped things turned out better than the last time they'd befriended a priest. He still felt regret that DeSmet Hawksclaw had sacrificed himself to save them.

Hughes recollected that he'd never told the priest about himself and Victrix. "Victrix and I share a telepathic bond," he explained. "I can sense what she does, and she has the ability to connect with certain non-human species."

"That's very unusual," the priest said, frowning. "And unnatural."

"The result of unrelated experiments," Hughes said.

The black shepherd trotted down off the crest. Having learned over the years that Hughes wasn't capable of canine speed, she adapted her pace to his. Rex, sensing that something interesting was going on, ran shoulder to shoulder with her, occasionally giving her a friendly nip to pester her.

"How far away, do you think?" Leina asked.

"Can't say for sure," Hughes replied, "but Victrix is picking up a strong scent, so probably close."

Victrix led them to one of the shallow streams, and followed it as it curved through a labyrinth of rock formations, dividing into a multitude of branches, most of which were narrow enough for both dogs and humans to jump with ease.

"It would be easy enough to get lost in here," Leina observed. "It all looks the same."

"That's one thing I never worry about," Hughes said. "Not with Victrix and Rex."

Victrix slowed as they approached a grove of pod-shaped plants with fern-like tops. Through gaps in the foliage, Hughes glimpsed a clearing dotted by several trees bearing yellow fruits. And just shy of the trees, a human-sized figure lay on the ground, partially hidden in some kind of stringy ground-covering.

"With me," he instructed the dogs, pushing his way through the pod-ferns to where he could see the figure more clearly—and what he saw made him halt suddenly. Victrix and Rex stopped as well, hackles and tails raised.

"It's a wolf!" Leina hissed from just behind him.

It was indeed wolflike, but—"It's twice the size of Victrix," Hughes whispered back, "if not more. The only wolf I've ever heard of that big was the Dire Wolf, and they've been extinct for millennia."

"This isn't Earth," Leina pointed out, as if he needed reminding.

"You researched this planet, didn't you?" he asked. "Did you read anything about large predators?"

"Nothing really big, and not on this continent," she replied, "there's not enough to sustain them. The Dragon Run has a high safety rating. Although…"

"Although what?"

"Sometimes runners have said they've seen things…"

"What things?" Hughes felt suddenly irritated.

"Nothing that the race organizers have ever verified," Leina replied, sounding defensive. "Sometimes runners get disoriented…have weird hallucinations."

"Or maybe there are *real* dragons on the Dragon Run?" he said sarcastically.

"Don't be silly. It's named both for one of the rock formations, and for the shape of the trail."

Hughes withdrew his neuraltranq from his running pack and held it at the ready. The creature hadn't moved or even showed that it was aware of their presence, but Victrix sensed that it was alive…

He edged closer. Something about its posture was odd…

<*Listen!*>

He craned his ears at Victrix's thought.

Nothing. Whatever she was hearing must be out of human range.

Victrix and Rex were moving towards the thing, canine curiosity aroused.

He took another step forwards, and then he felt it—a slight tingling in his arms, as if his hairs were raising—

"Back!" he exclaimed, startling both Leina and Stefan, as well as the dogs. "Everyone back!"

"What's the matter?" Leina asked.

"It's a stasis field," Hughes said. "Another step or two and we'll be as paralyzed as that thing."

They backed up until Hughes could no longer feel the tingling.

"I'm not familiar with stasis fields," Stefan said.

"I am," Hughes replied grimly, and Leina nodded as well. "They're used for trapping prey alive. The modern equivalent of ancient mechanical leg-hold traps. They paralyze skeletal muscles, leaving the victim immobile, able only to breathe." He was looking around as he spoke. "In military usage, you've either got a prisoner, bait for an ambush, or an immobile enemy you can dispatch with ease. When used for hunting game…" he motioned towards the creature. "It can lie here and die of starvation, exhaustion, or dehydration if the trapper doesn't feel like checking the trap regularly."

"Inhumane!" Stefan exclaimed.

"The darkness of the unredeemed human heart," Hughes said. He gestured with his hands. "The field will originate from a number of units. Most common are triangular or square fields because you need only three or four generator units respectively."

"Let's see if we can find them," Leina said.

"What if it's illegal to tamper with them?" Stefan asked.

Hughes' face clouded. "I don't know the laws of this planet—if there even are any. But I'm not leaving some creature to die in misery."

Leina took a deep breath. "I'm with you."

He flashed her a smile. "Good."

The first unit was situated on the edge of an eroded rock formation, at about waist height. It didn't appear impressive—merely a small black box with rods on two sides extending up another couple of feet and down to the ground. Its smooth surface was broken only by a pair of status lights—a green one, illuminated, and a red one, dark.

Hughes pursed his lips. Then he stooped over to pick up a slender stick. Carefully, he extended it and prodded the box.

"One piece of luck," he said. "It's a civilian model."

"How does that help?" Leina asked.

"A military one would be shielded," Hughes replied.

"Can we just move it?" Stefan suggested.

Hughes shook his head. "Moving one generator would cause fluctuations in the field which could be fatal. No, we'll have to disarm it."

"How?" Leina wondered. "We don't have any electronic gear."

Hughes remembered the neuraltranq he was holding. "Let's try this." He positioned it with its tip against the blinking green light. "Stand back."

He pulled the trigger.

The field generator sparked. The green light died.

"You did it!" Leina exclaimed.

"Almost," Hughes said. "If it's a quadrilateral layout, we'll need to disarm one more unit."

It took only a few minutes of careful searching to locate and disable a second unit.

"That should do it," Hughes said.

He took a tentative step forward across what had been the field's perimeter. He felt nothing. "The field's down. Let's take a closer look at what it caught."

Sensing his interest, Victrix dashed ahead. Hughes began to call her back, but changed his mind. Her curiosity often exceeded his own. Instead, he hurried after her.

The creature was breathing, as indicated by the barest movement of tawny-gray flanks. Victrix was busy giving it the once over—learning what she could from its scent. But Rex's reaction surprised him—the skaggit-cum-shepherd had dropped to his belly and wriggled close to the creature, until they were nearly muzzle to muzzle…and that muzzle…

"Look at its head!" Hughes whistled.

Whereas the extinct Dire Wolf had a smaller brain than later wolves, this creature's skull was enlarged; big enough, Hughes guessed, for a human-sized brain.

His scrutiny swept downwards to forelegs that were built more like arms and ended in human hands, to rear legs and a bushy tail that were pure wolf.

The creature stirred. Its eyes opened and struggled to focus. Hughes involuntarily took a step backwards.

"Hughes!" Leina breathed. "The eyes…they're human!" She clutched his arm. "What is it?"

"Something that shouldn't exist," Hughes said somberly. "Not on this world or any other."

"Now that it's free," the priest said tentatively after a few moments of shocked silence, "maybe we should leave it to recover on its own."

The creature's gaze passed blankly over them, and settled on Rex. Victrix, Hughes noted, was now sitting calmly, her inspection completed.

"It could be hurt," Hughes said, removing a medscanner from his pouch. It had been his long-standing practice never to venture planetside for any reason without basic medical gear. He never knew what he might encounter.

He moved slowly towards the creature.

"Be careful!" Leina enjoined.

"It won't be capable of movement yet," Hughes said. "And Victrix is sending calming signals." He could sense the reassuring emotions the black shepherd was projecting. Although whether or not the creature could interpret them was another matter.

"How long before it recovers?" Stefan asked.

Hughes shrugged. "Organisms take differing times to recover from the effects of a stasis field—the bigger muscles taking longer to regain function. Could be hours…could be minutes."

He ran the medscanner over the inert form. "Vital signs are unusual…some degree of dehydration…hypoglycemia…only mild signs of muscle damage…no kidney failure."

He put the medscanner back in his pouch. "It's either been lying here for a matter of two or three days, or, if longer, it's remarkably resilient."

"What's the plan?" Leina wondered. "Take it up to *Wolf-1*?"

"Ideally, perhaps," Hughes said.

"Is that safe?" Stefan asked.

The creature's eyes closed again.

"Probably not," Hughes replied, imagining the size of the thing's teeth, claws, and muscles, and the fright and disorientation it might feel on being removed to a starship. "So we'll have to do the best we can here. Do either of you have a spare BOSS?"

"I do," Stefan replied quickly, rummaging in his pouch and handing it to Hughes.

Once upon a time, long distance runners had carried nutritional supports—goos, gummy chews, tablets. Now, everyone wore a Body Surveillance and Support patch that monitored the athlete's metabolism, correcting glucose and electrolyte abnormalities automatically, advising the wearer of their fluid status, and alerting to any cardiac abnormality. Nobody had to worry about how their body 'felt' anymore.

Hughes removed the BOSS from its protective covering and applied it to one of the creature's humanlike arms.

"I'm giving it a mild stimulant as well," he said. "To try to speed the recovery process."

Leina snapped her fingers. "An Adlet, that's what it is. Sort of, anyway."

"What's an Adlet?" Stefan asked.

"Something from Inuit mythology," Leina said. "The upper half human, the lower half dog. Rather a grisly story. If you want the details—"

The priest held up a hand. "Not necessary."

Hughes laughed. "I doubt there have been any Inuit here."

"But somebody has been," Leina said. "Unless it's a native creature."

Hughes was studying the creature closely. "Not a chance," he said.

The amber eyes opened again. This time, they focused faster, and lit upon Hughes.

"It's beginning to come around," he said.

<*Curiosity…wariness…fear…*> Victrix relayed the sensations.

"It's not sure about us," Hughes said. "Let's give it some space."

"Is it telepathic?" Leina asked asked they moved back a few feet.

Hughes shook his head. "No. Victrix is picking up its feelings in the normal canine manner—pheromones and the like."

One of the human arms moved, the fingers scratching the ground.

<*Hunger…thirst…*>

"Toss me your water bottle, dear," Hughes said.

Leina, keeping a safe distance, pitched it to him. Hughes caught it, opened it, and from arm's length—and watched by a pair of wary, all-too-human-appearing eyes, let some of the water drip into the creature's mouth. He set the bottle down within reach, and backed away again.

The creature half-raised, extended its arm, picked up the bottle, opened its mouth—exposing wickedly long, gleaming canines—and poured the liquid in its maw.

"It's recovering quickly," Leina observed. "Hughes, don't you think we should—"

"*Hughes!*" Stefan exclaimed in loud whisper, clutching Hughes' shoulder. "Rex…!"

Startled, Hughes looked to where Rex had been lying. Concentrating on the creature's recovery and Victrix's impressions, Hughes hadn't been paying attention to the skaggit. Now, instead of a black and tan German shepherd, there was another wolf-human creature, a third or a quarter the size of the original.

"I should have warned you," he told the stunned priest. "Rex isn't really a dog. He's a metamorph—a shapeshifter."

The Adlet—Leina's name seemed appropriate—reached out to the unmoving Rex, stroked his muzzle, then the top of his head.

"It doesn't seem to be aggressive," Hughes commented. Victrix, he observed, was still sitting quietly, her head cocked to one side.

The Adlet stretched, extending muscular hindquarters, then in one swift movement that stunned Hughes, stood erect.

Hughes couldn't repress a shiver. It was a truly awesome sight. The rippling muscles radiated strength, and the lean lines promised immense speed. Coupled with deadly fangs and the intelligence shining from the eyes…

It could be a fearsome predator.

And yet, strangely enough, Hughes felt no fear. He didn't even raise the neuraltranq.

With one muscular arm, the Adlet picked up the unresisting Rex.

<*Go with friend.*> The thought, undoubtedly Rex's, came to him from Victrix.

Then the Adlet turned and bounded away.

"Hughes!" Leina screamed. "Rex!"

He swung to face her. "It's OK," he said. "Rex knows what he's doing."

"Are you sure?"

"Reasonably," he said.

They turned to leave the glade, and just for a moment—he couldn't be sure—he thought he glimpsed a figure in the distance, in the opposite direction from that which the Adlet had taken. Then it was gone.

He asked Leina.

"I saw something, too," she confirmed his suspicion.

"Let's get out of here," Hughes said.

Part of the allure of the Dragon Run was the rustic runners' camp erected not far from the starting line. The assemblage of stone and timber huts contained only the basic amenities and accommodations. The location, however—at the base of a range of jagged mountains—was spectacular, and the atmosphere…Hughes had never experienced anything like it.

There was something about being in a collection of runners from a variety of planets that engendered instant camaraderie. Interworld differences were of no account to people gathered for one purpose. Instead of politics, the talk was of runs—How many? Where? Best time?

Hughes found it inspiring.

But tonight, after they had returned from their training run, all he could think of was the Adlet.

Kalara was uninhabited for a reason—an eccentric orbit and unfavorable axis made it prone to extremes of both heat and cold. Only for brief periods of time twice per planet year was the ambient temperature congenial for human beings.

And even then…

He lowered his gaze from the broad rings arching across the night sky in a thousand bands of silver splendor to the crackling yellow flames in the firepit behind the hut he shared with Leina. Across from him, Stefan Tomislaw likewise stared into the fire, his angular face a sharp contrast of light and shadow. Victrix lay contentedly nearby, chewing on a treat.

Leina emerged from the hut carrying three steaming mugs. She handed one to each of the men, then sat down beside Hughes.

"Wirke tea," she said. "Brewed from one of the few edible plants here."

Hughes sipped it. The taste reminded him of spiced peach. "Quite pleasant," he said.

"Worried about Rex?" she asked.

"No…yes…" he said. "I mean…Victrix isn't sensing anything amiss…"

"But it's strange not having him around."

Hughes nodded. He'd become very attached to the skaggit.

The priest raised his eyes but didn't speak. He'd undoubtedly encountered more today than he'd ever expected—a telepathic dog, a shape-shifting skaggit, and a wolf-human. That was surely enough to boggle anyone's mind.

As if reading Hughes' thoughts, Leina asked, "Is it some kind of hybrid?"

Hughes paused before answering. "Not a true hybrid—the wolf genome is too different from that of the human to create a viable embryo. I'm not a geneticist—and it would require detailed genetic tests to be sure—but I suspect it's a chimera."

"They're mythical, surely," Stefan Tomislaw said.

"Lion, serpent, and goat, according to Homer," Leina said, always ready with a reference. "The offspring of Echidna, the mother of monsters."

"They're far from mythological," Hughes replied. "Some even occur naturally—although not to the fanciful extent that you find in mythology."

"What exactly *is* a chimera?" the priest asked.

"In contrast to a hybrid, in which genetic material from two species is combined into one genetic makeup—like a horse egg plus a donkey sperm forming a mule," Hughes explained, "a chimera is a combination of cells from two or more separate individuals of the same or different species. In this case, apparently a human embryo was combined with that of some sort of wolf. The wolf parts are fully wolf, the human parts fully human." He motioned with his mug. "It may have undergone other genetic alterations, as well—to deal with different blood types and such."

"You think it's man-made?"

"Undoubtedly."

The priest remained silent for a moment. "Saint Augustine wrote that he'd heard of a race of dog-headed people," he said.

"The cynocephali," Leina elaborated. "Such legends were common through the Middle Ages. They lived in remote areas and were often thought to be cannibals. St. Christopher was said to have been dog-headed until his conversion."

Tomislaw continued, "Augustine was skeptical, but said that if they existed, they were either not human, or they were descendants of Adam."

Hughes wondered where this was leading.

Tomislaw's voice was quiet. "So you think it was developed from a human embryo?"

"That's my best guess," Hughes replied, finishing his tea and setting his mug down.

"Then do you know what that means?" the priest asked, his eyes shadowed in deep sockets.

"What?" Leina breathed.

"That it has a human soul."

Despite the reassurance he received from Victrix—she sensed nothing amiss with Rex—Hughes didn't sleep well that night. He dreamed repeatedly of Rex being devoured by the Adlet—surely the skaggit would make a delightful dinner for a big predator.

Victrix would know, he told himself repeatedly. She would tell him. And Rex could shapeshift at will—surely he could escape easily enough if he wanted to.

Victrix curled in a ball, snoring on her mat beside him.

He needed sleep, he knew that—needed his body to be refreshed. But even Leina's hand perched gently on his shoulder didn't prevent his restless tossing and turning.

He also wondered about the figure they'd glimpsed when leaving the site where the Adlet had been trapped. It was too far away to distinguish clearly without a viewscope…and maybe it was only another runner. Probably that was so. But there was also the nagging possibility that the figure had been watching them. Perhaps it was whoever had set the stasis field…

He wondered what kind of mind the creature had—was it canine, or human, or some kind of combination?

And as if that wasn't enough, the priest's words circulated in his mind as well: It has a human soul…human soul…human soul…

Hughes and Leina picked a different route to train the next day. Father Stefan abandoned them to join a group of other runners on a swimming excursion. Hughes—on learning that the sea was quite likely to be very cold—had declined, despite the priest's assertion that it was good cross-training.

Victrix had, of course, picked up on the word "swim", and Hughes felt compelled to promise her a long swim before they departed Kalara.

Hughes would have liked to have gone in search of Rex, but Victrix didn't seem so inclined.

<*Rex happy,*> she replied when Hughes suggested that they go find the skaggit.

<*Rex play.*>

In the light of that reassurance, "He'll come back when he's ready," he told Leina.

They were ambling through a stunted forest when another runner caught up to them.

"Are you Doc Hughes the Wolfman?" the stranger asked.

He was thirtyish, fair-haired, and with just enough of a belly to give Hughes the impression of a casual runner. Hughes scowled; he'd never liked being called "wolfman", even though the nickname was well-nigh inevitable.

"Yes," he replied shortly.

"ID'd your ship in orbit," the other man said. "Figured you were down here somewhere. Didn't know you were a runner."

"Neither did I," Hughes said.

"Taking care of some wildlife?" the man asked.

"There's not much around here," Hughes replied carefully. "Now, who are—?"

The man stuck out a hand. "Tev Einbrok." He paused as if expecting Hughes to recognize the name. When Hughes made no response, he said, pointing to a logo on his shirt, "Writer and vidspec for *Galactic Runner*?"

Hughes shook his head.

Einbrok sighed. "Guess you're more famous than I am."

"Are you doing a story on the Dragon Run?" Leina asked.

"My wife, Leina—"

"Dickson," Einbrok interrupted. "Triple winner of the Winfryd Alliance Marathon."

"How do you know that?" Leina demanded.

Einbrok gestured. "I looked up backgrounds on many of the runners here." He grinned. "Maybe I can feature both of you in my story."

"Or not," Hughes said, finding Einbrok's breezy manner irritating.

Einbrok, not taking offense, gave a mock salute, said, "Don't let the dragons get you," and veered down a side trail.

When he was out of sight, Hughes said, "What do you make of him? Is he who he says he is, or—"

"Does he know more than he's letting on?" Leina finished.

"Could he be the trapper? Easy way to get close-ups of the local fauna." Once again the image of the mysterious watcher came to mind.

"I'll ask around," Leina offered. "I'd get in touch with some of my contacts in the Alliance, but we're so far distant…"

"We wouldn't hear back in time," Hughes concluded.

Every world, he knew, held its secrets. What was Kalara's?

Planets with rings weren't unusual—Saturn, Jupiter, Neptune and Uranus for starters—but habitable worlds with such a magnificent system as Kalara's were few and far between.

Seated on the stone bench hewn from native rock that surrouned the crackling campfire, with Leina nestled close beside him and Father Stefan, safely returned from his swimming excursion, directly opposite, Hughes gazed into the night sky.

He studied the bands of the broad, silver rainbow that arched from horizon to horizon. What did the Adlets make of the rings—could they appreciate its beauty like humans, or were they blind to it like animals? Was it a bridge to the incredible immensity of the universe, or merely a source of light? Did it raise feelings of awe and wonder within them, or leave them indifferent?

"The beast within," Leina commented, breaking into his train of thought.

"Come again?" Hughes asked.

"The Minotaur," she said. "The werewolf. The Chimera. The myths explored the idea of the beast within. They challenged the boundaries of nature."

"As have we," Hughes said.

She motioned for him to continue.

"Natural chimeras are fairly insignificant," Hughes said. "But beginning somewhere around the twenty-first century or so, there was an explosion of interest in creating them for research purposes, typically not allowing them to progress beyond a few hundred cells."

He spread his hands. "But once the genie was out of the bottle…Some worlds prohibited allowing human-non-human chimeras to progress beyond the embryonic stage to full maturity. Earth, on the other hand created-"

"Parahumans," Leina supplied.

"Exactly. Scientists wanted to test the limits of human evolution or to create humans with enhanced characteristics like those found in animals."

"Super-soldiers," Tomislaw added, stretching his legs toward the fire.

"Right. Or designed to survive in hostile environments. But there were problems, abuses, unforeseen consequences. Many developed mental instability. Not surprising, since they were shunned, outcasts excluded from society. There were cases of parahumans turning on their creators and officers. Eventually, at least on Earth's worlds, they were hunted down and exterminated, and further development prohibited."

Hughes puffed out his cheeks. "If you ever want to read a heartbreaking book, look up *The Killing of the Chimera*."

"The Church opposed the killing of parahumans," Tomislaw said, "as strongly as it had opposed their creation. Not that Earth particularly cares what the Church thinks anymore."

"So what is a parahuman doing here?" Leina questioned.

"What indeed?" Hughes replied, watching as a shooting star flashed beneath the rings, and wondering if there was any way to find out.

For their last training run, Leina had charted a short, easy course on flat ground encircling a lake. She'd also packed a picnic lunch.

"Plenty of rest today," she'd announced while they were eating breakfast.

Hughes, who'd slept in, was quite amenable to the idea.

"Did you learn anything about Einbrok?" he asked, as they set out in midmorning.

"He seems to be legit," she replied. "Several people here have either met him at previous events or are familiar with his work. He's apparently fairly well-known in the Earth-based running community."

They passed another miniature oasis, Hughes half-expecting Victrix to alert him to the presence of another stasis field. Unlikely, he told himself. Whoever was behind it surely wouldn't erect one this close to the runners' camp.

"What else do you know about Kalara?" he asked, changing the subject. "Whose territory is it?"

Leina shrugged. "Depends on who you ask. A number of systems claim it, but since it's so worthless, none have ever pressed their claim. Earth, the Alliance, the FarSuns…probably others."

Hughes absorbed that. "So it's one of those worlds where you could fly under the scanners, so to speak? If you wanted to conduct some illicit research…"

"Perfect," Leina replied. "If you could afford the expense of transporting materials this far off the trade routes, and didn't mind a climate generally inimical to life."

"Limits the number of visitors," Hughes pointed out.

The lake, an iridescent turquoise, came into view.

<*Swim!*> Victrix exclaimed, running ahead and plunging into the water in a shower of spray.

Leina fumbled for Hughes' hand and laughed. "Makes you want to be a dog, doesn't it?"

"Certainly fewer cares of life," he replied, slowing to a walk.

Today was warmer than the previous one, Kalara's sun shining pleasantly and making the rings appear even more brilliant. They found a weathered outcropping of sandstone above the lake that looked tailor-made for a picnic site. Hughes fished a ball from his pocket and threw it in the lake for Victrix to fetch while Leina unpacked their lunch.

They ate, and eventually Victrix joined them, curling up for a nap. Hughes decided to do the same, while Leina read a book. He was half-asleep when the sound of running footsteps brought him back to awareness.

He looked up to see Tev Einbrok and a pair of other athletes approaching.

Einbrok waved. "Fancy meeting you out here!"

"Fancy that," Hughes replied neutrally.

Einbrok slowed and walked over. "Thought you might like to know something," he said, "seeing that you have a dog."

"What's that?" Leina asked.

"Several people said they've spotted a strange guy around, out in the hills. Nobody seems to know what he's up to, but one person thought he might be setting up some kind of equipment. Couldn't tell for sure, though." He circled a finger by his temple. "Could just be some crackpot."

Hughes exchanged a glance with Leina.

"Anyway, I wouldn't want your dog to run into trouble," Einbrok continued.

"We'll keep her close by us," Leina said. "Thanks for the heads-up."

"Later," Einbrok waved. "And if you change your mind about doing that interview…"

When he was out of sight, Hughes commented, "The plot thickens."

"It does," Leina said. "Would you like a leg rub?"

Hughes nodded and stretched out again. "Please."

Feeling thoroughly refreshed by the day, and by a brief, cold swim that, by dint of relentless pestering, Victrix had persuaded him to take, Hughes almost didn't want to attend the group pre-race dinner that evening.

"It's tradition," Leina urged. "You don't want to go against tradition, do you?"

"Certainly not," said Father Stefan, answering for him. "Come along, Hughes. It's a part of—"

"The race experience, I know," Hughes sighed.

And, in fact, he enjoyed it. The food was good, and they actually met a runner who recalled Leina's wins on Winfryd.

"It was tough competition, particularly the third year, too," the woman told him. "A strong field."

"Tell me about it," Hughes requested, and for a good half-hour, she did. By the time she'd finished, Hughes felt almost as tired as if he'd run the marathon himself.

"We thought she'd be a contender for the quadrennial Alliance Games," the woman concluded, shooting a disappointed glance at Leina.

"Something came up," Leina said vaguely, "and I couldn't compete."

By which, Hughes knew, it had something to do with her employment with the Alliance Department of Justice. Work which, being frequently of a sensitive nature, he never asked about. She was still called upon, from time to time when they were in Alliance space, to utilize her professional skills.

Later that evening, Father Stefan said a special Mass for the runners. And before settling down for the evening, Hughes and Leina sat beneath the luminescent rings in quiet solitude.

Hughes slept surprisingly well, worrying neither about Rex nor the race; it was as if a supernatural calm had descended upon him.

He awoke to find Leina already up and dressed, and preparing a light breakfast for him.

"You're up early," he said, quickly putting on his running clothes. "Pre-race jitters?" he teased.

"Pre-race warm-up," she corrected, handling him a plate of bagels and jam, and pointing to a glass of orange juice equivalent and a cup of hot tea.

"Another tradition?" he inquired.

"You're learning," she said.

"You look really good this morning," he said, as she performed a stretching routine.

"I feel as if I could fly," Leina smiled. "Better than I have in years."

Victrix yawned, uncurled herself and padded out the door into a golden sunrise.

"She's certainly relaxed," Hughes said.

"Remember to keep loose," Leina advised.

Hughes slipped his Celtic cross over his head.

Victrix returned, and Hughes gave her some breakfast before fastening her running vest into place.

A knock at the door indicated Father Stefan's arrival from the communal hut he shared with several other men. "Ready to go, runners," he called.

Hughes clasped hands with Leina. "Let's do this."

"Let's."

Even though he was at the rear of the throng of runners gathered near the starting line, the energy washed over Hughes, adding to his own excitement. He performed a few last minute stretches, others around him doing the same.

Only a minute to go…

Beside him, Victrix was also soaking up the enthusiasm, the only dog surrounded by a forest of human legs. She wore a custom-made, lightweight running vest with an official race number—something that hadn't been easy to obtain. Dog-friendly marathons were few and far between. But Leina had managed to pull a few strings in the running world, and Victrix was participating as a representative—the mascot—of WOLF. Her time wouldn't count in the official standings, though—not that such a consideration would matter; she'd stay by Hughes' side, and his only goals were to finish and if possible, not be last.

He patted Victrix's shoulder, then scanned the sea of brightly colored shirts and shorts ahead of him, hoping to catch a glimpse of Leina.

Before leaving him to join the elite marathoners clustered at the starting line, she'd squeezed his arm and given him a big smile.

"I'll be waiting for you at the finish," she'd said.

"Save some food for me," Hughes had replied.

"Don't worry, there'll be plenty."

Then she'd planted a big kiss on his lips. "You can do it. I have faith in you."

He glimpsed a mane of reddish-blonde hair surmounting a white running shirt—one that was emblazoned with a howling wolf's head, the same as his own. He raised his arm, trying to wave above the crowd that separated them.

She spotted the movement and waved back, blowing him another kiss.

She'd offered to run with him, but he knew she'd be happier among the leaders, her lithe form practically skimming above the ground—possibly even placing—while he'd plod along towards the rear of the pack, content just to be part of the event. And so he'd insisted that she be at the front where she belonged, and run as she could.

BANG!

The sharp report of the starting gun—an anachronism that had survived for centuries—startled him as it shattered the stillness of the morning air, reverberating off the rock formations.

The pack of runners jolted into motion.

"Let's go, girl," he said to Victrix.

Hughes' adrenalin surged as he began to jog, passing under a large banner suspended between a pair of rock pillars that proclaimed START in giant red letters.

He caught a final glimpse of Leina, already well down the trail, as the runners strung out.

She deserves this, Hughes thought, as she vanished from sight.

For himself, he'd just enjoy the scenery.

The morning was clear and fresh—a perfect day for a run. The rising sun filled the rocks with a measure of its own radiance and they glowed, bathed in warm light. And the rings… he thought he'd never seen anything more magnificent. It was as if he was running under the gates of Heaven.

He spotted Father Stefan some ways ahead of him, before intervening runners blocked him from view. The priest wasn't going to attempt to keep up with Leina, but he'd still be far ahead of Hughes.

The trail began with a gentle downhill through a forest of what might have been petrified trees sculpted out of maroon, yellow, amber, and cobalt-blue crystals. Downhills were good—too steep and they'd rip up his thigh muscles, but a gradual downward slope made Hughes feel as if he could run all day. The temperature was perfect, and even the thin air didn't seem to be posing a problem.

He visualized the course in his mind's eye. This section of the course, a long curve, was the tail of the dragon. To his left, a waterfall splashed into an emerald pool, while to his right, the petrified forest extended for miles.

"We're going to enjoy this, girl, aren't we?" he said to Victrix, trotting happily alongside. To her, it would just be another long run.

The trail plunged into a narrow canyon carved by an exuberantly cascading stream and elaborated on by eons of wind-driven sand. Hughes was nearly mesmerized by the flowing curves and whorls etched into the variegated strata. Bands of subtle hues—tan, orange, rust red, topaz—twisted and twined in elaborate whirlpools of color.

If he craned his neck to look up—being careful not to lose his footing or bump into another runner—like the young woman dressed up like an Amazon who'd just cruised past him—the lavender blue of the sky was a flowing ribbon overhead.

He'd only covered three or four miles, yet already he could understand why Leina had wanted to run this race.

He exchanged a satisfied glance with another runner about his own age.

"My third time here," the man said. "I notice something different every time."

"My first," Hughes replied.

"Good luck," the runner said.

The canyon opened into a broad plain dotted by curious, mineral-encrusted pools, some of which vented puffs of steam, reminding him distantly of Yellowstone. He took his time crossing the plain, pausing to peer into some of the pools…and once or twice he thought he saw movement in their depths.

<*Swim!*>

<*Not here, girl. Not safe.*>

And then, to his dismay, all too soon the plain gave way to a series of hills, individually not very high, but cumulatively having a draining effect.

These, Hughes knew, signaled the end of the dragon's tail.

So much for the easy part.

"A little tougher, isn't it, mate?" A youngish man with a female companion, both wearing shirts proclaiming them to have run previous marathons, ambled past.

"Yeah."

Hughes puffed out his cheeks, glanced at Victrix, who didn't look the slightest bit tired, and pressed on.

He took the hills slowly, conserving his energy, not caring—except for one rather rotund specimen of humanity—that other runners passed him.

"You'll need your energy later," Leina had advised him. "One of the cardinal mistakes is to go out too quickly."

He remembered that as he saw another runner sitting beside the trail, rubbing his legs. He stopped to offer assistance, which was politely declined.

"Only a cramp. I'll be all right."

"If you're sure," Hughes said.

"Fine looking dog," the man said.

"She's a rescue," Hughes said, as he carried on.

Hughes decided to walk the next hill. And several more after that.

Finally, the last of the low hills was behind him, but ahead of him reared a greater challenge—a long, steep trail leading up to a rugged ridge known as the Dragon's Back.

This, Leina had told him, was where some runners gave up…not even completing half of the race. This was why she'd encouraged him to run hills in training.

Stamina and fortitude.

No guts, no glory.

He walked for a minute or two to catch his breath.

Then, fixing his eyes on the ground about six feet in front of him—"Don't look too far ahead," Leina had warned him, "it will depress you,"—he began the ascent.

It was, as he'd been warned, long and hard.

Somehow, he made it to the top of the Dragon's Back, with his lungs burning and his legs aching. He was greeted by a vast panorama, extending from an indigo-hued sea on one side to distant, mist-shrouded volcanoes on the other.

But what thrilled him most was a dragon-shaped sign indicating the half-way point, and some cheerful volunteers offering drinks and encouragement. Victrix was glad for some water, as well, not to mention the attention she garnered as the volunteers clustered around her to greet her.

"Hope she's not slowing you down," one of the visitors teased.

"Other way around," Hughes grinned, helping himself to a drink and some cookies.

It was the psychological boost that he needed. With renewed energy he pressed on along the ridge.

It was as he was reaching the end of the ridge that he happened to look off to one side, and saw…

A shadow? Or a figure?

Something that moved in the distance, too far away in the hazy air to make out distinctly.

One of the elusive—and perhaps mythical—dragons?

Automatically, although it hadn't registered an alarm, he checked his BOSS. He shouldn't be hallucinating. The temperature was still moderate, he wasn't overheating or dehydrated, his electrolytes were normal.

And yet he was sure that he'd seen something.

Something, despite the lack of details, that struck him as non-human. When he looked again it was gone.

A succession of steeper, quad-busting downhill switchbacks took him off the ridge and towards the base of the Dragon's Neck.

He was trying to keep himself from going too fast—a certain recipe for later disaster—and mulling over what he might—or might not—have seen, when a sudden thought from Victrix burst into his mind.

<*Rex!*>

Startled, he momentarily neglected to watch his footing, and stumbled over a loose rock. He pitched forwards, tried and failed to convert his motion into a roll, and tumbled awkwardly down the slope, coming to rest—thankfully—against a berm of sand and not a rock.

He lay there for a moment, mentally assessing the damage.

Victrix came and licked his face.

<*Hurt?*>

"I'm all right, girl," he said, slowly regaining his feet.

He'd skinned his knees and his left elbow, tweaked his right wrist and shoulder, and scraped his forehead. It could have been a lot worse. He looked ruefully at his now-grimy white running shirt, speckled with blood. The wolf logo looked as if it had bitten somebody.

He flexed his limbs. He'd be even more stiff and sore than anticipated tomorrow, but at least he could finish the race.

<*Rex here!*>

He'd almost forgotten Victrix's call that had precipitated his fall.

<*Where?*> he replied, looking around.

<*Come!*>

She led him to the base of the switchbacks, and there, to the side of the trail stood Rex, once again in German Shepherd form.

"Where have you been, boy?" Hughes said, bending over to hug the skaggit.

Rex gave him a quick lick, then turned and trotted a few feet away and stopped, looking back.

<*Go with Rex!*> Victrix urged, joining the skaggit.

<*Why?*>

<*Go see!*>

<*Now?*>

<*Yes! Important!*>

Hughes sighed. "I hope it's not far," he said. He'd planned on a marathon…not extra mileage.

Fortunately, it wasn't far. Rex led them down a defile, and onto a plain fringed by sandstone cliffs and riddled by gulleys. Looking back, Hughes could see the Dragon's Back arching away into the distance.

Rex followed the base of the cliffs, which gradually curved into a semicircle, obscuring the view of the Dragon's Back. He weaved around several house-sized boulders, and then halted, staring at the cliff.

Hughes studied it. The cliff face rose up for some eighty feet, and its base was blanketed with fallen scree that sloped down to the plain.

"OK," he said, "it's a cliff. Why did you bring me here?"

Rex remained staring.

"Show me," Hughes said after a moment.

Seconds later, Rex, now a wolf-human again, trotted forward, to the cliff face…and through it….

Hughes whistled. He edged ahead, one arm extended before him. He reached where his eyes told him was nothing but solid rock, and his hand disappeared…

He braced himself and, nerves tingling, stepped forward.

"My stars…" he said, when his eyes adjusted, and, as an involuntary prayer, "Dear God in Heaven…"

It was more than an hour later— closer to two— when Hughes returned to the course, his mind still in a state of shock.

Both Rex and Victrix now accompanied him up the final ascent of the race, to the promontory known as the Dragon's Head. It wasn't as steep as the hills he'd climbed earlier, but his muscles had stiffened up, and every step hurt.

Mile eighteen. The wall. The place where some people quit…and regretted it ever after.

Fight through it, he told himself. Leina's waiting for you…

The Dragon's Head was aptly named. It was a quirk of the human brain to see patterns and figures where none had been created—in cloud formations, on tree trunks, in rocks. He didn't know how many images of the Blessed Virgin Mary had been spotted in pieces of toast, in baked goods, and so on.

But this promontory really did look like a dragon's head, fiery breath emerging from a fanged mouth and everything.

He wondered how long it had taken the forces of nature to sculpt it, how long it had been there, and how long it would remain before those same forces eroded it beyond recognition.

The last few miles were another gentle downhill, meandering through a tranquil landscape of stunted trees and shallow ponds. He alternated walking with a slow jog. He saw no other runners.

And, he noticed, he heard nothing but the breeze…if there was any wildlife on Kalara, it was invisible or silent.

The miles grew longer, he was sure of that. Somehow, when they measured the course, they put short miles at the start, and long ones towards the finish…

Now, it wasn't just his legs that ached, it was also the places he'd jarred when he'd fallen.

It was with a rush of relief that he emerged from the forest to see the "FINISH" banner strung out ahead.

"Finish strong," Leina had told him, and he mustered enough energy to jog towards the finish line. At least there was no other runner wanting to sprint it out with him.

He spotted Leina on the far side of the finish. She waved to him; he waved back and the sight of her spurred him on. Victrix and Rex outpaced him to reach her.

He crossed the finish line upright, and then she was wrapping an arm around him to help keep him vertical as a race official draped a dragon-shaped medal around his neck—and one around Victrix's, as well.

"You made it! I knew you could!" Leina exclaimed, kissing his cheek.

He staggered, feeling slightly dazed and weak.

"Walk it off," she instructed, noticing, and directing his steps towards the refreshment tent. "I was getting worried…about ready to have a race official check on you. And you're all scuffed up—"

"Just a little fall."

"Are you sure you're OK?" concern filled her voice.

"Fine," he said.

"I'll get a medic to patch you up."

"Later, perhaps."

He looked back and noticed that someone was taking the "FINISH" banner down.

"Was I that slow—"

"Last," she said, following his look. "But what matters is that you finished." She touched his medal. "You got this."

She pointed him towards a chair. He slumped into it, and she fetched him an apple. He bit into it, thinking that he'd never tasted one so good.

"Rex is back," Leina observed.

"He met me on the way," Hughes replied.

"And Victrix looks very proud of herself."

The black dog was making a round of runners and volunteers, accepting any treat that was offered.

"Hughes! Good to see you." Father Stefan came over, looking as if he hadn't run a step; Leina appeared the same way. "Did you tell him?"

"Not yet," Leina said.

"Tell me what?" Hughes asked.

"You missed the awards ceremony," Stefan said.

It took a moment for his words to sink in. Hughes stared at Leina. "You didn't!"

She bent down and retrieved something from her pile of gear, and held it up for his scrutiny.

It was a golden statue of a dragon being speared by a muscular knight in armor—St. George, he supposed.

"You're looking at the women's winner—an official dragon-slayer."

"That's fantastic!" Hughes exclaimed, struggling to his feet.

"Still got it in me," she said.

"Quite a wife you've got there," Father Stefan remarked.

Hughes embraced Leina. "I always knew you could fly," he said.

"I'll leave you two lovebirds to celebrate," Father Stefan said.

Hughes reached out to hold him back. "Don't go far…I've got something to tell both of you…"

"When you're feeling better," Leina said, pushing him back into the chair. "Let me get you another apple."

"Or maybe I'll just show you…"

"In the morning," Leina said firmly. "You look done in."

"Hey Doc!" It was Tev Einbrok, striding over with a grin. "Glad I caught you. C'mon—you can't escape me now."

Hughes exhaled. He couldn't have run a step now if his life depended on it. "Well I'd rather not-"

"Great story," Einbrok insisted. "The alpha and omega—the first and last."

Beside him, Leina stifled a snicker.

Hughes groaned. "Let's get it over with, then. Just keep it short, huh?"

"Will do, Doc," Einbrok said, dragging over a chair and sitting down. "You look like you need a doctor yourself…"

Hughes wasn't about to retrace the route of the run the next morning. Instead, they took a flitter from the rapidly emptying runners' village to near the Dragon's Neck.

When first he woke up—sore, but not as bad as he'd anticipated, thanks to the ministrations of a race medic—the village was a hive of activity as the majority of the runners packed up and departed—either returning to the hum-drum existence of everyday life, or heading off to the next race. But the flurry of activity didn't last long, tapering off by the time Hughes and Leina had finished breakfast.

He kept a wary eye open as they traversed the fascinating terrain to the Dragon's Neck. But apart from two or three runners who apparently felt that the previous day's exertions hadn't been enough, the landscape appeared deserted. Still, he landed the flitter well short of the alcove to which Rex had led him the previous day.

"Around the bend," he said, pointing, before a slipping a pack over his shoulder. "Stay close, just in case."

"Where?" Stefan asked, looking at the sheer cliffs, as they scrambled across the scree. "You've brought us to a desolate place, Hughes."

Hughes halted. "Right here. Rex…"

No matter how many times he watched Rex shapeshift, the process always fascinated him. He'd love to know how it was done, but that would mean subjecting the skaggit to innumerable tests, some of which might prove harmful. He wasn't about to do that. The shapeshifting ability would remain a mystery.

Within seconds, Rex had assumed his new form, and Hughes nodded towards the cliff. "Go, boy."

He was enjoying the look of mystification on Leina's and Stefan's faces, which changed into surprise as Rex vanished into solid rock.

Leina caught on first. "A holofield!"

Hughes nodded agreement. He put his arm around Leina's shoulders.

"Prepare to be shocked," he said, stepping forward.

The shade of the alcove gave way to bright white light, doors that opened smoothly before them, and then Leina's hissed intake of breath and Stefan's whistle.

Ahead of them stretched a long, gleaming corridor punctuated by side-corridors and doors, and alive with the low hum of power. A glassed-in chamber situated near the entrance and filled with consoles was obviously a control room of some sort. Yet it was deserted—and the walls were dirt-streaked and the floor silted with piles of fine sand. The air had an almost animal-like quality to it.

"Who built this place?" Stefan wondered. "And why?"

"I don't know about the first," Hughes replied, "but I can guess the second."

Victrix barked and ran ahead. <*Rex!*>

From out of one of the side corridors emerged the skaggit, in wolf-human form…followed by a skittering, squirming, snarling mass of five or six others…

And behind them, a quartet of full sized wolf-humans.

"Hughes…" Leina whispered, backing away.

Encountering one such massive beast had been terrifying enough. But four…with young…

"Keep calm," Hughes whispered back. "It's all right."

The largest of the four—the one they'd released from the stasis field—broke away and approached them. It halted in front of Hughes, sat down, and extended one of its human arms. Hughes reached out and shook hands, his eyes holding the intense stare of the creature.

Behind him, Leina's giggle held a trace of hysteria.

The golden-brown gaze turned towards her.

"Shake," Hughes said.

Stiffly, she did as he instructed.

"And you, Father."

The priest complied, then said, "The cross."

Hughes hadn't at first noticed the crudely fashioned cross hung around the creature's neck. Instinctively his hand rose to his own.

"It must have copied mine," he said. "Perhaps he considers it to be the sign of the alpha male."

The Adlet—he still thought of it by that term—turned and padded away.

"Come on," Hughes said to his companions. They passed Victrix and Rex, busy playing with the pups, and the other three Adlet, who stood unmoving. Although he'd encountered them before, it was still unnerving.

They turned down a side corridor and entered one of the rooms. Several tables stood in the middle, which was ringed by banks of silent equipment. On one of the tables lay an adult Adlet.

"The alpha female," Hughes said, crossing over to her. "My patient."

Leina joined him, while Father Stefan inspected the banks of equipment.

The female Adlet opened her eyes, but didn't move as Hughes examined a long, shallow wound running from her flank to her chest.

"That looks like a burn from an energy rifle," Leina said, sounding much more like her usual, confident self.

"My diagnosis, too," Hughes replied, sliding his pack off his shoulder.

"The trapper?"

"My guess."

He ran his fingers gently alongside the wound, which glistened with the pink of regenerating tissue. "It looks a lot better than yesterday."

He pulled a tissue regenerator from his pack and directed it over the wound. "Yesterday I wasn't sure she'd make it. Today, I know she will."

"Do you want me to apply a fresh biopatch?" Leina asked. Living with Hughes, she'd picked up some of the basics of treatment.

"Please. And then if you could fill that bowl with water—and I brought food in the pack. She wouldn't eat yesterday, but maybe today..."

Leina bent to pick up the bowl, but the male Adlet was faster, picking it up with a human hand, carrying it across the room to a spigot, and bringing it back. Leina raised her eyebrows, and instead readied the food, watched intently by the male.

Father Stefan had finished his scrutiny of the equipment. "So what is this place, Hughes? I'm not much for technology..."

Hughes glanced up. "Isn't it obvious?"

"Not to me."

"I looked around a fair bit yesterday—it's a very extensive facility—"

"No wonder you came in last," Leina said.

Hughes gave a crooked smile. "It wasn't because of poor running form. A lot of this equipment here is ruined, but it's unmistakably a genetics research facility. No clue as to who was operating it, though."

He resumed working on the female Adlet. "Why it was abandoned, or whether the Adlets had something to do with why it was abandoned, we may never know."

He switched off the tissue regenerator and put it back in his pack. "Enough for today, I think. But with food supplies and the power source remaining operative, the facility enabled the Adlets to survive the planetary winters."

"It's like *The Island of Dr. Moreau*," Leina said.

"Where's that?" Stefan asked.

Leina laughed. "You've never read it? It's an old novel, from centuries ago, about a scientist who created animal-human monsters."

The female stirred, and reached up her arms. Quickly, the male embraced her, his muzzle close to hers.

"Those are no monsters," the priest said softly.

Rex and several pups skittered into the room, and as quickly dashed out again. Hughes hadn't seen Victrix in some time—probably off exploring, he thought.

"Hughes," Leina said pensively, "how can chimeras reproduce?"

"If these were true wolf-human chimeras," Hughes replied, "they would reproduce wolves if they had wolf gonads, or human if they had human ones. So they aren't pure chimeras. However they were created, they've undergone germline engineering as well to allow them to breed true."

"So they're truly a new species."

"Yes," he said. "They are."

"Created and abandoned."

"Heartless, isn't it?" he said. "Let's go now. I've done all that I can."

They headed down the corridor, watched once again by several of the adult Adlets, and trailed at a distance by Stefan Tomislaw. Walking slowly, with his hands clasped behind his back, the priest seemed to be lost in his thoughts.

Hand in hand, Hughes and Leina stepped out through the concealed entrance into the muted daylight. They'd taken several steps when, too late, Hughes felt the tingle of a stasis field. In mid-stride as he crumpled, he fell to his left, and landed looking up and to his right. He heard Leina give a squeak of pain as she too fell.

Barely in his visual field—since he couldn't turn his neck to look—he glimpsed a man, dressed in military-style fatigues, an energy rifle slung over one shoulder, and a small control unit in one hand—probably for the stasis field, Hughes guessed. He stood in the few feet that separated the holofield concealing the facility entrance from the stasis field.

The man grinned. "Look what we have here. Meddlers. Fancy that."

Hughes couldn't place his accent; couldn't even see his face clearly—but something about the man's voice.... He struggled to move, knowing it was useless. He couldn't even tell if Leina was all right.

"I saw three of you go in there," the man said. "Where's the other?" He raised his voice. "I know you're in there! I've got your friends. Come out slowly, unless you want something very unpleasant to happen to them."

Don't come, Stefan, Hughes thought. Completely encased in the field, he was unable to speak. Even breathing was an effort.

But a moment later, he heard cautious footsteps, and realized the priest had exited the facility.

"Very smart," the man said. "Stop where you are. Who are you?"

"More to the point," Stefan said—he obviously hadn't come out far enough to be trapped in the stasis field—"Who are *you*?"

"That doesn't matter."

"You've no right to assault us—"

"Oh, is this *your* facility?"

"Is it *yours*?" Stefan countered. "This is an unregulated planet—"

"So my right to be here and do as I please is every bit as great as yours," the man said. "Perhaps greater, since I'm armed and you obviously aren't. Now answer my question." He raised the energy rifle.

"We came here for the Dragon Run—" Stefan began.

The tip of the rifle inched higher.

Don't play games with him, Stefan! Hughes thought.

"My name is Stefan Tomislaw. I'm a priest."

"A priest?" their captor laughed.

"This is Hughes and his wife. Founder of Wellness for Other Life Forms—"

The man laughed again. "I should have guessed. You do-gooders are everywhere." His voice hardened. "Why are you here?"

"I told you, for the run-"

"*Here.*"

"We were tending to an injured creature."

"Of course. What else would you be doing?" He waited, then repeated angrily, "*What else?*"

"What else is there?" Stefan rejoined.

One part of Hughes' mind was listening to the conversation, while another was trying to think of a way out.

<*Victrix!*> At least the field couldn't interfere with his connection to the black shepherd.

<*Victrix,*> he called again.

<*Here.*>

<*Stay inside. Get Rex.*>

"Helping monsters. How noble," the man sneered.

"They are children of God," Stefan replied.

"You're nuts. An experiment gone wrong. Subhuman freaks."

"What are you going to do with them?" Stefan demanded.

"None of your business."

"Kill them? Enslave them? Sell them on the black market?"

"I said, *that's none of your business*!"

"Look," Stefan said patiently, and Hughes realized the priest was trying to buy time, "They care for one another, they feel compassion. Can't you see the humanity that is in them?"

Hughes visualized the controller in the man's hand.

<*Rex get bad man's toy.*>

<*Not Victrix?*> She sounded disappointed.

<*Rex get!*>

<%&**$%#>

<*Tell him!*>

"I'm not going to argue with you, priest."

"They were made from human embryos! They're human!"

"I don't care if they were made from your grandmother. Even if they were human, it wouldn't matter. They're mine, and I'm going to—"

A black *something* burst through the holofield—Hughes glimpsed only a flicker, but it reminded him of a misshapen bat—straight at the man.

He cursed and instinctively raised his hands to shield his face.

The thing snatched the controller from his hand, and was gone.

<*Push the green button,*> Hughes sent to Victrix, making as clear a mental picture as he could. <*Tell Rex.*>

<*Rex push.*>

The tingle vanished.

Hughes struggled to his feet, although the brief time in the field had left his legs feeling weak and rubbery. But even before he was upright, Stefan leaped on their captor, trying to wrest the energy rifle away. But his opponent was too big and strong. He felled the skinny priest with the butt of the rifle.

"Nice try," he snarled. He motioned with the rifle. "All of you. Over there."

Hughes helped Leina to her feet, and together they hoisted the stunned Stefan, blood trickling from a gash on his scalp. They lined up against the rock wall to the side of the concealed entrance.

Now that he could see the man's face, he was able to place the voice. "Vach!" he exclaimed.

Their captor laughed harshly. "You've met my brother, have you?"

"We had dealings. Your brother?"

"Twin. The good one."

"Good one?" Hughes repeated, his heart sinking.

"The one who has scruples, who works for other people."

"And you –"

"Call me Kron if you like. I work for myself. And I keep what I find—especially if it's valuable. And I most certainly don't have scruples. Now, tell your animal to bring the controller back," Kron directed, facing them. "Or one of you gets it. Perhaps the pretty lady."

"Look," Hughes began, "surely there's some way to resolve-"

An energy bolt gouged a hole in the rock between him and Leina.

"Negotiations aren't in my vocabulary."

Hughes sighed. "Come, Rex," he called. "Bring the toy."

Rex, back in canine form, came trotting around the corner, the controller held in his mouth.

"Drop it," Hughes instructed. "Then lie down."

Rex complied, and Kron bent over, picked up the controller, and reactivated the stasis field, but left them free.

"Better," he said. "Perhaps there's a chance you'll leave here alive. Now, since you're buddy-buddy with those freaks in there, tell them to come out."

Hughes stared. "They don't understand language. I can't call to them—"

"They didn't eat you. You can communicate with them well enough."

"I can't—"

Kron loosed a shot from the energy rifle that impacted the ground inches from Hughes' sneaker-tips. "Do it," he said, "or I'll start taking off feet."

Hughes glanced helplessly at Leina.

"Please," she said, "we really can't—"

This time, the shot was closer to Hughes' toes. The burst of energy made him wince.

Hughes thought about throwing himself at Kron—but he'd probably have no better luck than Stefan. Still, he had to try something –

"I'm losing patience," Kron said.

Pebbles skittered down the cliff-face.

Kron's gaze jerked upward, followed by the rifle—

Hughes' foot lashed out, catching Kron's arm and sending the bolt harmlessly skyward.

And then two furred forms—one black and one gray—who must have exited the facility by an air shaft partway up the cliff face—slammed into Kron's chest.

The combined weight of nearly three hundred pounds flung him backwards into the stasis field. He hit the opposing field generator, dislodging it, and fell forwards. Man and generator tumbled down the scree, Kron jerking like a dog's toy being ripped apart—which, Hughes knew, was exactly what was happening to him as the stasis field fluctuated wildly. His scream reverberated off the cliff face.

"Everyone stay put!" Hughes said, snatching up the energy rifle.

He destroyed the nearest field generator, then made his way cautiously down the slope to where Kron lay twitching and spasming. The second and third generators went up in bursts of flame and smoke.

It hadn't taken long.

But for Kron, it was too late.

After some discussion they buried Kron's body in a crevice and covered it with rocks.

"Let's hope his brother doesn't know he was here," Hughes said. "I have no desire to meet up with Vach again."

"We shouldn't linger," Leina said.

"Agreed," he said.

"But what about them?" Stefan wondered, pointing back to the concealed entrance. Rex had disappeared—gone back to play with the kits—or were they children?—while Victrix and the male Adlet sat next to each other in some kind of canine harmony.

"We can't simply load them onto *Wolf-1*," Hughes said. "There are too many. Even if we did, where would we take them? Where could they go where they wouldn't be hunted down or exhibited as freaks?"

"Yet we can't just leave them," Leina added.

"That's the other horn of the dilemma," Hughes agreed. "The Adlets can't live here undetected forever. They're bound to be rediscovered sooner or later. As their numbers increase, the facility won't be large enough for them…the food supply will be exhausted."

"And if other hunters come…"

Hughes motioned assent. "But Kalara is, in a sense, their homeworld."

"Can it support them?"

Hughes shrugged. "Impossible to say without a proper ecological survey. I rather doubt it."

Stefan interrupted. "You're talking as if they're simply another species of endangered animal." He looked between Hughes and Leina. "They're *people*, I tell you. With as much right to life, to freedom, to self-determination as you and I have."

"What do you suggest, then?" Hughes asked.

Stefan spoke forcefully. "They are God's children. They need to learn that. I am going to stay here with them."

Hughes stared. "Are you serious?"

"You can take a message to my bishop for me, seeking his permission. But I'm certain that this is my calling—my mission field."

"But…there's no common language—" Leina began.

"There is," Stefan said. "The language of love. You've already demonstrated that, Hughes. Begun the process. I will carry on. I can also help protect them."

"But the weather..." Leina said. "The temperate season will be over soon..."

"If they can survive in the facility, I can, too," Stefan pointed out.

"For the time being," Hughes said. "But we—they—need a long-term solution. Earth won't help them, not if past history is anything to go by—rather, the opposite. I doubt that the FarSuns will care. That leaves the Alliance. Leina, you have connections..."

She was nodding. "I can take the question to the requisite authorities. But do we recommend they establish a protected enclave here, or move them to another world...?"

"Let's not jump the gun. I'll have a full WOLF ecoteam do an assessment. An official recommendation might go a long ways."

"Plus, the Adlets will be under the protection of the Church," Stefan said. "My bishop will agree. If society won't protect them, the Church will."

Hughes clapped him on the shoulder. "You'll be the spiritual father of a new race of humans."

Stefan blushed. "I wouldn't go that far—"

"I'll leave you all the supplies I can spare," Hughes said, his mind already moving on to practical matters, "and give you a crash course in basic medicine..."

Wolf-1 was outbound from Kalara. Victrix and Rex were lying on the deck, nosing a ball back and forth in a low-key game that both considered immensely entertaining. Hughes and Leina reclined on a couch. Her trophy gleamed in a display case next to Hughes' finisher's medal.

"Next time," Leina said, wagging a finger, "I'm running with you to keep you out of trouble."

"Next time," Hughes replied, "I'll try to be faster."

She raised her eyebrows. "Is there really going to be a next time?"

"I can't leave it at just one," he said. "Maybe some time - not immediately, mind you..."

"You're not going to beat me." Her smile was mischievous.

"Being on the same course will be good enough," he grinned. He reached for her hand. "I'll be happy to run in your footsteps."

Victrix and Rex barked in tandem.

<*Victrix and Rex run!*>

<*Yes. Both of you.*>

<*Fast?*>

"What's with them?" Leina asked.

"Just the competition gearing up," Hughes replied.

"Dr. Hughes?" the voice was Sofi's.

"Yes, Sofi?"

"Distress call, Doctor, from the Extinct Species Re-creation Project on Aafedt III."

"This promises to be interesting," Hughes said to Leina. "I wonder what sort of trouble they've got?"

<*Work?*> Victrix was on her paws and heading for the bridge, Rex on her tail.

"Don't just sit there," Leina said, poking Hughes in the ribs. "Let's go find out."

"Set course and initiate, Sofi," Hughes said, climbing to his feet and following Victrix. " Tach 7."

"Affirmative, Doctor."

"Aafedt III," Leina mused. "I wonder if there are any good marathons there…"

THE END

TALES OF A TIME-TRAVELING HISTORIAN

IN THE ROMAN EMPIRE

www.ingramcontent.com/pod-product-compliance
Lightning Source LLC
Chambersburg PA
CBHW030134180626
46812CB00002B/692
9781927154441